M000104959

PROFILE OF A
KILLER

A SUSPENSE/MURDER MYSTERY

To Shantrize with my very best wishes.

Brent W. A. Henderson

BRENT W. A. HENDERSON

Library of Congress Control Number:		2013903626
ISBN:	Hardcover	978-1-4836-0116-8
	Softcover	978-1-4836-0115-1
	Ebook	978-1-4836-0117-5

This book was printed in the United States of America.

Rev. date: 5/16/2013

To order additional copies of this book, contact:
Xlibris Corporation
1-888-795-4274
www.Xlibris.com
Orders@Xlibris.com
129972

This book is dedicated to my four grandchildren: *Big Guy, Sluggo, Best Friend and Pretty.* How I wish you all could live in a world where there were no "bad guys."

ACKNOWLEDGEMENTS

If the saying goes, "It takes a village," then that saying goes for books as well. I have several people who played major roles in this story. First to Mary, my soul mate and wife for over forty eight years. Writing a book is no easy task and she was always there to encourage me, help me, stay home when I went to conferences and help me over the pain of those always arriving rejection letters. She is the best.

Several people read the manuscript, corrected grammar, added comments, thoughts and ideas. Linda Muszynski Compton read the first draft, written so many years ago. She read and wrote in pertinent comments. It was not until I looked at and began re- reading that first draft that I could imagine what a difficult job that must have been for her. My daughter Hilary Barr also read that first draft. I should have known by her comment, "Yeah Daddy that's pretty good," that that first draft was not much, and indeed it was not. My deep thanks go to both of them.

On a more current level my thanks go to Phil Scala, Billings, Montana who dropped his other tasks, read my manuscript, made comments and sent it back almost by return mail; and Jennifer Scala, Bud Cross, Gail Collins and Dina Robertson Kehne, who is like a daughter to me, for reading and making comments. Pat Collins, who for a time was a proof reader for the Christian Science Monitor read the book for both content and grammar, while riding AMTRAK cross country. Pat has always been there to help me and has been, and still is, my computer guru. In short he has been a lifesaver. When I panicked he always had a steady hand as well as a calming word. Tom Nunnally (Sgt. Major, U.S.M.C. Ret.) wanted the story to be a movie and did all he could to bring that about. My wonderful neighbor, Cindy Cross read the book for grammar and put off packing for a winter in Florida just to meet my deadline. She is a very dedicated and true friend for helping me. Michael Brunson told me it would take him a week to read the manuscript. He called me the next day telling me he could not put it down, nor could he get the story out of his mind. He has always been my biggest fan. David McCready was a big help trying to get me to understand a computer. He was in Poughkeepsie, NY at the time. After I finished this book he retired and moved to Florida. I have no idea if working with me had any impact on his decision.

Donna Peerce, Nashville, Tennessee did a professional edit and added a little here and a little there and made the book as good as it is. She did a wonderful job and continued to work diligently even though I hounded her. She always had time for me and she became my best sounding board.

I owe a great deal of thanks to my medical advisor Danny Perkes, M.D., Fishkill, NY. It did not make any difference what time or date, he was ready to answer all my questions. More importantly, during this time we got to be wonderful friends and our friendship is worth more than anything.

I met Dr. Perkes through my New York daughter Brooke Fedigan. She has a feel for those sort of things. While she did not read the book I had my work with me when we visited. Brooke made an area for me to work where I would not be interrupted by little voices. Of course those little voices did interrupt on occasion from little people, but what grandfather could get upset at his grandchildren asking for a story to be read to them. I read to them but not from this book.

PROLOGUE

White Man put on his jeans, slipped on a tee shirt and stepped into an old pair of Nike cross trainers. He put an Atlanta Braves cap on his head pulling it down to partially hide his face. Careful to make sure the door was locked as he stepped onto his porch, down the steps and made his way to the well-worn path that led to the entrance of Stone Mountain Park.

When he reached the entrance he walked directly to the sidewalk that surrounded the mountain which also ran parallel to the road that went around the mountain as well. He walked with a steady gait and was happy to see very few runners or walkers. *It was too early for them* he thought. He continued until he came to a fork in the road, one way continuing around the mountain, the other crossing a small bridge that went past a small part of the cove which was a part of the lake. The road eventually led to Evergreen Lodge, Stone Mountain's convention center.

There was no sidewalk on this road so he walked in some small weeds and grass that edged the road. This area was a part of the park that few runners or walkers took. Most preferred to take the five mile route around the mountain.

He walked until he came to that part of the cove he knew so well. Being careful not to slip on any bushes he walked down close to the water. His eyes scanned the spot where he had placed the body. The water was still and mirror like, reflecting the new spring growth of the trees near the cove. It did not take him long. He saw the body in the water by some logs, just as he had placed it. Leaning closer, his right hand lifted to his mouth in both amazement and frustration. His lips tightened and he muttered "Jesus," out loud. Then he thought to himself, *If somebody does not find her soon her soon she will be just so much food for the fish and turtles.*

Quickly he made his way back to the road. Giving the area a quick scan and seeing no sign of anyone he retraced his steps and shortly was back inside his house. He looked at his watch. The little excursion had taken him just about an hour. An ugly twist came to his mouth as he thought how "dumb" and unobservant people were.

APRIL, THE FIRST MURDER

It was the best of everything for Mose Ellard. The morning air was still a little crisp, but normal for mid-April in Atlanta. And the early morning sun, well, it was what his Mama had always described as a southern sun: big, full, and a deep coral red with brilliant rays wrapping their arms around the entire sky. He loved when the sun was bright and vibrant, as it was in the spring. Sometimes, in the evening during the long summer months, even with the Atlanta smog, the setting sun would become beet red. Mose loved it.

This morning was one of those idyllic times; the crisp air, the red sun and the calm waters of Stone Mountain Lake. His johnboat hardly moved the waters of the cove were so still. Mose sat there, alone in his boat, line in the water, his eyes scanning the scenery that he so loved. Every once in a while, he would let his eyes wander to the bobber on his line hoping that a small bass or crappie would take the bait.

"It don't get much better than this," he whispered to himself. Mose turned, looking toward the shore, near Evergreen Lodge. The trees were dressed in their new leaves, several shades of lime green.

The redbud trees were in bloom and the dogwoods would soon paint the landscape with brilliant white flowers.

Such was the ritual of Mose Ellard. He had been coming to Stone Mountain Lake to fish since he was a boy. Early on, when he was a little boy, it had been almost forbidding. His father told him the stories of the Ku Klux Klan gatherings at the mountain, a large crowd of creepy hooded men chanting and raving about "niggers and Jews," about the Kennedys and what they wanted to do to the South and the southern way of life. And then, there was the huge cross wrapped in burlap and soaked in kerosene and erected on what is now the great lawn. A torch was set to the base of the cross and the flames, snaking a path, soon engulfed the entire structure in a huge fire.

Mose had asked his father, "Daddy, why do they wear masks?" and his father replied, "Son, when you are a coward you don't want folks knowin' who you are. Always be proud of who you are and don't be afraid of it." Mose had always remembered that. Mose had treasured those time with his father.

His father had also told him of the completion of the 1960's carvings on the mountain. It was a monument to the heroes of the confederacy, a Civil War that continued to be fought for many years after the surrender at Appomattox.

Mose had never married. Always a dutiful son, he had lived with, and taken care of his mother after his father had died of "the high blood" so many years ago; Mose was still a young boy when this happened. His mother had died just a year ago when old age finally got too much and her body simply wore out. She had gone in her sleep and for that, Mose was grateful. He had never wanted anybody, or anything, for that matter, to suffer.

For years, Mose had worked for an animal hospital. A jack of all trades, he did janitor work, cleaned the exam rooms after each appointment, wiped piss off the tables after a frightened animal was given an exam, and swept the floor regularly. He was also the one who went in every Saturday and Sunday to feed the animals and walk the dogs being boarded. Among his favorites was an iguana, a pet of one of the vets. He loved to watch the big lizard, its throat undulating as it breathed. Mose would take the animal out of its cage and place it around his neck where it would stay as he made his way from room to room doing his chores. It was not unusual for Mose to rescue a stray or unwanted pet, brought in to be put down, back to his home.

"Lordy God," his mother would say. "What we goin' to do with another animal?" But in no time, she was as attached to the animal as he was. It wasn't until a neighbor made a call to the police to complain that this practice was stopped. Fortunately, the officer who responded, knew Mose, and talked to the vet who, in turn, talked to Mose. Mose understood, but it had been difficult for him to give up his rescue missions. From that time on, he refused to dispose of any animals. The vets accepted and honored Mose's decision and from that point on, Mose was never asked to take part in any euthanasia of any animal.

Suddenly Mose realized he had not caught any fish. *If I'm going to have a fresh catch for dinner, I'd better concentrate on the task at hand,* he thought to himself. Sometimes, he was successful catching crappie by the shore. They were smaller than what you might catch in the deeper water, but Mose realized that soon it would be too warm and the fish would stop biting. Taking his oars in hand, he began navigated the johnboat closer to the shore.

With fresh bait on the hook, Mose cast his line a bit too close to the shore. By the time he noticed the log, it was too late and the new lure he had just bought last night at Wal Mart was hooked into the wood. Using one oar, Mose moved the boat closer to the shore.

Steadying himself, he stepped to the front of the boat. Then, getting on his knees, he took the line from the fishing pole, and followed it to the log so he could dislodge his new lure. As he did this, he glanced toward the water

"*Whoaaaa, Lordy!Good God Almighty!*" he said out loud. Mose fell back. The sudden jarring and shift of weight almost caused the boat to capsize.

That was most unusual for Mose. A deeply religious man, he never took the name of the Lord in vain, thinking he could be condemned to hell, or *perdition,* as his mama and the preacher man often called it.

His heart thudding a million beats per second, Mose slowly got himself upright and crawled to the front of the boat. Again, following the line from his fishing pole, Mose gazed into the clear, shallow water. What caught his breath was the location of the lure. It was not caught on a log at all. Before him was the body of a person. Scared, but a bit curious, Mose looked more closely at the human remains lying in the muck in front of him. It was difficult to tell if the body was a man or woman, adult or child. The bloated face was staring at him with hollow orbs, the eyes having been long since nibbled at by fish that found soft tissue an easy meal. The skin was dark, but Mose could not tell if this was from discoloration or race.

He was unable to turn away from the body. It was bloated except for the toes, which were just bones now, with no tissue left, and were sticking out of the water. Looking at the foot of the body, Mose was aware of the sweet, but putrid smell coming from what were now stumps.

Finally, Mose reached for his line. With trembling fingers, he grabbed it and cut it loose, leaving the lure still attached to the body. Dropping his pole in the bottom of the johnboat, Mose grabbed the oars and paddled as quickly as he could for the spot where he had parked his old pickup truck. He had to get help.

———————

The coroner said the body was that of an African-American female, perhaps in her mid- teens. The cause of death was probably downing. He could not tell due to the time the body had been in the water, which he estimated to be approximately one week. The water, the fish and other conditions made it difficult to tell much more.

———————

Mose scoured the paper every day for news about the investigation of the dead girl. Unable to find anything, and having seen nothing of the dead body on the TV news, he decided somebody had to do something to at least acknowledge that a human being had been found dead and deserved some sort of investigation. That someone was him.

Early the following morning, Mose drove to the police station. When the officer at the reception desk was finally convinced that Mose was not to be dismissed, he made a phone call, then directed Mose through a locked door where he was met by a detective. After inviting Mose to sit down, the detective, who never introduced himself, rattled off a litany of things the police had done to identify the girl. He also gave a list of reasons why the case remained unresolved.

The police had conducted an investigation, Mose was told. It was hindered by the fact there were no reports of missing girls, at least no reports that fit the circumstances. Certainly, there were missing girls all around the Atlanta area. Most were runaways. Some left the city and state, some turned to prostitution or became dancers at some "titty club," according to the detective.

Checking the juvenile court, the general consensus among the juvenile officers was that runaways were not that at all, but were throwaway kids, coming from such dysfunctional families that it was pointless to try to find and return them to parents who did not care. If they left town, fine, then they could become the problem of some other jurisdiction. If they stayed, they were bound to get into trouble again and would be handled some other way, sooner or later.

The detective told Mose the fact that the body was that of an African-American, contrary to what elected officials would admit, the reality was that race did have an impact on a criminal investigation. It was no secret that black children were more vulnerable to crime. Black girls got pregnant often, and the fathers, for the most part, were totally out of the equation. The mothers were not ready to settle down and the result was that these fatherless, and to a great extent motherless children, were pretty much left on their own. These children grew up pretty much as street children, accountable to nobody, and nobody accountable to, or for, them. It was a shame, and a problem that had been present for years. But, until society owned up to its responsibility, it was a problem that would only continue.

Standing up, the detective made a move to help pull out the chair for

Mose, who realized it was time to get up. The interview was over. The detective showed Mose to the door and thanked him for his interest. He promised to call as soon as he knew anything. Walking out the door of the police station, Mose mumbled under his breath, "Bullshit, ain't nuttin' gonna be done. That case is cold as a crab's ass."

Perhaps there was nothing else that could be done. No missing girls fit the description; no alarmed mother was hounding the police; there was no real evidence of a murder, nothing. Then again, it could have been the fact that the chief of detectives was at a month-long FBI National Academy retraining session at the FBI Academy at Quantico, Virginia, and wasn't there to direct an investigation into the death of the girl found in the lake. But one thing was certain. There was a dead body, a human being who had just one week ago been a living, breathing, human being. She was somebody's daughter.

One week after Mose Ellard visited the police, nothing had been done about the girl. Mose Ellard said, "That poor girl. It's a damn shame. Ain't nuttin' gonna be done about her."

Mose made one additional call to the police department inquiring about the investigation. He was told the detective who had talked with him was out. Insistent, Mose was given the name of another detective who had no recollection of the case, but promised to find out, and call Mose back. Of course, no return call was ever made.

Thoughts about the young girl haunted Mose. *Who was she? Who was her mama? Where was her family?* It made him very sad. Finally, he decided he would think about the girl no more.

The result of the cold case was a distorted body stored in the locker of the DeKalb County Coroner. A nondescript body on a slab, soon to be buried in a grave without a real headstone. A body with a toe tag that simply said *Jane Doe*, with the date of her discovery underneath the name. In the space marked *Next of Kin*, it was blank.

As he had done on a daily basis White Man perused the paper for news about the girl. One morning, after finding nothing, he, once again decided to don jogging clothes and went for a run. *Well, actually,* he admitted to himself, *it was more of a walk beginning at Stone Mountain Park.* As he had done in past days he walked down by the cove of the lake near the Evergreen Center. Once at the cove, he looked around to make sure he could not be seen.

"Jesus," the guy mumbled. Across the cove, a heavyset black man sat motionless in a johnboat. His fishing pole and bobber bounced gently in the water. White man stared at the fisherman, not sure if the old coot was even awake. *Could he chance it?* White man could not stand there all day waiting for some geezer to take his shit and go home. He could walk around the mountain, but he didn't want to take a chance of being seen, not today.

White Man looked around. People were running not far away on the sidewalk. As he turned back toward the cove, White Man noticed the fisherman was looking up at the sky. *It must be almost noon,* White Man thought to himself.

Slowly, the fisherman reeled in his line, put his pole on the bottom of the boat and began rowing toward the opposite shore.

Waiting patiently, which was against his nature, White Man watched until the fisherman reached the shore on the other side of the cove. Slowly, the old black man muscled the johnboat out of the water and pulled it up to an old pickup. Pushing the boat into the bed, the black man secured the boat with bungee cords, then hobbled slowly to the cab, climbed in and puttered off down the road.

"Finally," White Man whispered. Looking to make sure no one was around, he walked down by the lake. In the relatively short period of time, the scenery had changed. The leaves were now mostly in full green on the trees, and the dogwood flowers were almost gone. The lake seemed fuller, covered in a brighter shade of green with the trees' reflection. It was a sign that summer was near.

It took White Man a few minutes to look through the moss and lilies and locate the exact spot. When he found it, he walked closer to the water, concentrating, his eyes searching. Then he knew he had the spot. His eyes narrowed. *The body was gone.* She had been found!

"Fuck," White Man whispered to himself. He climbed back up to the road and began to walk home. Not only was he disappointed, he was angry. Furious.

"Fuck this," White Man said aloud, "next time people will notice. Next time, I'll get a white girl. That will get the bastards' attention."

MISSING

Beverly Langford squinted into the last shades of red and purple in the deepening twilight, so characteristic for the Deep South. Twilight was just a fleeting intermission between daylight and darkness. A pause of gentleness before the great darkness spread over the land. Plus, currently, the humid August haze blurred the edges of the great lawn in a mist where spectators sat to watch the laser show. It was almost impossible for her to see the concession stand area, which was beyond the lawn, over near the railroad station and the village. She could swear the girls had been gone at least half an hour, far too long for a simple trip to the restroom.

Of course, Beverly knew it probably hadn't been a simple trip to the restroom in the first place. The family had arrived at the lawn well in advance of the start of the laser show, which was projected across the granite face of Stone Mountain.

Forrest, Beverly's husband, always believed in getting anywhere early to beat the crowd. Naturally, their daughter Paige and her friend Holly, weren't quite as patient. Both girls had started to fidget while waiting to watch the laser show. Twelve year olds didn't have the world's longest attention span. The two girls finally insisted that they couldn't wait until after the show started to go to the restroom. Moreover, they argued that it was better if they went now, rather than stand in endless lines afterwards, when everybody else had the same idea.

"Good friends," Forrest said. "I don't blame them for wanting to go now. It'll be much easier."

"O.K.," Beverly said. "I'll go with them."

Forrest said, "No, Bev, stay put. You're bushed. We can practically see the building from here. The girls are old enough, they can go by themselves. They'll love being let off their leash." Forrest winked at the girls. He regularly contended that Beverly was overprotective.

Beverly was exhausted and had to admit that she didn't want to walk another step. Hearing Forrest's comments, the girls looked at each other and giggled. So, against Beverly's better judgment, she agreed that the girls could go by themselves. Beverly strongly suspected that they would be looking for boys to flirt with at the concession stand. Even though they were only 12 years old, they were already interested in boys and often stayed up late at night, experimenting with their hair and clothes, and discussing Justin Bieber and any new pop artist on the scene. The girls giggled and strategized over every teen magazine and had pictures of boys plastered all over their rooms. Beverly thought that it was inappropriate behavior for twelve year olds. Kids just grew up so much faster these days.

Holly, a nice girl, but more worldly than Paige in many areas, already had quite a following, and she wouldn't even be in middle school until next week! Of course, she looked older, with small round breasts clearly apparent under her T-shirt. And Holly already had nice long legs and a curvy butt that she managed to accent in cute, tight jean shorts.

Beverly wished the girls weren't in such a hurry to grow up, but she knew it was a lost cause. That was probably why they were so late in getting back from the restrooms, too. Doubtless they were hanging on to every word of some seventh-grade heartthrob. Beverly smiled to herself as she remembered some of her seventh-grade crushes.

Forrest was right, of course. You could practically see the concession stand from where they sat on the lawn and the girls were responsible, obedient kids who never gave her any grief. Let them have a little fun by themselves. It was the last outing of the summer vacation, after all.

She slipped her shoes off and rubbed her weary feet. Since noon, when they had arrived, they must have walked miles! Somehow the park hadn't seemed so daunting when she was Paige's age. Of course, there had been less to do in the park thirty years ago. The enormous *Confederate Memorial* sculptures hadn't been finished when Beverly was in high school, so there had been no light shows then. And, many of the current major park attractions: the antebellum plantation, the paddle wheeler replica, the tennis courts, and the village itself weren't built either. Beverly could remember scrambling up the mountain effortlessly, and not thinking twice about it. Of course, when you're 12 years old, scrambling up mountains is fun and easy.

Today, they had taken the tram to the top instead and she was exhausted, still. *You're getting old, Bev, baby,* she said to herself, putting her sturdy Nike tennis shoes back on her feet. They provided good support. She remembered her mother telling her, "Now remember, you're no spring chicken."

You're right, Mom, Beverly said to herself. *You're right.*

The girls appeared to be having a great time, which was the point, after all. Holly, whose family had recently moved to Atlanta from Omaha, had never been to Stone Mountain before. Holly had acted impressed by the park attractions, but Beverly suspected it was only because there were lots of boys there. But Holly even listened politely while Forrest played tour guide, though it was clear to Bev that Holly wasn't much of a geology or history buff. *What 12 year old girl was?* Beverly thought.

"The mountain is one single piece of granite," he explained. A native, he loved to show off his city. "It's five miles around the base. The entire area covers 3,200 acres right here smack in the middle of Atlanta. And, three million people come here every year just to see the mountain and the carvings."

"That looks like Mount Rushmore," Holly said, pointing to the bas reliefs of the rebel icons, Jeff Davis, Robert E. Lee and Stonewall Jackson, which loomed above them. "We went to the Black Hills last summer to see Mount Rushmore."

"Well, it should," Forrest replied enthusiastically. "See, the same artist designed both places. Don't misunderstand, though. Stone Mountain has been a landmark for 200 years. That's a long time before the boys got themselves up there."

Bev added, "One of Forrest's relations had a lot to do with the history of the mountain." Forrest loved talking about his Georgia roots.

"Indeed, he did," Forrest said, then continued, "One of the greatest Confederate Generals, Nathan Bedford Forrest, was my great-great-great grandfather. I was named after him, in fact."

Paige rolled her eyes at Holly. She was embarrassed by her father's bragging. Especially because of what he was going to say next.

"Yes sir, it was right here on top of the mountain, after the war, that my great-great-great grandfather accepted command of the Ku Klux Klan!"

Paige could have died. She felt her face turning beet-red.

Holly didn't seem particularly impressed. "My Daddy was in Desert Storm and Afghanistan, too," she replied.

"Remember, honey, Holly's not a southerner," Bev interrupted, knowing their daughter, Paige, was embarrassed. She was almost as tired of Forrest's views on States' rights and the "glorious cause" as her daughter was. "Perhaps we can go over Atlanta history another day when we have more time. The girls just want to have some fun right now."

To keep Forrest off his favorite topic, Beverly suggested that they take the tram to the top of the mountain. Kids loved trams. And since Holly had lived in Nebraska, where the land was mostly flat, compared to the hills and mountains in Georgia, Beverly figured she'd love it. Even with the heavy summer haze that obscured most of Atlanta's skyline, Holly had been excited as she was able to make out what she thought was Tennessee, Alabama and the Carolinas from the lookout point as the sun began to set.

Beverly jumped as if someone had stunned her as the music introducing the show began. *Where were the girls?* They were missing the high point of the day. Even a jaded twelve year old would love this spectacle and Holly had never seen it before! Beverly scrambled to her aching feet and looked around. It was thoroughly dark now. She could see the lights from the village area and the village which had grown since she had last seen it. Now it was concessions, and old time village with glass blowing and a blacksmith along with accompanying rides that go along with amusement parks. The last riders were departing from a rail trip around the mountain. Beverly could no longer make out faces in the crowd, though.

Forrest had turned toward the carvings that the lasers danced across. He was oblivious of his wife's distress.

Beverly grasped his arm. "Forrest, I'm worried."

"What?" He half-turned. "I can't hear you over the music."

"The girls haven't come back yet," she shouted. "Should I go look for them?"

Forrest turned completely around to face her. "In this crowd? In the dark? Nah, you'll never find them." He didn't look particularly concerned. "They probably ran into some other kids, lost track of time, and just stayed where they are to watch the lights when the show started. They know where we are. I made Paige point out all the landmarks to me before they left. I wouldn't worry too much about it."

Knowing Forrest made Paige recite their location back to him helped calm Beverly's nerves. It was unlikely they were lost and Forrest was probably right about the rest of the story. She knew the girls had other interests besides the restrooms in the first place. And, as Forrest regularly reminded her, the buddy system worked. They were both smart sensible children. *What could happen to the two of them together?*

Beverly could have kicked herself for not bringing her cell phone along. Forrest hadn't brought his either. He had insisted they leave all technological devices at home so they could sit and enjoy the moment. "Too many people have their cells with them all the time and never take a moment to just relax," he had said that evening. Even the girls, who had cell phones for emergencies, had left their cell phones home, as well.

What the heck! It was a beautiful night. Beverly inhaled the thick, green smell of the humid August night as she sat watching the lasers bring the mountain to life.

The horses of the three icons reared and galloped across the face of granite as Elvis sang *Dixie*, the *Battle Hymn of the Republic* and *Hush Little Baby* into the summer darkness around them. At the climax, as General Lee broke his sword over his knees and peach blossoms rained down from the top of the mountain upon the emblems of the Southern cause, Beverly felt a moment of utter contentment. She had always been a big fan of Elvis, and they had enjoyed a lovely day. Beverly smiled to herself when she thought of Paige and Holly who thought she was terribly old-fashioned and "retro" in her music choices, especially when the girls loved Justin Bieber, Katy Perry, Lady Gaga, and a few similar others on the pop scene.

The show continued with Ray Charles's *Georgia on My Mind*, which was Forrest's favorite, to the concluding fireworks accompanied by Lee Greenwood singing *God Bless the USA*.

Taking advantage of the light from the fireworks, Beverly looked around again for the girls, half expecting to see them walking her way, wearing smiles and a little guilt on their faces for having been gone for so long. This would be a logical time for them to come back while they still had some light from the show and before the crowd disbursed, clogging the paths.

Beverly didn't see them. As the smoke from the last fireworks dissolved, Beverly grasped Forrest's arm to get his attention. He turned and looked around, puzzled. "Where are the girls?"

"Forrest, they never came back!"

Under any other circumstances, Beverly would have gained a certain amount of satisfaction from the shock she saw on Forrest's face. He was always so sure of himself. But now, she only wanted reassurance and comfort.

The lawn had become a mass of milling people, the park lights on the periphery were dim, and the girls, gone. That's when the enormity of it hit her. "Forrest, what on earth should we do?" She anxiously looked around at the crowds of people.

Forrest's right arm circled her shoulders, squeezing them hard. He said, "Let's not panic, sweetheart," he said soothingly. "They're smart girls. They'll wait 'til the lawn empties out to find us. We just need to sit tight. Remember, they know where we are."

Twenty minutes later, when Forrest and Beverly were the only two people standing at the north end of the exhibition lawn, his confidence had faded somewhat. "Maybe Paige forgot," he said. "Look, you go to the railroad station. I'll go to the car. They probably went to the car, but let's cover all bases. You wait for me. I'll come get you."

Seeing her husband's confusion and fear, Beverly started to cry.

"Bev," he said gently. "Keep your head. We'll find them."

They didn't. The stands were closing when Beverly got there. There was no one she could ask about the girls. The restrooms were deserted, too. Beverly walked in circles around the station and stands, shouting, "Paige, Holly! Come here now! Paige, Holly, where *are* you?" She yelled into the woods behind the train station, "Are you all out in the woods? Come on back, now! We're going home?"

Beverly felt sick. If they could hear her, they would have come by now. Finally, ignoring Forrest's instructions, she ran toward the parking lot. She had spotted a police officer there earlier, down by the exit, directing the last few cars from the lot to the public road.

"Help me. Please! Help!" she cried as she ran up to him, grabbing his arm.

It took forty-five minutes – minutes they could never get back – to unscramble the situation. Bev was hysterical.

The patrol officer called for backup, unable to figure out what the crazy woman hanging onto him, was talking about.

After thoroughly searching the far parking area where he had parked the car, Forrest drove around the lot near the concession stands and the train depot several times before he saw Beverly. He realized his wife was involved in an altercation at the far end of the parking lot. He quickly drove over and joined his wife. By now, another police officer had shown up. Beverly and Forrest insisted that the police officers needed to do something *immediately*.

The officers continued to assure Forrest and Beverly that teenage girls were infamous for wandering off with friends and were probably at one of those friend's houses by now. In the general confusion, the officers hadn't listened very well when Beverly and Forrest told them exactly how young Paige and Holly were. Neither of the officers seemed unduly concerned.

When Beverly realized Forrest had no idea what to do next, she insisted that the cops call the Langford home on their cell phone. But there wasn't an answer, just the voice-mail telling the caller to leave a message. Beverly then demanded they call the house a second time. Still, no answer.

"See, they're not there! *You have to do something.* Paige is barely twelve. She wouldn't go joy riding with other kids. She doesn't even know anybody old enough to drive! They're both children!" she screamed.

The two cops looked at each other, suddenly understanding the severity of the situation. Seeing their hesitation, Forrest joined Beverly in demanding immediate action, starting with a search of the woods around them. This response terrified his wife. At that moment, she knew beyond a shadow of a doubt that her baby was in deep, deep trouble.

———————

LOCATED 3

Todd Warren and B. J. Weaver enjoyed their early Sunday morning runs around the mountain. The five mile workout served several purposes, not the least of which was keeping B.J. breathing. He had had fairly severe asthma all his life. While jogging was difficult, without regular exercise, his lungs lost their elasticity. If he hadn't had asthma, however, he would have had to invent some other pressing health reason in order to spend an hour or two enjoying the peace of the mountain before the tourists arrived. The asthma also gave him a reasonable excuse to skip the early church session. B.J. let his wife deal with spiritual matters of the church. The morning run was spiritual to him.

The humidity seldom let up in Atlanta in August, but if the two men were careful to be on the trail by 6:30 a.m., they could complete the circuit before the summer heat and the accompanying high humidity made serious exertion impossible. The five miles around the base of the mountain made a comfortable circuit for the weekend warriors. Some of it was quite demanding – fairly steep hills – but there were also a number of fairly flat parts where they could catch their breaths to prepare for the next incline.

The Stone Mountain Police patrolled the area regularly, which meant runners, walkers and bicyclers felt safe. This also meant that a red-blooded American male could study a wide variety of female joggers and walkers as he clocked off the miles. The police presence encouraged women to feel safe alone. Neither Todd nor B.J. would ever admit it, of course, but ogling the ladies was part of the Sunday ritual, along with rehashing the week's sports and stock market movements and the latest shortcomings of the President.

The men, both alumni of the University of Georgia where they had been fraternity brothers, religiously attended all the Georgia Bulldog games, which is why they did not run on Saturdays. In the summer, they spent their Saturdays with the Atlanta Braves instead, either attending home games at Turner Field or watching away games at a favorite sports bar.

This particular morning though, they talked about the signs they had spotted at the entrance to the park. Beverly and Forrest Langford had spent Saturday printing hundreds of "Have you seen these girls?" posters at Kinko's. They had managed, with the help of their church, to get them up on every bulletin board and power pole around the Stone Mountain parking lots.

Both the Langford's and Holly's family, the Putziers, belonged to St. Jude's at the Mountain, which was quite near the park; in fact, it was on the road leading to the entrance to the park. Thanks to a phone tree that a friend of Bev's and the church youth minister had organized, 50 people had turned out to plaster the lower part of the mountain with the lost children announcement, hoping that someone – a jogger who ran at dusk, a concession worker, a park gardener – might have seen the girls after they left the exhibition lawn.

"I'd be wild if Brandi just vanished like that," Todd commented, overlooking the fact that at four, his daughter was a long way from catching a bus to the park or any other place outside the boundaries of the home. An afternoon in her paddle pool was still hot stuff to her.

"Well, you know teenagers," B.J. commented. B.J. was short for

Billy Joe, which B.J. thought was a little ingenuous, even for Georgia, for a 30 year old attorney who would soon make partner. Atlanta was New South, after all. Answering to a double name once you were twelve seemed, well, a tad redneck. "They get upset over the damndest things. Take off on you if you look cross-eyed at them. You better hope they wise up quick before somebody moves in on them. I can tell you that white slavery is alive and well. The Russians are making a pile of money exporting women now that their borders are open."

"Shit man, the Russians aren't the only ones doing this stuff. Just look at what's available on the Internet when it comes to kids. I mean, you read about it all the time in the papers. And TV is full of it," Todd commented. "Makes you sick to think a man would want a twelve year old. Both of them are twelve, for Christ's sake! Strikes me as pretty young to be runaways."

"Our criminal specialist has a case right now, a stat rape case, where a twelve year old could pass for eighteen real easy," B.J. replied. "It's his defense, in fact…" B.J. paused, trying to take a deep gulp of morning air as they started up another incline and feeling his lungs tighten, refusing to admit any oxygen at all. He wobbled, stopped and then doubled over in a coughing fit.

"You okay?" Todd asked. He was used to B.J.'s breathing difficulties, but this was a particularly acute attack.

"Yeah," B.J. gasped after he had deployed the inhaler he always kept in his fanny pack. He stood a moment, panting ragged breaths. "Goddamn summer and the shitty, smoggy air that comes with it. You don't know how happy I'll be to see the first of October." His breathing had evened out. "Listen, I was about to piss on my foot anyway. Wait a minute. I'm going to take a whiz."

The two men stood in a parking lot across the road from the big playground on the backside of the mountain.

B.J. clambered off the asphalt parking area as Todd jogged in place. "Don't take too long," Todd yelled after him. "Don't want to knot up." Todd halfheartedly bounced on the asphalt another few seconds, then decided to rest. No question that the day would be a scorcher. His t-shirt was already soaked and his sweatband, which he removed and wrung out, was full of perspiration and it wasn't even 7:00 a.m. Todd sat down on the stone wall that separated the parking lot from the path. Resting his elbows on his legs, he let his head drop; hoping some small amount of breeze would cool his sweaty body.

B.J. pushed through the bushes by the parking lot and down an embankment, taking him in the direction of the railroad tracks that lay between the mountain, the path and road. A large green-eyed fly buzzed around his head, then attacked his neck and shoulder, biting him hard. Slapping continuously at the bothersome insect, he wondered how one bug could find him in such a large area. He hurried to a spot close to the tracks where the insect population might be a little thinner. He didn't relish exposing his tender flesh to additional flies or mosquitoes. Preoccupied, he tripped over a tree root, fell heavily, and then rolled out of control downhill. He screamed like a baby.

Todd hadn't heard B.J. yell like that since the day a 300 pound household appliance named Junior Tharp sat on his back in their intramural days in college. Startled by the scream, Todd ran from the wall down the embankment, expecting to find his friend lying in the bushes below, clutching his arm or leg. Instead, he saw B.J. kneeling on the ground by a bundle of old clothes, vomiting.

"What happened? Can you talk?" Todd called to his friend.

B.J. just shook his head, wretched again and, making a guttural sound, beckoned him over. When Todd reached his friend's side, he saw that the bundle was not old clothes, but an obviously dead person, a young girl. *Oh my God!* Her mouth and eyes were wide open. In fact, the eyes themselves weren't there anymore at all, just gaping holes. Some animal had helped itself to the tasty parts. Flies swarmed around the body. She was young and slender, the August heat doing her no favors. Todd recoiled from the stench, then tried to brave it to examine the scene more closely, but as he leaned over the girl, saliva filled his mouth and like B.J., Todd threw up all over the corpse.

That's when Weaver's already ragged breathing turned into a fullscale asthma attack. As he wheezed, he turned blue. Todd dragged his friend away from the body to fresher air and stuck the inhaler between his lips. Minutes passed as B.J. desperately struggled to breathe. His friend held him upright to help open the airways in his lungs.

When B.J. could finally stand, he leaned on Todd, and the two scrambled back up the embankment. They headed back to their cars for their cell phones. In their haste to escape the smell and the horrid scene of the dead body, they failed to see the second body, another girl, stripped nude to the waist, lying approximately ten feet nearby in the clearing.

CRIME SCENE 4

Theo Reed heard his cell phone ringing at his mother's house.

"Do you have to answer that?" his mother said while they were finishing the big Sunday breakfast she insisted he eat with her every weekend.

"Mama, it might be important."

"Isn't it set to go to your answering machine?" asked his mother.

Theo's mother, once a slender beauty who looked very much like Erykah Badhu on her wedding day, had shrunk into a bony, almost bird-like woman with a forward stoop and a perpetual frown. Theo could remember her singing around the house, but no more. His mother had become isolated, lonely. Her remaining friends were forced to come to her because she seldom went out.

"When my friends and I get together, I just want to cry," she confided once to him, "They remind me how it used to be. We had such good times when your daddy was alive."

Now, practically a hermit, Theo's mother jealously begrudged her son's time.

Theo got up to answer his cell phone which he had left in his suit coat, draped on the hall tree. He had shed the coat as soon as he came in out of respect for the hot Georgia morning.

"Mama, you know I have to answer. I'm off duty, so if they're calling it's important." Theo tried not to sound too impatient with her, even though he knew damned well that she understood the ground rules. He was a second-generation cop. She had lived with interrupted meals all her adult life.

As soon as he answered, he was instructed to call the station back on the landline. Cell phones were not secure.

"I need to use your phone, Mama," he said, walking toward the front hall and the walnut telephone table that she had Johnson paste-waxed once a month for the last forty years.

She sighed, "It's bad, then, I know it. You'll have to leave. I *never* see you anymore."

"You see me every week, Mama," he said. "And sometimes more!"

The woman's memory grew more selective by the day. Frankly, he was relieved to be called away from a heavy southern breakfast consisting of gravy, biscuits, grits and country ham. It didn't help his waistline one bit.

As Theo dialed the heavy black rotary phone that was ancient, he fought his annoyance with his mother who staunchly refused to replace it with a more efficient digital phone.

His desk sergeant was cucumber cool, as usual, but the news wasn't. "Theo, remember those two girls the Stone Mountain Police reported missing Friday night? The ones that seemed too young to be runaways?"

"Yeah, I remember," Theo replied. Usually he didn't get involved in missing persons situations, but he had felt different about this case. He had a gut feeling about it.

The park police had made a point of passing on this report saying the girls' parents were more believable than most when claiming how reliable and well-behaved both of the missing children were. In addition, the two fathers had been adamant about not waiting the usual 24 hours before considering the disappearance a police issue.

In response, the park police had said that, at twelve, the girls weren't quite teenagers yet. Missing children got attention immediately. Theo hadn't liked it when he heard the girls' ages, but since there were two of them and they had last been seen together, he had figured there would be a good outcome. He had hoped, anyway.

A couple of healthy nearly young adult-sized children were generally difficult to kidnap together. It was far more likely that they had gotten lost or maybe one had sprained an ankle or something, and the other had stayed with her. Parts of the mountain were surprisingly wild for an urban park. In summer, a night in the woods was no immediate life or death problem. Still, if they were lost, they should have turned up by Saturday morning. There were thousands of people in the park on weekends.

"Two joggers just found the little girls' bodies in the woods by the railroad tracks near the playground on the back side of the mountain."

"Shit. Shit." Dead children were administrative nightmares with the parents half-crazed, the chief's office pressed for immediate answers and the media howling for blood. Theo could feel the sweat trickle down his neck, even in his mother's dim, air-conditioned hallway. It was a helluva hot day for a park crime scene.

"That's Stone Mountain's jurisdiction. I take it the girls didn't have an accident?" Theo asked. The Stone Mountain Police capably handled traffic control, car crashes, liquor violations, vandalism, and general day-to-day mayhem on their own but they were a very small department attached to the State's Parks and Recreation Department. They had no means to investigate a major murder case. If they had called Theo's office so quickly, the situation at the mountain was at best, equivocal, or more likely, a clear case of homicide.

"No way. The uniform on site says it's violent, probably a multiple rape. The chief wants you up there to secure the scene. I called him already because one of the fathers is old Georgia. According to Stone Mountain, he was already screaming yesterday that nobody was doing anything. It sounds like he'll call everybody from the governor on down once the girls are officially identified and that's going to happen soon. The ME's on his way."

Theo sighed, not eager to meet the parents. He had observed that the fathers of violated children expressed sorrow by channeling all their feelings into blind anger. He could just imagine the father ranting, "*Somebody must be to blame for this and we'll damn well find out, goddammit!*"

At least Theo didn't have to pussyfoot around ancestral worship and idolization as practiced in Savannah or worse, Charleston. Old family ties never meant much in Atlanta in terms of clout. Too many transplants in Atlanta. Some of them weren't too happy with a black chief of detectives, either. Between the devil and the deep blue sea, maybe he would be happier having a quiet breakfast with Mama after all.

Mama came into the hall just as he had shrugged into his suit coat.

"Theo, *must* you go? I'd think that in your position you could delegate."

"Mama, there's two twelve year old girls who disappeared at Stone Mountain Friday night that are lying dead up there."

His mother gasped, "Oh dear!"

"I've got to go," Theo continued.

"Raped?" she asked. "Murdered? Were they black girls? Theo I always worried so much about Coretta at that age."

"I don't know anything yet, Mama," he replied. "They were white girls. That's all I know." He leaned down to kiss his mother goodbye. Theo, built like his late father, towered over his mother with shoulders nearly twice the width of her waist.

She reached up and hugged him. "Please, please be careful," she said, "In my dreams, sometimes, I see you lying dead."

What a cheerful way to send me out the door, Theo thought as he walked out the front door. He knew his mother was dreadfully lonely, but when the blues really hit her, which they did more and more lately, she could give a saint a nervous breakdown. Her life had been difficult. The problem was that her suffering was not enabling, just annoying.

If he could find five free minutes, he could talk to his sister, Coretta, about finding Mama some useful social outlets. *If Coretta ever had five free minutes, that is.* Theo sighed again. A sad, dependent lady like their Mama needed children who didn't have busy, professional lives. And she needed grandchildren to love and dote on. Lots of them.

On the way to Stone Mountain, Theo passed a billboard with the coming football schedule of Morehouse College. Theo had been planning to go over to Morehouse later that morning to watch an intra-squad scrimmage. Football had been his sport in high school. He knew he had talent and his plan had been to go to Grambling University to play football for Eddie Robinson, but that all came to a screeching halt with the death of his father. Now missing that scrimmage seemed less important. He wondered where on the mountain he was supposed to go. As he neared the park, he felt the adrenalin kick in.

"Don't ever believe a cop, or a fireman, for that matter, if he tells you that excitement means nothing to him," his Daddy told him once. "Gotta be the rush that keeps a man on the job, for it surely isn't the pay."

Theo looked a lot like his father. He had a medium-brown skin tone, and was six feet., two inches tall. He had to admit he was not as trim as when he thought he was going to play football. As a uniform officer, he had been able to work out regularly. But since he was promoted to detective, his schedule in the gym was not as regular. And, once he made Chief of Detectives, he hardly had any time for exercise at all except for the once or twice a month he was able to play tennis. The result was a waist line that had gone from a 36 to a 40 in what he felt like was no time at all. His weight had gone from 190 to somewhere around 215. He was not sure anymore since he refused to step on a scale. Theo sported a thin mustache and was considered by some to be extremely good looking. He couldn't see it in himself though. He always dressed in a tie and suit, or slacks and a blazer, just like he demanded of his detectives. There would be no walking around without your coat off and no public display of side arms.

Naturally, the detective squad room and all the cars in the fleet were air conditioned. Theo demanded that his troops looked and acted like the professionals they were. He told every officer who came into the Detective Division that if he or she wanted their pistol to show, then he or she needed to stay in uniform. And there were no shoulder holsters. Those were good for Hollywood, but not in real life. Regular officers carried their sidearm on his or her side. This held for female detectives, as well. He was not going to have a female officer scrounging around in her purse if the need ever arose that she needed her pistol.

A Stone Mountain officer met him at the gates to the park to escort him to the crime scene. Theo knew Stone Mountain Park as well as he knew Mama's backyard. From childhood on, he had spent hundreds of hours in the park. Despite that, protocol between the two police departments demanded that he accept an escort.

The girls had been killed near a playground that bordered the path around the mountain, the most popular jogging route. Theo remembered the playground clearly. He had run the circuit himself five times a week when he was still a patrol officer. He believed that a cop on the street owed the city a sound, fit body. It was the soft, fat cops that got lazy. But since he had made detective, it had been a lot harder to go to the mountain and he had a new empathy for those overweight cops. He could not recall the last time he had been for a jog. Whatever his size, Theo Reed was every bit a professional.

He hoped his crime scene wasn't too screwed up. An outdoor site could hold so many small things that were so easy to overlook – or accidentally destroy. Footprints, cigarette butts, drag marks, a drop of blood in an obscure place. The fewer people there were, the better until the area had been secured and photographed.

It took all of five minutes to arrive at the spot of the joggers' discovery. The playground, which was a proper architecturally-designed fantasy of geometric steel bars, towers, barrels, and a bi-levellog fort with a handful of old-fashioned swings built in one corner to satisfy classicists, swarmed with children, most of them under six and most of them gleefully screaming. For them, it was just another day at the park. For their parents, it was something else altogether. Every adult present stared across the road at the parking lot now filled with patrol cars. The lot was entirely ringed with yellow crime scene tape.

The DeKalb County Police crime scene van had already arrived. This gave Theo hope that they might have a relatively pristine scene to deal with. If they had been able to defend the parking lot and area below from bystanders and road voyeurs, he would be ahead of the game. You never knew though. The police themselves had been known to plow up the ground like charging rhinos. You had to train people and educate them in the correct protocol. The responding officer's job was to administer aid to living victims, to secure the crime scene and then sit tight for the detective. But, some smaller departments had education budgets that looked like petty cash. Sending even one of their men to the Georgia Public Safety Training Academy to learn crime scene preservation was a stretch. For that matter, even experienced people could screw up, particularly if they encountered a child victim. The social taboos and stigmas surrounding the nature of a crime involving children often derailed objective professionalism. People simply had a hard time dealing with crimes involving children. And then, of course, murder was just plain ole fascinating. That might be why a detective had made it his or her business in the first place.

All of Theo's analyses fit right alongside his daddy's comments about the excitement of police work. Theo had never met a firefighter who didn't like to watch things burn either. Once in awhile, the urge to satisfy curiosity and poke around the site would get the better of the responding officer, and almost always, a detriment to the case.

There was a hot, heavy smell around the periphery of the parking lot, a mixture of melting asphalt and forest duff rotting in the high humidity. Theo wiped his forehead with his handkerchief as he started downhill to the bodies. It had to be over 90 degrees by now. He hoped this high heat was not an omen of what to expect for the summer. He prayed the girls wouldn't be too ripe yet. Then, 25 feet down from the road, the smell of death hit him like a solid wall. Bad. The putrid, sweet smell of decaying flesh. Theo could almost see the stench rising before him. *Grin and bear it.* Theo breathed as shallowly as possible, longing for a bad cigar or someone's heavy perfume to blunt the miasma.

Theo stood outside the second circle of yellow tape that the crime scene unit had used to rope off the dead girls – a circle within a circle. The child positioned closest to the railroad track, and the one who had gone unnoticed by the joggers, lay on her back as if sleeping. The illusion was preserved by her closed eyes and mouth. The body had been neatly arranged, back and arms straight, arms folded over her stomach. She looked quite natural from the waist up unless you noticed that her head was pillowed on her neatly folded shorts. From the waist down, she was quite naked, no sign of her panties anywhere. Consulting the initial missing person's report that the crime scene guys had supplied, Theo concluded that his victim was Paige Langford, the younger of the two girls.

"Dark blond hair, pink shorts, lilac t-shirt, small for her age." Theo shook his head as he mentally amended the stock phrase. *And she will never get any bigger,* he thought. *Not now.*

Still outside the line, Theo walked over to the other body. In contrast to Paige's peaceful pose, this girl, who had to be Paige's friend, Holly Putzier, had suffered gross indignities. For one thing, somebody, probably one of the people who found her, had hurled on the body. For another, animals had already started to dismantle the corpse. Theo himself had to fight to keep from vomiting as flies buzzed through the vomit and about the child's empty eye sockets.

But even before Holly had been violated by the joggers and the local wildlife, her murderer had displayed a far different attitude toward her. Her mouth gaped open. Her eyes, obviously, had been opened, which allowed the bugs and flies to crawl inside her body.

She had been wearing shorts with a Tweetie-Pie appliqué on one pocket and pink nylon panties underneath. Both garments were twisted around her ankles with damp, rotting leaves stuck to them. Her whole body lay contorted as if she had been tossed awkwardly on the ground. The killer had made no effort to straighten the corpse or arrange her extremities, which accounted for the child's final indignity. As she fell, her matching Tweetie-Pie t- shirt had apparently caught on the fallen tree branch that lay at a right angle to her torso. The branch had pulled up the right side of her shirt to disclose one small, vulnerable breast.

Theo had been so preoccupied gathering first impressions that he failed to notice the Stone Mountain Police sergeant standing just outside the tape, obviously waiting for Theo to finish. Theo introduced himself, apologizing since he should have gone to the sergeant first, and then the bodies. No sense stepping on toes. "I've too much of a one-track mind sometimes," Theo explained. "You did a good job holding off the hordes. It could make a big difference."

"We try," the sergeant replied. "I've been here awhile. A jogger called it in at 7:30 this morning. There were actually two guys running together. The one that literally fell over the body had an asthma attack. They both upchucked. It was a real mess. We had to call for medical aid for the joggers, would you believe? I ended up sending the one who couldn't breathe to the E.R."

Still keeping outside the crime scene tape, Theo led the sergeant toward the girl by the tracks, the one identified as Paige Langford.

"There's no question these are the girls reported missing from the laser show. The clothes are identical," the sergeant continued as they reached her.

After asking the sergeant to continue guarding the line, Theo ducked under it and cautiously walked over to the Langford girl's body. He kept his eyes on the ground ahead of him to keep from stepping on anything foreign to the scene. Seeing nothing, he knelt beside the body. There were fingermarks on both sides of her small, fragile neck, a textbook strangulation. He saw what he thought to be faint ligature marks around her wrists and ankles, though there was no sign of what she might have been tied up with.

As he leaned closer, Theo gratefully realized that his nose had overdosed on death and decaying vegetation. He could no longer smell much of anything. He saw a small droplet by the child's left eye. It rested on the slope of her cheekbone. Odd. A tear would have long since slid to the ground and dried. Theo took his Swiss Army knife out of his pocket, unfolded the longest of three blades and poked at the clear little tear. It was hard, set like sap on a tree truck. Instead of peeling off the skin, it pulled it. Very gently, Theo reached down to her left eye and tried to open the lids. They did not move. Neither did her lips, he discovered a moment later.

"Jesus!" Theo muttered to himself as he sat back on his haunches, forking up his knife. "The son of a bitch glued her mouth and eyes shut!"

Theo cautiously walked away from the body using the same path he had when he entered. The sergeant joined him at the tape. Together, they approached the Putzier girl's body. Theo was less concerned about the contamination now because the joggers had already completely thrashed the ground around it.

"I figure there had to be two people," the sergeant said. "The bodies were treated so differently. Besides, I saw fingermarks on this one's neck." He nodded toward Holly. "If there's only one of you, how can you strangle two girls?"

The sergeant was right about the fingermarks. It looked like the killer, or killers, had also wrung Holly's neck. Her eyes and mouth were open though. *She might have been choked in mid-scream,* Theo thought. There were ligature marks on her wrists and ankles also, more clearly defined than on the other body. *She fought more? Longer?* Unfortunately, there was no sign of whatever had been used to truss her up either.

An immediate part of the investigation would be to canvass for twine, wire maybe, since the marks were thin, and anyone who might have heard Holly scream. They were pretty deep in the brush though, with the only nearby public landmark, the playground, where it was unlikely that anyone would have been lingering after dark. Theo thought that finding a witness, even just someone who had heard noises, was slim.

As he scanned Holly's body for a second time, he saw the string – just a couple of inches of it hanging between her labia. *A tampon?* Holly, heavier and curvier than little Paige, could have been old enough to menstruate. Theo made a mental note to ask the medical examiner if she had been having a period at the time of her death. This reminded him of another unpleasant task ahead of him. He would have to attend these two autopsies. Usually you sent the detective with the least seniority over to the examiner's office, particularly when the bodies were ripe, but for a double child murder (and Theo recognized the killings as indisputably murder), Theo had to go. He would need every scrap of information, if not to find the killers, then to defend his conduct of the case from the parents, the media, the county CEO, the Chief – no question. Kids were hell.

Keeping that in mind, he devised a plan of attack for the Stone Mountain Sergeant. Calling him to one side, he said "We need to get everybody extraneous" – he nodded toward other uniforms – "out of here so the crime scene people can finish up as fast as possible because when they're done, I need a grid search. I'm also going to need every warm body available to canvass for witnesses, but the first thing we have to find out is whether they were killed here or brought in from somewhere else so that grid search is extremely important."

The sergeant nodded his agreement. Theo thought he detected the sergeant's relief at being presented with a clear-cut task. "There are ligature marks on both girls. Did you find anything that might have been used to tie them up?" Theo continued.

"Not a thing," said the sergeant. "I'd swear there was nothing here except their own clothes."

"I'm going to need your help to get a command post set up over by the crime scene van. We've got a mobile CP unit I can call in for you."

The sergeant nodded again, but more hesitantly.

Theo doubted that he had ever participated in such a setup. Fortunately, he could trust his detectives to actually get everything started while keeping the sergeant busy. This killed two birds with one stone. The sergeant would get useful homicide training and Theo would have an extra body to protect the scene.

Actually, Theo had another agenda in mind, too. With the sergeant busy in the command post, he would be free to walk the area alone. Theo worked best that way. He needed quiet and he needed to look at everything one more time in silence. Something he missed initially might have import. Walking a scene alone while it was fresh had made all the difference on more than one occasion in Theo's career. This case was already looking like he would need every break he could get.

Eventually, Theo returned to his car just as the medical examiner's van arrived to transport the bodies. Nothing surfaced as Theo took his solitary stroll around the now deserted playground, down the embankment, over the tracks and along the right-of-way for the parks excursion train. He doubted the girls had been moved for he saw no signs of dragging and no foreign objects on the brush, which was thick enough to pose a problem for the murderer anyway, if he had tried to haul the bodies from elsewhere. It also seemed unlikely that their attacker had encountered the girls at the death site. The spot was a long way from the concession area and not a normal congregating place for teenagers. That meant that the killer had managed to lure not one, but two responsible, well-disciplined girls away from where they were, into the woods after dark. Very bad. The girls weren't afraid of him and trusted him. Theo saw planning, intelligence and cunning in what was shaping up as the homicide's modus operandi. Also – he hated to think about this, but it was logical – the scene was professional. This guy knew what he was doing. He had done this before. *Where was this guy from? And, what had he done before?*

––––––––––––

THEO REED 5

Theo's desk sergeant was prescient, as usual. There were two calls on his voice mail when he finally made it back to his apartment, midafternoon. One from his sister, the other from his chief. As the sergeant had so accurately hypothesized, the parents had identified the bodies, the father screamed at the county CEO, the CEO screamed to his Chief of Police, and now it was Theo's turn.

Usually, he would put off replying to Coretta as long as possible because when she called on Sunday, it was almost always to respond to their mother's complaints about Theo's shortcomings. His sister really didn't understand how much more demanding Mama had become since Coretta had moved to New York to complete her residency.

Mama, immensely proud of her little "orphan child," as she called her doctor daughter, was always cheerier when Coretta managed to fly home to Atlanta for a visit. Theo got the brunt of Mama's depression the rest of the time. He didn't rate "orphan child" status either. Well, maybe that was fair. He had been a senior in high school when Daddy died. After that, Theo finished growing up in a hurry. Coretta, only ten then, really was a child.

Theo learned a lot in a hurry the first few months after his father died. Despite being married to a cop for nearly twenty years, apparently Mama had always ignored the possibility that something could happen to Daddy. She hadn't even acquainted herself with the family finances before his daddy's death. A seventeen year old in a watch cap with a nylon stocking pulled over his face just like in TV, had killed Theo's father a block from the *7-11 Convenience Store* that he had robbed moments before.

Daddy didn't know that, of course. He had pulled the car over for speeding. When he approached the driver's side window, the kid shot him in the face, point blank and drove away. Daddy died before he hit the pavement.

Theo started, suddenly aware that he had been standing unmoved by the phone for five minutes, remembering all that ancient history, the football scholarship he had to turn down after Daddy's death, the community college he attended for the two years instead, in order to get on the force as quickly as possible. There had been just enough money for that and no more.

Fortunately, Theo had wanted to be a cop as long as he could remember, so he wasn't giving up all his dreams, though he regretted not being able to play college ball and the end of his football career. He remained passionate for the game, attending those Morehouse open scrimmages whenever he could.

Mama had done the best she could. To supplement Daddy's pension, she got a part-time sales job while Coretta was in school. She really hadn't been trained for anything so there was no question that the burden of support would eventually fall on Theo. Even then it was obvious that Coretta was smart as a whip. That mind demanded an education.

Theo recalled that Mama hadn't been a burden the first years after Daddy died. She had worked five mornings a week, participated in the Shiloh Baptist Church choir, gone shopping with friends, even packed picnics for the three of them to take to Stone Mountain once in a while. She had sad times, but not like she suffered now. The bitterness and isolation gradually overwhelmed her after Coretta had gone to college. What Mama referred to as "the nervous chills, like somebody's walkin' on your grave, but it lasts..." had finally forced her retirement. Her slide downhill into ever present gloom began shortly thereafter.

Theo understood the gloom. He lived with it himself far too often, clearly his mother's child. Coretta was the one who took after Daddy.

He stared at the phone. He had to return those calls. The Chief would want to know a thousand things that his head detective couldn't yet answer. Theo took the path of least resistance. Blood was thicker than water. He punched in his sister's New York number.

Coretta sounded cheerful, as always. Daddy used to say she was born happy. "So what did you think of breakfast today?" she asked as soon as he said hello.

"The usual, Coretta. Except that today, Mama told me she dreamed about me lying dead," Theo replied tartly. "She really knows how to cheer me up."

Coretta laughed ruefully. "Too true, Big Brother." She paused a moment and then broached the real subject, "Could you spend more time with her, Theo? She sounded just devastated that you had to leave early today. I understand you're busy, but..." Coretta's voice trailed away. She knew what she was asking. "Oh, Theo, I realize what a drag Mama can be, but remember, we talked about this before I left. I wouldn't have come to New York if I'd realized just how much time she would have alone. I could have stayed at Grady Memorial Hospital instead! You promised me that it was okay for me to come here, that you would take up the slack."

"And then I got promoted and I couldn't turn that down, Coretta. That would have been professional suicide. Besides, I need the money," Theo responded, trying not to get angry. "Daddy's pension doesn't go up with the cost of living, you know. He died before those cost of living allowances came into play. So the pension barely covers Mama's taxes, the house note and her medications." Theo fell silent, seizing the moment to cool off. None of this was his sister's fault. He continued in a softer tone, "Coretta, today I had a double homicide

— two twelve year old girls — at Stone Mountain. It may make the national news. There was nothing I could do except what I did, which was to leave Mama early. And she does see me at least once a week, always. Whether I like it or not. Mostly not, lately."

"Theo, don't lie to me," Coretta said. "Mama says you've hardly been by in months, that she's not left her house for days at a time."

Theo took a deep breath and he could feel his chiseled jaw begin to tighten. This was a new development. Mama always complained, but she had never made things up before. Maybe her memory was going.

"Coretta, she may not have left the house, but that's her choice. God knows, I've tried to get her out more often. Believe me, it would be easier for me to take her to a movie than to sit and listen to what's wrong with her life. I go over every Sunday. *Every* Sunday, rain or shine. If for some reason I cannot make breakfast, I get there later. And I talk on the phone with her nearly every day. Once a month, *at least*, I insist we go to dinner somewhere, though that gets harder all the time. You practically have to bodily haul her out of the house now. And I know for a fact that she told Florence Johnson she was going to be out of town the last three times Florence tried to come visit. *Our mother travel?* And pigs fly. Florence knows that, too. She finally called me to ask if she had done anything to offend Mama."

Florence Johnson was Mama's most faithful friend, a member of the same Sunday School class in the days when Mama still went to church. It was Coretta's turn for silence. Finally, she responded, worry clearly apparent in her voice, "Oh my dear Lord! Is she exaggerating, do you think? Or, does she have dementia? Does she really believe you don't come by?"

Theo didn't know what to think. He would have sworn that their mother was just miserable and complaining more. It hadn't occurred to him that she might be slipping into dementia, even Alzheimer's.

Suddenly Coretta was all business. "Theo, I'll call Dr. Freedman, get Mama scheduled for a complete workup, neurological, psychiatric, the whole nine yards. Once I know the dates, I'll arrange a week's family leave here, come home and take her to the procedures myself.

We'll get to the bottom of this," she said reassuringly. "You know, even severe depression can cause delusions sometimes. It's treatable these days. This could be a blessing in disguise, a way to get Mama to face her problems. In the meantime, I'll call more often, just to check and see if everything is going okay. And Theo, I'm sorry for getting on your case. I didn't handle it right. I love you. I'll be in touch. Bye!"

Theo felt both alarm and relief at his sister's conclusions. On the one hand, Mama might be really ill. A wave of guilt assaulted him. He should have noticed what was going on instead of blaming Mama for whining constantly. On the other hand, he wouldn't be entirely by himself with the problem anymore.

For the first time, he realized Coretta was finally an adult. He had been her surrogate parent for so long that it never occurred to him that she could now lend a hand. Theo noticed a moment of regret as he contemplated the reality of his sister, Dr. Coretta Reed, consulting on a case. Then he smiled at the contradiction. Coretta had always contended he was a control freak. Guess she was right. The idea that she was taking charge would take some getting used to.

Theo's second call, the one to the Chief, did not proceed as well. "*Now* I've heard from the Governor too," Malcolm Ballard stated. "Forrest Langford is a shirttail relative. And a heavy contributor. We got to look busy on this real fast. What have you got?"

Theo's boss was not pleased to that hear that his department had squat. Theo liked Ballard. The man played as much politics as was absolutely necessary to stay Chief. He was, underneath the title, a career officer who put his men first and had more than once stood up to the county administrator who appointed him. Nevertheless, when you were fielding gubernatorial intervention almost before the bodies were cold, the situation demanded diplomatic response and hopefully, some prompt results.

"So what's the game plan?" Ballard queried. Theo was grateful that he asked for Theo's plan instead of devising one of his own.

"Stone Mountain seems happy to let us direct them."

"That's a relief," Ballard replied. "One less damn thing to waltz around."

"I've got a mobile command up and running, I should have the results of a grid search soon, and we're canvassing for witnesses," Theo responded. "I'll go to the autopsies myself. They are the first two on the ME's schedule – I got them pushed up as a priority. When I've got the findings, I'll know more about where to head next, though obviously, if the search turns up anything or we find a witness, we'll be running with that."

Ballard wasn't fooled. "Theophilus, you got any ideas at all?" he asked. Chief Ballard was the only human on earth, other than Mama, that Theo would tolerate using his entire given name. Mama had had highfaluting aspirations for her firstborn.

"Not many, and I don't like the ones I have, to tell you the truth," Theo responded. "This surely does look like a random attack. The girls were a little too young to have lives of their own. The parents say they didn't hang out with older kids either. The first problem is that the bodies were treated very differently. One was almost ritually laid out, the other tossed on the ground like trash. That makes it seem like two killers. On the other hand, two random killers working together are scarcer than hen's teeth. But if we've only got one guy, we've got another whole set of questions. How did one guy strangle two girls? Wouldn't one child high-tail it as soon as she saw what was going down? It looks like the girls were lured to the murder site, too. It's in the middle of nowhere. That says preplanning to me and that, I hate. Preplanned murders are done by more organized, experienced killers and organization makes them harder to ID. Then again, it also indicates that the girls may have known their killer and willingly gone with him. That might make him easier to find. Just on the face of it, there's a lot of contradictions."

Ballard sighed. "That's something the governor does not need to hear. Let's see what the autopsies turn up. I'll make nice to our Fearless Leader. Call me tomorrow."

THE AUTOPSIES 6

Theo could read the headlines on the *Journal-Constitution's* front page: *Killer in the Park,* without bending down to pick the paper up out of his doorway. That alone told him it would be a very long day. Bad enough that Theo had a double homicide. Worse, the victims were children.

This Monday was obviously a slow news day, and that was bad news for Theo. The *Journal-Constitution* covered almost nothing else on its front page. Ballard had released what Theo had recognized as the most noncommittal statement possible, "Both Stone Mountain and DeKalb County Police are exhaustively examining the murder scene and the evidence. Both organizations have every reason to believe we will quickly and see developments..."

Ballard seldom told a straight lie either. "Examining the evidence" came powerfully close. *What evidence? The man must really be pushed,* Theo decided. There were photos of the death scene, the playground, the parents, the girls, interviews with one of the children's teachers, one of the joggers who found the body (the asthmatic lawyer) and a friend of Paige.

Theo concluded her parents must have oatmeal for brains. Then he scanned the three separate sidebars on other notable Atlanta child murders. Two of them unsolved, he noted gloomily. The reporters had far, far too much information on the actual murder scene, too. Somebody was talking who shouldn't. Nobody reported the glue on the eyelids, a detail Theo fervently hoped to keep quiet, but otherwise, the descriptions of clothing, location and probable cause of death seemed disturbingly accurate.

Theo looked again at the sidebars where the paper had listed the three child murders. The biggest solved case was the Wayne Williams child murder case. That had been a particularly brutal case with a large number of young missing boys. Fortunately, Williams had been caught and convicted. Officials had set up a task force among several metro Atlanta jurisdictions. That task force was still loosely intact and was the reason Theo had been called in on this case. Investigation of potentially big cases involving children was set up to rotate among the few larger police agencies in the Atlanta area.

His answering machine had logged six calls from reporters since yesterday afternoon. They would probably manage to corner him today, but the longer he put them off, the happier he would be. Fortunately, he could sneak unnoticed into the Medical Examiner's Office using the freight elevator.

That would buy him time with the press but it didn't make attending the autopsies any less disagreeable, of course. No matter how many bloody messes he dealt with in the street, nothing shocked him as much as watching the pathologist apply a power saw to somebody's skull like it was firewood. Try as he might to think of the lifeless body as just the meat left behind, when Theo observed a post-mortem, he could not get past the feeling that he was watching the work of a civil servant from hell. The examiners scooped the entrails from the victim as if it were dressing out a deer. They were, of course, much more precise than sport hunters. They measured organs, sectioned tissue, looked for gross and fine bodily markers, but to Theo it was still horrifying, particularly the moment the pathologist began to reassemble the remains, using large, utilitarian stitches that left nothing to the imagination about how dead his patient was. Theo wondered darkly how much of a "nervous spell" Mama might have if exposed to this aspect of his job. Advanced decay made the experience even worse. Paige and Holly were ripe. Theo put a tube of Vick's Vaporub in his suit pocket. He never used the stuff when he had a cold, just when he had to go to the Medical Examiner's Office. The menthol cut the smell.

A person could not have asked for a lovelier late August day, Theo noted ironically as he walked out of his townhouse door to the double garage for which he paid an extra fifty dollars a month. A minor front had blown through in the night, sweeping out Atlanta's humidity and lowering the temperature a good fifteen degrees. It was a great day to go anywhere other than to an autopsy.

Inside Theo's garage were two vehicles, a five year old Camry, the one that usually ran as a dull, but dependable workhorse, as *Road and Track* described it, and one that usually didn't, Theo's beloved Avanti, which he was slowly restoring to pristine condition. Since his appointment as chief of detectives, he had gotten nothing done on the Studebaker. *Maybe this winter when, hopefully, things slowed down a bit,* he thought, knowing quite well that he was indulging in wishful thinking. Still, a man could dream.

When he arrived at the Examiner's, the grief counselor offered him a cup of coffee. Not only was Theo never comfortable with autopsies, but his stomach disliked them even more so. Theo declined despite the fact that the woman made excellent coffee, the best he ever got in a governmental office. Theo suspected the skill was included in her job description. He applied a thick moustache of Vick's as he entered the autopsy room. Having been through several autopsies throughout his career, he was familiar not only with the smell of formaldehyde but also the smell of bodies in several states of decay. He knew the Vicks would help mask the smell.

As always, the entire room had a smell of death. It was always creepy. Theo was pleased to see that Harley Ewing, the senior pathologist, had drawn the task of autopsying the two girls. Harley's twenty years' experience couldn't hurt. He seldom missed a trick.

He was doing Paige first. She lay face up, tiny on the steel table designed to accommodate larger bodies. The little girl still wore her lilac tank top. Each of her hands were enclosed in a lunch-sized paper bag, a routine procedure done at the scene to prevent the loss of any material that might be lodged under her fingernails. Below the waist, the victim was naked, her shorts and shoes already cataloged and sent to the Georgia Bureau of Investigation Crime lab. The wisp of remaining clothing – and her encased hands – emphasized the child's vulnerability. Theo would have been more comfortable, the picture more natural, if she had no garments on at all.

The examiner carefully removed the tank top. Speaking into an overhead mike, he recited Paige's gender, external measurements, weight, height, color of hair, state of nutrition and muscle development, then he made his initial observations of the surface of the body, looking for obvious abnormalities. He described the neck bruises Theo had spotted at the scene. He also found the faint lines around Paige's wrists and ankles, but found nothing else of note. An old, well-scratched mosquito bite on one forearm, a small birthmark on the right shoulder blade. As the pathologist worked around the body, the department photographer snapped a series of close-ups of the child to document each finding. Only after he was finished with the basic description did the examiner attack the first real anomaly about Paige's glued-shut eyes.

"Epoxy, most likely," Ewing said, carefully slitting open the child's eyelids with a scalpel. "And strangulation," he continued, pulling one down to disclose the evidence. Theo saw the small hemorrhages, petechial, on the eye's inner lining, a classic indicator of asphyxia. The ME found another when he slit open the glued lips. Paige had badly bitten her tongue.

He checked the interior of her mouth and ears, looking for signs of trauma, and then took swab samples from the mouth and cheek looking for presence of semen. Theo backed away from the body for a moment to regain equilibrium. The Vick's wasn't doing its job. From the somewhat less intimate vantage point, he watched Harley run a laser over the body. The ruby light brought out marks unnoticeable to the naked eye. In Paige's case, it clearly showed fingernail marks on both sides of her neck. The photographer moved in on those while the doctor progressed down the little girl's torso. On her belly, the laser illuminated a large patch of a dried foreign protein, almost undoubtedly semen. Harley carefully scraped off samples, transferring the evidence to slides, which he would use for DNA, and secreter/non-secreter testing anything else he could culture from the dried fluid that might make a case.

Ewing completed his non-invasive procedures by swab-sampling the child's vagina and anus as part of a pelvic/rectal exam that disclosed Paige's intact hymen and the absence of foreign bodies in her rectum. Their boy committed sex crimes all right, but penetration didn't seem too high on his list of desires. Theo was both relieved and disappointed at the last finding. Anal violations sometimes turned up evidence still lodged in the body.

Ewing washed the child's body. Theo thought he detected an uncharacteristic tenderness toward Paige's remains as the ME gently cleaned her. Usually, the pathologist brusquely scrubbed as if he were cleaning vegetables. Theo unobtrusively backed another couple of feet from the autopsy table. He knew what was coming next. He never got used to it. Ewing peeled the skin back from her skull so he could saw through to the brain. Finding nothing of note, he moved down to the abdominal cavity, making a large incision on the child's median line. As Ewing proclaimed to the overhead mike that the subject's ovaries were immature and the uterus non-gravid, Theo fought his rising gorge. Exposing the guts always loosened an odor that he could never quite tolerate, a stomach turning mixture of feces and decay. He fumbled for an ammonia capsule (his second line of defense after the Vaporub) and broke it under his protesting nose.

Looking at Theo, the pathologist asked, "You okay?" Embarrassed, Theo just nodded.

The pathologist uncovered nothing further that was useful. All they had were the semen samples, which would be invaluable if they ever had a suspect, but until then, Theo had zilch. Ewing thought the glue had been applied after the girl had died because it had been so precisely and tidily done. "Like the son of a bitch was putting on eyeliner," Harley commented. "That would have been damn near impossible if she were thrashing around." He also hypothesized that the killer had masturbated over the corpse, then smeared the ejaculate. *It didn't take a genius to figure that out,* Theo thought. He hoped Holly's corpse would disclose more.

In the interim, Harley had regained his usual cynicism. "I believe your boy got really pissed off at this one," he said to Theo as he proceeded to examine Holly. "The hemorrhaging is more pronounced, the fingermarks deeper. See?"

Theo was forced to take a closer look. Ewing was right. The bruises on Holly's neck stood out clearly, nothing like the faint marks they had noticed on Paige. "Wrung her neck like a chicken's," Ewing continued, his dissection revealing deep trauma to the older girl's trachea. Unfortunately, while the killer had been more brutal, he had been more careless. She had not been raped (in fact, there was no semen present at all, not even on her skin), the debris that clung to her clothes was characteristic of the location where the girls had been found and none of her clothes appeared missing.

"This one either fought more or made her move before he tied her up," Ewing said, pointing at one of Holly's ankles. Theo could clearly see the ligature lines. "The bindings left deeper marks. And I'll bet you he used electricians' ties. I saw the same kind of damage last week on a prisoner who died in that county sheriff's custody, the one down in South Georgia. They used that plastic stuff, too."

As the pathologist concluded the internal exam, he noted that the Putzier girl, although an intact virgin, was sexually more mature and had been menstruating when she was killed. Theo suspected that had a bearing on the difference in the way the bodies were treated. He couldn't exactly say why – purely a hunch, so far – but Theo believed that there was only one killer who had, for reasons that might eventually get him caught, treated the two girls very differently. He would explore this further.

The nausea caught him unprepared. He felt the bile begin making its way into his stomach. Theo did not make it a habit of throwing up at autopsies. It was amateur and embarrassing. And, in this case, very necessary. He barely made it to the men's room, his mouth already full of vomit as he leaned over the toilet.

7

SATURDAY

*H*e sat mesmerized in the dark, quiet cave of his living room. Covering the windows with that brown curtain fabric he bought at Sears did the trick. The stuff was almost as thick as awning canvas. On sale, too. He had never much cared for bright light. So it was ironic that he had, once again, settled in the sunny south.

White Man liked the West, the open spaces, the drier air, but Atlanta had its advantages. Winter was bearable, for one thing, and for another, he had a pleasant job. Couldn't ask for things to be much better. Work he liked, a nice house, idiot co-workers.

The girl's panties were nylon, his favorite. Cotton might be more hygienic for their little bottoms, but nylon was the stuff for him. Smooth. Soft. It draped over his hand, over his balls. Legs spread, leaning back in the Lay-Z-Boy he stroked himself, first slowly, then inevitably, faster. Friday's caper had been so very exciting. *So easy.* At first, he had planned to avoid the two because they were together. *What a pity.* Separately, they would have been ideal candidates. Then he had reasoned, "So why don't I spend money on a little insurance?" which he had. Then, he struck up a conversation with them. It was easy to be interested in what they had to say because, of course, he was interested in what he planned to do. A bit of patience with twelve-year-old gossip and it yielded big, big dividends.

He tilted back further in the recliner, enjoying the moment just a bit too much. "Slow down, kiddo," he said to himself, forcing his nylon-sheathed hand into a lighter, more languid motion. That was better. He had all afternoon. *Make it last.*

The little bitches said they came to use the restroom by the concession stand, but he knew better than that. They walked down by the depot looking for boys. The restroom was a convenient excuse. See, they were all hunters together. He was just better at it. Apparently, the girls' quarry had strayed because they seemed quite willing to talk to him instead. In the intervening minutes, he discovered that Paige didn't have the hots for anybody specific, but that somebody named Mike Gordon, a mature lad of nearly fourteen was deeply interested in Holly. Holly was borderline. Next year, the breasts would be too big, her scent too female to really interest him. Paige though, now there was a Georgia peach.

He gasped, his hand having involuntarily speeded up as he visualized the smaller girl. He forced himself to breath deeply, savor the moment, skate on the edge.

Such delicious subjects. They even pretended obedience, seemed dutiful, the best kind. *Who wanted obvious sluts?* He liked the babies' genteel veneer. That so excited him. Once they finally said they had to go back to Paige's parents, that the adults would be worried, he had controlled his ecstasy and buckled down to work, played them like the barely hooked trophy fish they were.

"I'll come with you," he volunteered. "After all, you can't be too careful." He continued to ask them questions, even about the dreary Mike Gordon, as he herded them along the railroad right-of-way that dissected the park's exhibition lawn. If he could keep them moving, he might get them past most of the crowd before they realized they were not headed to quite the right location. If they did notice his detour, he would simply apologize for his lousy sense of direction. *Nothing ventured, nothing gained.*

Fortunately, the girls apparently had no sense of direction at all. In only a couple of minutes, they were nicely confused as to exactly where Paige's parents might be waiting for them.

When they had walked well beyond the laser show – and the girls were completely turned around – he suggested that they all go to his car and he would drive them to where the Langford's had parked. He even volunteered to stay with them until Beverly and Forrest arrived. Being lost upset the girls. Paige said her Dad was going to kill her. He patiently soothed them, "I'll vouch for you," he reassured them. "You just got turned around in the dark. It happens to everybody sometime." He assured them that it was better to wait for the Langford car than to wander around a crowd of 20,000 people in the dark, that Daddy Forrest would understand such a sensible action. It occurred to neither girl to return to the concession stand instead, where it was not so dark, *and why should it?* They were safe with him.

So they walked east on the railroad right of way. He took out his little Maglite, the one that fit into his pocket, and directed its beam on the tracks ahead. The train didn't run during the show. He knew an excellent spot. It looked quite legitimate from the roadbed – there was a small parking area nearby – but after dark, nobody came near the place.

As they walked, Holly foolishly questioned him about how far they had to go. *Whiner!* He fought his temper, didn't want to spook them now. That one was gonna be a little ball-breaker real soon. Where he was going was none of her damned business. A good thing she had come to him this summer. Another six months older and he might have hit her. That would, of course, have scared the tastier prey, his little peach.

"Not to worry," he said to them. "We're just about there. It's right this way." He led the girls off the tracks and down a path into the bushes. They walked in single file. He took the lead, guiding his tender morsels to their destiny. *They were really remarkable,* he mused to himself. The night was very dark. Holly stumbled.

"Up you come," he said, helping her back to her feet.

"It's really dark. Are we lost?" Holly asked. She sounded nervous.

Briefly, he showed the Meglite on her instead of the track. In the beam, he could see that she was chewing her lower lip apprehensively.

"Not at all," he said cheerily as he led them back into the trees. Behind them he heard the laser show's heavy duty ordinance kick in, the fireworks that ended the show. *Good.* He would have half an hour of noise and confusion in his favor as the crowd scattered, heading to their cars.

"This is far enough," he announced, stopping in the middle of the little clearing, the flashlight making a small pool of light at the girls' feet. There were irregular flashes overhead from the exploding shells, faintly lighting the clearing.

For the first time, he saw the fear in their faces.

Instinctively, they huddled close to each other. *Little lambs. The big bad wolf's gonna eat you all up. Starting now.*

"Take off your shorts," he said.

"You've got to be kidding," Holly replied. Paige looked frightened.

He had become a bit nasty then, needed to at some point, or they got too feisty.

"Shut the fuck up," he told Holly as he backhanded her. Remembering the moment, there in his chair, he almost lost it. He took a breath, regained control. *Savor the moment, boy.*

The blow had knocked Holly down. She was terrified, her eyes big like a deer's caught in the flashlight's beam. *Spotlight hunting! So unsporting, but oh, how he loved it.*

Out of the corner of his eye, as the fireworks finale lit up the night, he saw Paige edging away toward the trees. *Time for insurance.* Keeping the flashlight in his left hand, he pulled the little revolver, his ladies' gun *for young ladies only,* out of his right hand pocket.

"Get over here, Paige, and behave yourself," he instructed firmly. "Otherwise, Holly will get hurt. Obey orders and you'll both be on your way home an hour from now."

He held the gun up to the light for just a moment so Paige could see it. She crept back toward him, head lowered, then stood next to her friend, sobbing. Holly, bravado gone, joined her in tears.

"All right, that's better. Take off your shoes and shorts."

Holly was first, he thought. He planned peaches for dessert.

"Paige, stand right there," he directed. "Holly, lie down on your back and spread your legs like a good girl. I need to examine you." Holly whimpered, her terror making it clear that she was still very young. Obedient now, she lay down, oblivious to the twigs and leaves beneath her. That's when he spotted the string in the little flashlight beam.

"Shit. Is that a tampon up your twat?" he asked.

Holly looked dazed, not comprehending what he was saying.

"What have you got stuck up you?" he repeated, moving closer.

"Don't hit me. Please," she answered. "I'm having my period."

Rage flashed through him. *Filth. Decay. Women were sewers.* It was the punishment of God that man had to stick themselves into something so unclean to maintain the race. He would forego that pleasure, thank you very much. *Careful though, now. Don't scare the pretty.* Fortunately, he always had Plan B. Always. That's what separated common thrill seekers from a true enthusiast and professional such as himself.

He directed Paige to his right hand pocket where he kept his electrician's ties, then ordered her to bind Holly's feet together at her ankles with one of them. Gun trained on both of them, he told Paige to give Holly another tie from his pocket. Then he made the older girl lash up the ankles of the younger one. Finally, he instructed Paige to put her hand behind her back, and had Holly firmly tie Paige's wrists together.

"Put your panties in your mouth," he instructed. "Stuff them in." Paige locked her jaws. "Open your mouth or I'll blow it open," he said, gesturing with the little lady's gun. Paige opened her mouth. Frantically, Holly stuffed her underwear between her friend's teeth.

With his peach secured, he could deal with the housekeeping tasks, dispose of the dirt. He walked to Holly, told her to turn away from him. She awkwardly hopped to do his bidding. Then he told her to put her hands behind her back. He tucked the gun into his pocket, then with the flashlight in his teeth – it was such a nice size – he bound up her wrists, too. Then he let the light drop. Meglights – so sturdy – were worth every penny.

He casually grabbed Holly by the throat with both hands, picked her up off the ground and shook her like a Rottweiler enjoying a toy poodle. *It was all in the wrists, don't you know, that breaking twist that snapped the neck.* When she had been satisfyingly limp for two minutes, by his count, he let her fall and retrieved his light.

He would love to see the face of his sweet dessert, start to finish, but he needed both hands. She knew what was going to happen by then. He would always remember her look of fear as he flipped off his light. *Raw, primal fear. A bunny rabbit just before the wolf took it in his mouth.* He almost couldn't wait to touch himself, nearly came in his pants as he lovingly squeezed her fragile throat. *Two for one, even if one was a dud, was so stimulating, so satisfying.*

Afterwords, he took his time. A succulent treat demanded respect. He unbound the hands and removed the gag. Then he laid her out neatly before him as he very gently closed her mouth and eyes forevermore. Hair had just started to sprout on her pubis. He almost cried from the beauty of it as he sprayed her belly with ejaculate. Then, with shaking fingers, he painted his tribute across her tender skin.

White Man pressed himself deep into his chair, the memory of the night making his orgasm now inevitable. Afterward, he held the dead girl's semen soaked panties to his nose, inhaled the combined scents and licked the crotch clean. She had been a true Georgia peach.

THE PSYCHIATRIST

Theo called Aiden O'Brian as soon as he got back from the autopsies. Theo's disturbing impressions of the murder scene – the tidy lack of trace evidence, the beautifully isolated site near thousands of people – had solidified his grim suspicion as he watched Harley Ewing examine the bodies. Theo believed that there was only one man. Two people would have had a hard time maintaining the level of control he had observed at the site. His boy had managed to tie up the girls by himself without much of a struggle on their part and then had removed the ligatures before he left the woods. *Remarkably good planning.* He left Theo nothing to trace. There wasn't so much as one usable unmatched fiber on the bodies. The guy's semen was wonderful evidence, but only if Theo could reduce his possible suspects to a manageable number.

At the moment he didn't even *have* suspects. The easy solutions – violent boyfriends, vindictive ex-husbands – didn't apply. This left Theo thinking darkly about random sexual murder. He feared he was about to have every cop's worst nightmare, a motiveless stranger who killed children.

What he wanted right now was a drink in a bar full of friendly strangers, someplace where he could sit wrapped up in a tipsy goodwill, remote from the outside. What he was stuck doing instead was arranging a consultation with a forensic psychiatrist as soon as possible. In Theo's view, the best around was Aiden O'Brian. Theo had met him at Quantico, Virginia, when he took one of the FBI's advanced training programs for police officers.

O'Brian also consulted for the Bureau's National Center for the Analysis of Violent Crime. He specialized in sexual predators, an area that frequently overlapped serial murder. In the years since Theo had met him, O'Brian achieved his ten minutes of fame as a profiler who helped nail the "Congressional Rapist." O'Brian had always been good. His dead-accurate hypothesis about that rapist, a real character who preferred bestowing his favors on female Representatives, was just the frosting that upped his fee.

O'Brian had accepted a professorship at the Emory School of Medicine a couple of years before. Theo ran into him, literally, on the tennis court shortly after Aiden moved down from New York. Until recently the two had played together twice a week, their mutual interests complementing their athletic relationship. The two men loved fast, demanding games. Theo supposed that he should be grateful that somebody of Aiden's stature was local and a friend. Instead, he dreaded the meeting. Theo was a long-term, very attentive student of homicide. He already knew that Aiden was going to tell him things he didn't want to hear.

Aiden's secretary said he was with a class but that she would get him the message by noon. "You've been a stranger lately," she continued, teasing. "Shin splints? Tennis elbow?'

"Just too busy," Theo said. "I haven't been on the court once in the last two months."

"Oh," the secretary said in a more sober tone, "this a professional call, right, Detective Reed? I can call Dr. O'Brian out of class if it's urgent."

"No, no. After class will be fine, but yes, it is a professional call. I'd like to meet him as soon as possible. Today if fact, if that's an option."

"Sure thing, I'll get on it. One other thing, Detective..."

"Yes?"

"Go back to the courts. All work and no play. Well, you know the saying."

"I know," Theo said, his shoulders slumping and a heavy sigh coimng from deep in his lungs. Between Mamma and the Atlanta murder rate, he wasn't getting any exercise. *Oh, Lord! Mamma.* He had forgotten to phone her Sunday night to reassure her that he was just busy, not dead, injured, indifferent. He started to call her, then put the receiver back down. By this time he might as well be hung up in a noose somewhere. His mama would kill him. He would call tonight, without fail. Besides, he needed to take time to explain to her that the case was going to be very demanding, taking a lot of effort and time. Maybe he could forestall her inevitable disappointment over his absences. He wouldn't elaborate the details. That would definitely bring on one of Mama's chills. Perhaps he could convince her to visit with Florence Johnson. Nah, that was asking an awful lot of Florence after Mama's sorry behavior.

"It's the girls at Stone Mountain," Theo said to Aiden's secretary.

"I figured that was it. I've got you down for two this afternoon," the secretary said.

"See you then," Theo said as he walked out of the office.

Walking down the stairs from Aiden's office, Theo thought to himself, "To hell with it, I'll just go get him." There were times Theo did not take well to waiting. Especially when it was something he felt was important.

Aiden's "sex lectures" revolved around sex practices at the House of Wax or perhaps the Rue Morgue. He illustrated them with crime scene slides, autopsy photos and videotapes of perps who ranged all the way from Florida to Michigan.

There were all kinds of stories and descriptions. Stories about perps who claimed God had told them to send to heaven some poor little innocent girl who had been violated weekly. Or what about the stories of a pleasant rooming housekeeper who shared her bed with elderly clients until they agreed to sign over management of their social security checks. And there were cool sociopaths who raped when convenient and then killed their victims to shut their mouths.

The story of Alice Gandarte, the rooming housekeeper, was always a favorite at presentations. The police eventually found 41 of the former boarders buried in her large, lush back garden. The lady regularly won prizes for her flowers, especially the Iris. Her green thumb was a neighborhood legend.

Next was Richard Trenton Chase, who was known as the vampire killer. He murdered his victims, then drank their blood. Aidens' subjects were not nice people. Despite that, the theatre was always packed on lecture day. Many of the attendees were not students. *Strange,* Theo thought. It was his job to study remains. He hated it. At the same time, he was fascinated by such behavior. In contrast, an amazing number of apparently normal people who could have gone to a movie, slept in or studied for something else instead, enjoyed the gore, the lunacy and the recurrent amorality of forensic psychiatry.

Aiden encouraged them. He lectured cleverly and loved using a certain shock value. "They remember it better that way," he explained to Theo.

Aiden's own appearance, a shock of red hair that he apparently combed with a fork – added to the illusion of controlled mayhem, along with his casual wardrobe. In the summer, Aiden wore jeans, a t-shirt and the latest Nike running shoe. Running shoes were one thing in which the psychiatrist indulged himself. In winter, he added a tweed blazer for warmth. The Nikes were a sign of his addictions. Besides playing tennis, Aiden ran marathons.

"Developing a profile is like making any other diagnosis in medicine," Aiden was saying as Theo slipped into the back of the lecture hall. "You interview, you observe symptoms, you order lab work and, most important, you use your accumulated experience and that of your colleagues – *always* talk to your colleagues – to hypothesize, diagnose and treat. The difference in forensic psychiatry is that what you are diagnosing is the *nature* of the murderer and successful treatment is identifying him or her. Don't discount ladies, by the way. They get better all the time."

Aiden glanced at the clock in the rear of the hall. "And that's all folks. Feel free to email me with questions or you can come in and see me. I'm a unique specimen. I *do* honor office hours." A small giggle rippled through the audience.

Theo knew the constant complaint at the Med School was that the professors who were doctors – never a humble group – tended to blow off their drop-in hours by claiming that their time was too valuable given the small number of students that usually showed up.

O'Brian greeted Theo with a bear hug, then put his arm around the detective's shoulder. "Come on, pal," he said. "I ordered a Mellow Mushroom Special pizza. There's plenty for both of us. You look like hell. In fact, you look like you were shot at and missed and shit at and hit. That worry line above your nose could be permanent. How's your mama?"

"I'd rather talk about the case," Theo said, sighing.

"That bad, huh?" O'Brian looked questioningly at Theo as they walked out of the lecture hall doors and toward Aiden's office. "You know, there are new drugs that really work well on depression and anxiety without the side effects we used to struggle with."

"The side effect with Mama would be the number of bones broken by our trying to get the pills down her," Theo replied bleakly. Saying it, he realized his pessimism now rivaled Mama's. He forced a bit of attitude adjustment. "My sister Coretta – you remember her – she's a doctor now?'

O'Brian nodded.

"She's going to come home for a visit and get Mama evaluated. Coretta can usually sweet talk Mama into leaving the house. I'm hoping for some answers."

"Good," said O'Brian. "I know that will help you a lot."

They reached O'Brian's office. He unlocked the door then said to Theo as they walked inside, "Let me know how it goes. I was actually thinking of the pills for you. When Coretta gets some results from the tests, I might have some referrals for you and your mother. Aging can be touchy."

Aiden's secretary had left the large pizza box in the middle of his desk. The tantalizing smell from the rich tomato sauce and all the toppings wafted through the room. Theo's stomach growled and his mouth watered. He realized he had missed dinner the night before and then failed to keep down his breakfast. He was ravenous.

"So what have you got?" Aiden asked. He handed Theo a hefty slice of pizza piled high with various meats and vegetables.

Theo explained the girls' disappearance, the isolated murder site and the apparent lack of struggle, all the time wolfing down large bites of the pizza between sentences. He touched on the autopsy findings – the semen, the lack of penetration, the glue of Paige's eyes and lips.

Aiden listened and ignored his lunch. While Theo extracted another slice of pizza from the box, O'Brian asked, "How exactly were the bodies laid out? You said they were different?"

"The older girl was sprawled out haphazardly. She looked like she had been thrown down on the ground. Her eyes were open. Her clothing was scattered around. Everything had been trampled into the dirt, but that doesn't mean the killer did it because the joggers who found her, pretty much destroyed the scene around the body. That's why I keep saying *apparent* lack of struggle, but I think that's accurate because the younger girl's scene was pristine. The joggers didn't get that far. There's one thing I think is important. The older girl was menstruating, had a tampon in her vagina. It hadn't been disturbed. The younger girl was on the other side of the clearing and was more prepubescent. Now she had been carefully laid out, almost lovingly, like she was sleeping, hands folded across her chest. He tucked her shorts under her head for a pillow and not only did he close her eyes, but he glued them shut with Epoxy. Did the same with her mouth. Actually, as I think about it, maybe she wasn't supposed to be sleeping. Any mortician would lay her out the same way, you know, like on a bier." Theo paused for a moment, disturbed by this new insight.

Then, hunger won and he reached for another slice of pizza, then continued, "The killer obviously masturbated over her body because there was semen spread across her stomach. I think maybe he finger-painted her body with it. I brought you the photographs. It's a fairly bizarre scene. The two bodies were treated so differently."

O'Brian picked up the crime scene photographs. He stood up, still ignoring his lunch, and paced the room while staring at the pictures. Then he returned to the table, laid the pictures out and picked up the box with the remaining pizza, obviously intending to pitch it.

Theo stared wistfully at the disappearing pizza. O'Brian glanced up, saw his interest. "I'm sorry. Did you want the rest of this?" he asked. "My secretary shouldn't have ordered it. I'm in training. Pizza is not on the recommended list."

Theo thought of the five pounds he had recently put on, but reached for the pizza box anyway. "Thanks. It's delicious pizza," Theo said, "And I'm starving." As he opened it to pick up another piece, he resolved to get back to the tennis courts as soon as possible.

O'Brian studied the crime scene photos in order, first one girl, then the other. Then he minutely examined the autopsy shots of both victims' necks. He spent over an hour on the gristly collection, a great deal of that time going over all the views with a magnifying glass. Finally, he put the glass down and sat staring at the wall over Theo's left shoulder. Theo was used to this with O'Brian.

Theo thought, *I talk to walls. O'Brian stares at them.*

Another five minutes passed, then Aiden leaned back in his chair, locked his hands behind his head and propped his feet up on a blank spot on the table.

"You've got one killer, Theo," he said. "The girls were treated differently but the scene wasn't. It's very tidy, very controlled. I'm sure the guy picked the spot out long before the event. I know you're thinking what I am about that. Two girls each treated so differently."

Theo nodded. The suspicion had been nagging him all day. Such an organized solitary perp meant a veteran killer. Practice made perfect. Worse, serial murderers usually worked alone.

"I believe the second girl repelled him because she was menstruating. He probably sees her as dirty, defiled – he had no use for her which is why he threw her aside, probably literally. He's angry at her too." O'Brian paused, put his feet back down on the floor and then passed the autopsy neck shots across to Theo. "See how much more trauma there is to her trachea and esophagus compared to the other girl's. They both have ligature marks from where he restrained them, but the younger girl was strangled neatly, swiftly – with only as much force as was necessary to kill her. The menstruating girl has all kinds of bruising. I think he shook her by the neck, like a kitten who just messed on his rug."

O'Brian paused again and looked at the crime scene photos once more. "Theo, there's one bright spot in this. It's possible the girls knew the killer or at least one of them did. Could be that's just how he managed to kill them without more damage. This just doesn't look like a stranger murder to me. Oh, and he is almost undoubtedly Caucasian, probably in his thirties. I'm very much afraid he's done this before."

O'Brian closed his eyes, massaging them with thumb and forefinger. Opening them up again, he concluded, "I'd follow up on all the girls' contacts, their friends, you know, who they hung out with, but quickly, Theo. This probably wasn't a stranger murder, but there's no reason why the next one won't be. This one may give you the most coherent evidence that you'll ever get."

O'Brian glanced at the clock, winced and stood to leave. "I've got a class in five minutes. If I run, I'll make it. Leave me the photos. I want to look at them some more."

"O.K.," said Theo, eating the last of the pizza. "Thanks for your help, and the pizza."

"No problem," said Aiden. "And good to see you, Buddy. We have to get out on the tennis courts soon."

THE SEARCH BEGINS

9

Theo made it back to the office by 2:00. Wilma, his administrative aide, took one look at his face as he walked in and said, "I'm afraid it's not going to get any better this afternoon, either, Theo. You've got a pile of messages. Most of 'em from reporters, but the Chief called twice. He wants an update."

Although Theo was used to Wilma's warnings and had come to expect them, he still felt his stomach knot up when she made her announcement.

Theo appreciated Wilma's sympathy. She had been with the department for most of her adult life, starting in the secretarial pool just out of high school. Her expertise was by far the best perk that came with the Chief of Detective's title. What Wilma didn't know about the internal pecking order was not worth knowing. Theo suspected that she could also run a homicide investigation herself – start to finish, without any assistance.

As Theo paused to pick up the messages, she proved this yet again. "I called around the funeral homes this morning," she said. "The girls are both at McLaughlin's. Apparently they attended the same church.

They'll be buried at St. Jude's by The Mountain on Wednesday. It's an Episcopal church. McLaughlin's grief counselor thought it was a little unusual, a double funeral when they were not related, but they were best friends, and that might make your job easier."

Theo looked gratefully at Wilma. "Wilma, I'm not just talking when I say I don't know what I would do without you. Thank you."

"Want me to call the Chief's office?" Wilma asked.

Theo inwardly winced. Time to dodge and feint. "Not yet. I want to talk to the pastor at St. Jude's first."

Wilma nodded. She was Theo's age, unmarried, and although Theo knew it was wrong of him, he hoped she would stay that way. A change in her marital status might encourage a job change, too. Theo knew his office routine would degenerate to chaos without her. It was strange, actually, that Wilma hadn't married – she had the face of an Egyptian princess, Cinnamon colored skin, all high cheek bones and slightly slanted eyes. She was tall and slender. Quite beautiful, actually. Once, in an uncharacteristic moment (as a rule Wilma kept her private and professional lives strictly separate) she had mentioned to Theo how demanding she was about a choice of mate. "Your mother was lucky," she had said to him.

Theo had thought to himself, *If you only really knew my mother*, but he had kept his thoughts and comments to himself, perhaps out of embarrassment. His relationship with his mother was something he guarded closely, talking about her problems only with Coretta and Aiden O'Brian.

Wilma interrupted his reverie, "The rector of St. Jude's is Father Stephen Bainbridge. So, you want me to call him?"

"Father?" Theo asked.

"Yeah," she replied. Those Episcopals are sort of like Catholics except they can marry. You know it's all that Henry the 8th stuff."

"Er...right," Theo said, chuckling. "I doubt that has any bearing on our case. Don't call him. Just make an appointment for me to see him some time this afternoon."

Theo steeled himself for the visit. He hated this particular duty, which was trying to persuade the presiding minister into letting the police observe the funeral of the victims. Usually, he tried to get it done by phone and frequently, he failed, but in this case, it was extremely important that the department have a presence at the funeral. Sex murderers relished attending last rites the same way arsonists liked to hang around and watch the fire. If the girls were to be buried at the same time, the services would be more tempting for the perp.

Wilma stuck her head in the door five minutes later. "You're on for 4:00 p.m. today," she said. "Should I call the Chief, tell him you're still mopping up?" She stood on Theo's threshold, awaiting orders. Once upon a time, there had been a working intercom between the outer desk and Theo's office, but like many other things in Homicide Division, when it died, far more pressing things demanded the available discretionary funds.

At the time, as Theo had apologized for the inconvenience, and Wilma said the exercise was good for her. Theo couldn't see that she needed it. Wilma stood a willowy 5'9" tall. As far as he could recall, she hadn't varied a pound in nearly twenty years.

"The chief?" she repeated.

"Oh yes. Tell him I'm still in the field, that I'll get back to him this evening. And, Wilma?"

"Yes?"

"Run interference for me as long as you can. I'm really backed up on this."

Wilma nodded without comment. She knew the score.

St. Jude's At-the-Mountain was located a block off the road to Stone Mountain Park on an intersecting street that was primarily residential. The church, which sat on one or two landscaped acres, could not have been more than a half a mile from the entrance to the park itself.

Theo drove into the large, almost entirely empty parking lot that bordered the chalet-roofed main church building. Theo suspected the church's architect had been heavily under the influence of the 1970's when the place was put up. There were ships' prow windows for and aft on the main A-frame from which jutted two equally forward look wings at right angles to the center structure. The sign beside the left one said *Parish Office.* Theo pulled up in front of it.

Once inside what felt to him more like a ski hut than a house of worship, the church secretary, a brisk young Chinese woman, escorted him to an inner office. Theo had expected the secretary to be like the one he remembered from when he was a child and went to church with his mother. A retired lady who worked part-time and didn't type very well. Of course, Theo hadn't been to church since his father died. Obviously, times had changed.

The secretary tapped on the door. "Father Bainbridge? Your 4:00 is here."

A slender, dark-haired man in a clerical collar who was obviously no more than 45 years old, opened the office door and waved Theo inside. "Please come in, Detective Reed," he said as he escorted Theo to the chair in front of his desk.

He turned to his secretary. "Rose, could you please fetch Father DuPree? He may be more help to the Detective than I can be."

The Rector sat down at his desk. "I'm assuming you are here regarding Paige and Holly's deaths," he said.

Theo nodded.

"I asked Rose to get Father DuPree because he is our Youth Director," the Rector continued. "Frankly, he knew the girls much better than I. In fact, he helped the Langford's get the missing posters printed and distributed that last day, before we knew the truth. Father DuPree must have nailed up a couple of hundred notices. He was at the park most of the day. I've been counseling the parents. They are devastated, in shock, as you might expect." The rector paused a moment, looking at Theo. "You never expect to outlive a child, you know, even if the child is gravely ill. When children are simply slaughtered, out of the blue, well..."

Theo met the rector's eyes and nodded silently, agreeing. He and Father Bainbridge were both in businesses that sometimes dealt with the events most people didn't want to think about.

"What can I do for you?" Bainbridge continued, smoothly changing gears. He was interrupted by another discreet knock at his door, then Rose came in again. She was accompanied by another priest in a clerical collar. He was fairer in complexion than Father Bainbridge, a bit shorter too, and as evidenced by the fit of his shirt, he was obviously quite muscular. He appeared younger than Father Bainbridge, perhaps in his mid 30's. The main difference was the new priest sported a dishwater blond ponytail. Of average build, and about as tall as Theo, he was probably 6 ft. in height.

While Bainbridge was wearing a clerical collar, the second priest was dressed in jeans, a clerical shirt with a collar and black shoes that had not seen an application of polish since they were carried out of the shoe store, all probably having to do with getting more in touch with the youth of the church. For adults, it was helpful to talk with your priest especially if he or she was wearing a collar. He was a representative of God. It was a much different story for youngsters. They preferred and trusted someone more like them. The second cleric held out his hand as Theo stood up.

"Hixon DuPree, Detective. I'm the Youth Minister here at St. Jude's."

"Good to meet you," said Theo.

"Pull up a chair, Hixon," Bainbridge said. "I had just asked Detective Reed what we could do for him."

The younger man shook Theo's hand vigorously and then drew another chair close to the desk. Two things which struck Theo about Father DuPree were his ponytail and his intense dark eyes which Theo found a bit penetrating when the priest talked directly, while looking someone in the eye.

"Terrible thing," he said in a remarkably loud voice that took Theo aback. It seemed unpastoral. The Youth Director was a bit deaf, perhaps? Of course, Rose the secretary, St. Jude's mountain cabin architecture and even the Rector's buff physique seemed odd to Theo, too. He needed to get to church more often, he guessed. Definitely more than once a decade, at least.

"Paige and Holly were beautiful young girls. Best friends too, you know. That's why the families decided on a united service," DuPree said.

Theo took the opening offered. "Actually, that's the reason for my call today," he said, plunging directly into the problem. "Father DuPree, I *do* want to meet with you about anything you might know about the girls, but in the meantime, I understand that the funeral is tomorrow. I have a delicate problem."

Theo looked directly at Bainbridge. "I want to station men in the church at the funeral," Theo continued.

As he expected, the rector frowned.

"May I speak in confidence?" Theo asked.

Bainbridge and DuPree both nodded.

"These were sexual murders. They are random in that the killer chose victims that simply happened to be there. For them, they were in the wrong place at the wrong time. For the killer, they were in the right place at the right time. We know that it is typical, very typical in fact, for this kind of criminal to attend the funeral of his victims. I need men in the church where they can get a close look at the congregation. Ideally, I want to videotape the funeral. I want photographs and videos of every person, then afterwards go over the tapes with someone who is familiar with the parishioners. Most likely, we will be looking for a strange face in the crowd."

Bainbridge looked down at the blotter on his desk, then back at Theo and shook his head. "I'm sympathetic, Detective, but I just can't go along with that, I'm afraid. It would violate the privacy of the families to have strangers roaming the church with cameras," he said. "This is a nightmare, a tragedy for them. They are already under siege from the media. They are depending on the support of their faith. They expect their church to be a place of sanctuary. More cameras, more outsiders at the service is the last thing they need. It would be far too disturbing and in no way what anyone would expect in God's house, especially under these circumstances. I'm sorry, I just cannot allow it."

It was silent in the room. The Rector pushed his calendar around his desk, then turned to a small cross sitting on his desk. Picking the cross up, he looked at it and fingered it smoothly and lovingly.

To Theo, it was obvious Bainbridge was dealing with turmoil. He did want to help, but a church service was done in the presence of God and nothing should take away from that. Bainbridge looked up. "Perhaps if you just taped outside in the parking lot? You know, in the parking lot as people come and go, where you would not be seen, providing it can be done in a covert fashion and uphold the dignity of the families. I could go along with that," he said.

Theo sighed. He hated the hard sell and he knew the struggle Father Bainbridge was dealing with. "Father, I *do* understand your concern..."

"Steven, perhaps we *could* assist Detective Reed, very discretely?"

Amazed, Theo realized that Dupree, the youth minister, had come to his defense.

"Couldn't we accommodate them if they were to set things up so that the police wouldn't be apparent? And if we got the families' permission? I could speak to the Langfords and the Putziers. In particular, I think Forrest Langford might just be willing. He's been very concerned about the effectiveness of the police efforts so far. Sorry, Detective. I don't mean to be disrespectful. I know you are doing all you can with a most difficult matter."

Bainbridge continued to frown.

"Do you tape Sunday services for shut-ins?" Theo asked the Rector.

Bainbridge nodded. "We have a camcorder in the ceiling."

"It's not the ideal location, but could we station a man there," Theo continued. "That would feel normal to the congregation, wouldn't it?"

"We can do better that that," Dupree again interrupted. "We could put a policeman in the choir. That way, he could be looking out at the congregation. We could also put someone in the sound system room. You get a good view of the sides of the nave from there, Detective, and there's a louvered door. You can tape from behind it, but no one can see in. Another thing..."

Theo looked at DuPree, encouraged by his enthusiasm.

"St. Jude's owns the building across the street from the church. I think one of the second floor rooms looks down on the narthex doors. You could set up a video crew there, as well. A remote unit, like on some of those criminal shows?" DuPree smiled ruefully at Theo. "I must admit, I'm a big police procedural fan. I don't miss an episode of CSI."

Father Dupree turned back to Bainbridge. "A crew across the street behind the curtains certainly wouldn't be visible to the mourners, but they could get clear shots of the mourners leaving..."

Theo nodded. "Father DuPree has a good take on this," he said to the Rector. "I think we could be entirely unobtrusive and still get good pictures. In fact, I'd volunteer for the choir position myself. Take full responsibility. Believe it or not, I'm a former choirboy. I'd be willing to rehearse a little and look more convincing. Perhaps Father DuPree could run me through the paces." Theo hesitated a moment, then forged ahead. "In fact, if Father DuPree could look at the tapes for unfamiliar faces afterwards, I'd have what we need without disturbing the families at all."

Bainbridge remained silent, staring thoughtfully at his hands, fingers intertwined. He was clearly mulling over the proposal.

DuPree pled his case, "Father Bainbridge, I had Holly and Paige every week at youth group. They went to camp with us this summer, too. Paige was baptized here. These were *good* girls, angels. What happened was monstrous. We should do what we can to help the police find them. And I believe the families would want this, too."

Theo found the youth minister's advocacy unprecedented. He could never ever recall a clergyman actually helping him at a funeral before, but he certainly wasn't going to look a gift horse in the mouth. This could be a real piece of luck. The fact that Dupree loved crime dramas might actually succeed in getting him a lead or two. In the meantime, he could assure the Chief that they weren't sitting on their hands. Theo looked hopefully at the Rector.

Looking at DuPree, Father Bainbridge asked, "What will we tell the Altar Guild? They use that room to prepare the altar and store the palls for the caskets."

"Leave that to me," DuPree replied. "I can handle those ladies with kid gloves and still keep everything secret. I'll just tell them that due to certain circumstances, they must set the altar the evening before the service. Then they can place the palls on the caskets when they are brought in the narthex the day of the funeral. This will not be an issue. I'll see too that."

Bainbridge spoke to DuPree first, "Hixon, talk to the Langfords and the Putziers. If they are willing to allow a police presence, I will defer to them providing..." Bainbridge turned to Theo, "...you can set this up so that the order of worship, the mourners, nothing is disturbed. I want your word on that Detective."

"You have it, Father Bainbridge," Theo assured him, gratefully.

———————

AIDEN'S MEMORIES 10

Aiden O'Brian worked late into the night. From the large table in his office, he had cleared the collected, but organized mess of student papers, journal articles sent to him for review, his own research projects and a collection of other cases sent by various law enforcement agencies from around the country for evaluation.

Taking the photographs left for him by Theo, O'Brian began to study each one, paying particular attention to the details in each photograph. As he studied the gore from the crime scene and the more tolerable, but equally upsetting autopsy photographs, he dictated his impressions and thoughts into a small handheld mini-recorder.

He then put the photographs in order, crime scene photos of the bodies of the two girls, crime scene photos of the surrounding area and the autopsy photos. He tacked them in order on a large corkboard attached to the wall of his office. Sitting back in his chair, he stared at the photos individually, then in their organized groups.

"Talk to me, you bastard," he whispered softly as he studied the collection. "Come on, tell me about yourself," he repeated as he continued looking from photo to photo.

Finally, with a huge sigh, he slowly raised from his desk. Glancing at the Regulator clock on the wall across from his desk, he saw that it was well past midnight. He hadn't realized so much time had passed since he had come back from class and had begun to study the photos and to contemplate the murders of the two girls. He simply had lost track of time.

Of course, time had always been the problem. "Time was always been the problem," she had said. Ever since they married, she had felt as though she was competing with death, corpses, cops and killers. She had cried, begging him to stop this macabre work he was doing.

"God, why can't you just be a normal psychiatrist and just see neurotic housewives with depression and middle-aged men having midlife crises," she had pleaded with him.

In spite of his best intentions, he had for some reason, been unable to make the changes she wanted and that he had promised. Perhaps it was due to the continuing demands with what appeared to be an increase of extremely violent crimes. More honestly, maybe it was that he enjoyed the hunt to identify the perp, enjoyed the notoriety he received when one of his profiles led to the arrest of a heinous killer, rapist or child molester.

He never had to answer the question of why he could not stop work. Eight years ago, Margaret had brought the issue to a head. She reached her decision before he could honestly begin to deal with it.

He had come home, late again, an evening at the theater, with pre-theater dinner reservations at her favorite Broadway restaurant forgotten. Walking into their upper west side apartment, he could tell immediately that something was amiss. He did not have to read the note on the floor; he knew she was gone. The furniture, china, books and all those other items that had seemed so important to them at the time were still there. The only thing missing were her clothes and the silver given them by her parents when they had married.

He had met Margaret when she was a social work graduate student at Columbia and he was in his residency in Forensic Psychiatry at Columbia, as well. By this time, he had already honed his interest on the intellect of murderers, rapists and molesters.

From a small fishing village in Michigan's Upper Peninsula, Margaret was intelligent, funny, and, in his eyes, beautiful. She had a wonderful curiosity about human behavior that was woven with a genuine desire to understand and help people who were down and out. But her small town, country naiveté had made this a struggle for her. While she had been able to develop an understanding of life among the poor, of racism, of the ravages of drugs and street crime that haunted the poor neighborhoods, she had never been able to approach any level of understanding of the work Aiden did with the people, or "Animals" as she called them, that Aiden studied, worked with and tried to understand.

They had married the summer after they met. The wedding had been in her home church in Michigan. Their honeymoon at a lakeside lodge was not too far from her hometown. Their honeymoon had been interrupted by a series of prostitute murders on the west coast.

A helicopter had taken him away and he had been gone for two weeks. That had been the beginning of the end. Try as hard as she did, she could never adjust to, or learn to accept, the world in which Aiden lived. Finally, she had no other alternative. As she had told him time and time again, "I'm drowning in loneliness, Aiden. I need something, something more than I'm getting now."

Since that time, there had been no other women. Not that there had been no opportunity. In a curious way, some women almost threw themselves at him when he was on the road speaking or working on a particularly heinous case. He had always wondered what it was about him and his work that these women were so attracted to. If only Margaret had been able to have just a bit of that – whatever it was.

Aiden turned off the lights, locked his office door and set the deadbolt as an added protection. Slowly, he walked down the dark hallway and down the stairwell, lit only by campus streetlights coming through the window. He smiled as he walked past the sleeping security guard seated at the desk at the building entrance. At the parking lot, he unchained his Harley, started it and headed for home, the warm August wind blowing in his face.

———————

THE SERVICE

I am the resurrection and the life, saith the Lord; he that believeth in me, though he were dead, yet he shall live, and whosoever liveth and believeth in me shall never die," began Father Stephen Bainbridge, the Rector of St. Jude's by the Mountain, for the dual funeral for Paige Langford and Holly Putzier.

True to his word, Hixon Dupree had convinced Father Bainbridge of the necessity of cooperating with Theo by allowing the police to be strategically placed throughout the church building and the surrounding area to observe and photograph the funeral and those attending the service.

Dressed in a red choir robe, Theo had been allowed to join the choir and to have a prominent, but unobtrusive spot, sitting on the back row, with the other basses. He would have an unobstructed view of all those who went to the altar rail for communion. He would also have a view of the nave and all those sitting in attendance. While he was sure he would not know any of those attending the service, his position would give Theo the opportunity to view everybody and to be on the lookout for anybody who, in Theo's opinion, might look out of place at the funeral.

Hixon DuPree had been more than helpful. He had set up an area for the video camera between the chancel and the nave, in a room where the clergy would vest for the service. There were louvered windows that looked out on the congregation. These windows would easily accommodate a video camera which could run during the entire service, yet remain unseen to the undiscriminating eyes of the congregation. This did require some reconfiguration of the room and DuPree had given Theo and his men free reign to set up a stand that would allow the camera to sit high enough to be able to view the middle of the congregation.

Theo asked Aiden if he might be able to spare some time to sit in the room and view the congregation. Luckily, Aiden was able to rearrange his schedule and was posted in the room with the officer manning the video camera. The camera stand had been arranged to accommodate O'Brian, giving him a clear view of the congregation as well as those going up for communion.

The church-owned structure, directly across the street from the church building, was also made available to one surveillance team which was equipped with a video camera. Another team of officers with a second video camera were stationed at the side window to observe and videotape people as they approached and later, left the building.

Luckily Theo, in his younger days, had sung in his church choir. He knew some of the music and was able to hear the bass next to him well enough to get through the other hymns. He was not used to all the kneeling, sitting and standing up of the Episcopal church, but the location of his seat in the choir section located in the chancel did give him a good opportunity to look out over the congregation.

The service was led by Father Bainbridge, but when it came time for the homily, it was Hixon DuPree who took his place in the pulpit. DuPree took a few moments simply to look over the congregation before he began.

"Two precious lives. These girls were among the most precious I have ever known. There have been, as you may know, so many beautiful ladies who have, over the time I have served as Youth Minister, come to me for care and instruction. They come to me at the brink of womanhood, when the questions about love are plentiful. These two girls though, were exceptional. Most of the questions of their lives so far had already been answered. They talked to me with the wisdom I expected in women far older than the twelve plus years they had lived. I could not account for the maturity of these two souls. Perhaps those of you who were close to them, understand. They were little women, already mature in many ways.

"If you have not followed the information provided by those investigating this tragedy, let me tell you a little of what they have learned. Both girls were brutally murdered in Stone Mountain Park. They were taken to a desolate area and strangled. Interestingly, each body was treated differently. They were found by two joggers last Sunday morning."

Theo, while trying to appear as one of the choir, while at the same time viewing the congregation, only caught bits of the sermon, but his ears perked up at the description of the murders. He did not recall ever saying anything to the press about how the girls were found; nor did he remember saying any such thing to either set of parents. He certainly had not disclosed this to the two priests and he thought it a little strange that a priest would talk about the grisly murders at their funeral. It was a time for grieving, not rehashing the murder, for God's sake! He made a mental note to follow up on this.

DuPree continued with his sermon, talking of the maturity of the two girls, their hopes and ambitions, their boyfriends and their dreams of being a teenager.

"But I am not here to preach them into heaven! Their faith took them into the presence of Jesus. Although he who ended their lives certainly did not know that he did them *great good* in that crime! We know from the word of God that 'to be absent from the body is to be present with the Lord.' They are now free of the difficulties of this world. The difficulties, the disappointments, the tears of earthly life will not touch them. From what we see in the world today, we can imagine the horrors of tomorrow! Such horrors will hold no grip on Paige and Holly. As we lay their beautiful bodies to rest, let us do so with hearts full of joyful memories of those precious lives. Let us also remember their parents as they suffer the unspeakable loss of their precious daughters. Only God can heal their broken hearts, but we can love them and remember them fondly.

"Let us pray for the tormented soul of the person who took these precious girls from us. For his mind must be wrecked with evil. And let us live our lives to help change the world so that there is no more such tragedy and no fear to haunt the hearts of all other precious youth. Let us so live that instead of fear, they may know the fulfillment of all their wonderful dreams."

There was nary a dry eye in the congregation. Even Theo was trying hard to swallow the lump in his throat.

THE REVIEW 12

Prior to the funeral service, Theo and Hixon DuPree had decided to meet in Theo's office the day after. Theo was anxious to get all the film reviewed in order to determine if the killer had, in fact, shown up for the service; or at least someone present who could not, in any way be accounted for as a legitimate and interested party. He and DuPree had agreed on 9:00 a.m. Then they would go to a conference room where all the audio visual equipment was set up. Theo had made arrangements with the A-V Tech prior to the funeral.

Theo bounded into his office early. He had several things to get out of the way prior to the meeting with DuPree. Number one was a synopsis of the investigation to date. The Chief wanted it yesterday; however, that had been impossible. Theo was well aware that the Chief was taking some hard heat on this one.

The company who held the contract to all the concessions, rides and games at Stone Mountain was complaining that attendance was down at the park due to the murders. The company was a large organization with operations at several parks and recreation areas in the United States. Their issues and complaints were made from their

CEO to the governor who, in turn, put the strong arm on the Chief. Of course, Theo was at the bottom of that pecking list and thus the one to receive the brunt of everybody else's frustration.

Using a rear door to his office he had just settled down to his desk when Wilma knocked and opened his door. *Shit, I can't even get into my chair without being bugged,* Theo thought to himself. With an irritated look on his face, uttered "What?"

Maintaining her usual calm, Wilma's replied, "Theo, Father DuPree is here for his appointment."

Glancing at his wall clock, Theo could see it was just 8:15 a.m. "Christ," was his reply. "We're not even supposed to begin until 9. What the hell is he doing?"

"I have no idea," Wilma said. "He was here when I came in, which was just before eight. I guess he can tell you. I'm sorry, Theo." There was a note of compassion in her voice. Wilma was well aware of the pressure her boss was experiencing and she was most empathic to what Theo was experiencing. In fact, it reminded her of the Atlanta Child Murders, the Wayne Williams case. Those murders caught international attention and the city was inundated with press for months. While Theo was not the lead investigator, Wilma was the administrative assistant at that time, as well, so she was well acquainted with the stress and pressure of a big investigation.

"Okay," Theo said, "send him in, and, Wilma, can you set aside some time for me today to do the synopsis? I simply must get it done for the Chief. If that means both of us need to stay late to get it done, we'll just have to do that."

There was a pause, then Wilma gave Theo a look between empathy and *Deal with it yourself, Boss.*

"Will your staying late interfere with something you've planned?" Theo asked.

"No," Wilma replied, "no problem at all, Theo."

"Thanks, I'll owe you one. Say how many 'owes' do I owe you, now?"

With a chuckle in her voice, Wilma said, "Too many. I stopped keeping a tab several years ago. I'll bring Father DuPree right in."

Almost immediately, Wilma stepped in with Hixon DuPree right behind.

Without even a greeting, DuPree began talking, "I know I'm early, Detective, but the anticipation of our work today simply kept me wide awake last night. Finally, around six, I just simply told myself enough already, so I got dressed and came down to police headquarters. I am most hopeful we can find our perpetrator in the pictures."

Theo gestured to a chair and the priest took a seat. Again, almost without a pause, DuPree was talking, "One of the things that went through my mind was the issue of volunteering as a police officer. I mean, this is a very personal issue for me and I want to do all I can to bring this person to justice. So, I was wondering...I mean I know the sheriff's department and the local police have volunteers, and I was hoping that I could volunteer and help on this case."

This was not something Theo had expected from DuPree. A man with a full-time job plus a part-time job, which Theo assumed, required him to devote a lot of time to activities outside an office... well, it was a strange request. But he was not caught off-guard.

"Well, Father DuPree, both our department and the police department do have auxiliary officers who volunteer their time. Their main use is traffic control before and after big events. The state requires that volunteers in law enforcement have a certain amount of training prior to the time they are allowed to do any type of work with uniformed officers. That said, there is an issue, especially in big cases, of liability. A murder investigation is the biggest type of case we do. With all due respect, Father, untrained officers simply become a liability in such cases. I thank you for your offer and respect your interest, but it simply cannot be done." Theo was in hopes what he had said would put the matter to rest.

"Understood, Detective!" said the priest.

"Okay, should we be about our work for this morning?" Theo stated.

"Detective, I am at your disposal," said DuPree. "However, if there is ever a time I can volunteer my services in a capacity greater than I am doing now, I would appreciate it. I hate what has happened to those two lovely little girls. It has cast a terrible pall over our congregation. I don't know that our parish will ever recover. Quite frankly, I am angry, very angry. I am frustrated, very frustrated, and I am incensed about the entire issue. I guess it is like a crime show on TV. I want it solved in an hour and everybody to be happy at the end."

"I understand. We all feel the same way," Theo said.

Ushering the priest out of the office, both men headed down the hall to the conference room. Theo walked fast just to insure Father DuPree did not talk anymore. He had no time for idle chatter.

Walking into the conference room, Father DuPree said out loud, "My God, who are all these people?" The room was practically full of men and women.

Theo took the priest by the elbow and led him to the front of the room. The room, which was buzzing with talk when they walked in, became instantly quiet. "Ladies and gentlemen, may I present Father Hixon DuPree, the youth minister at St. Judes. He was the one who arranged things for us yesterday during the funeral. Father DuPree, this is the task force working on this case. All these people, in some way, were involved in the funeral, either by taking pictures or videos, sitting in the congregation and even doing road work and telephone and power work while hoisted up a light pole, or from a truck parked by the side of the road."

"My, oh my," Dupree said. "I had no idea. Thank you all from the bottom of my heart and the heart of our church, and congregation. I shall pray for you all for the work you do, as well as the time taken away from your families."

With that, the lights were dimmed. Each officer who had taken either still photos, videos, or simply scrutinized the congregation got up and went through each image. It was a long session. In each instance, Father DuPree was called upon to give his input and to identify the images on the screen. "That is the Senior Warden and his wife. Those are the members of the vestry, the girl's Sunday school teacher, the director of Christian education and on and on. There was not a person DuPree did not know. Theo was impressed because the church had been filled to overflowing, and yet DuPree seemed to know them all.

Theo asked DuPree how he did it. "Well, knowing the members of the congregation is part of my job. As a priest, I see myself as an extension of every family in our congregation."

"But what about those people who came who were not members of the church?" asked someone from the group.

"As the youth minister, it is part of my role to know each child as intimately as I can. They all feel comfortable coming to me with their various issues. Adolescence is a difficult time for these people. They have so many roles to deal with and there are some parents who simply cannot deal with this or do not understand this. So the kids come to me for advice on any number of issues. I have always made it a part of my job to do as much as I can to understand *my children*," he said. "So I spend time at their schools. I'm at as many extracurricular activities as I can. I'm invited to their parties and get-togethers. It is no small task, but one I love. I guess it is with that in mind that I did so much with the missing persons' flyers. I spent a lot of time at the park trying to find out everything I could about the murders."

The upshot of the meeting was that, as far as anybody could determine, there were no strangers at the funeral. Everybody was identified by the priest. Theo had hoped that the killer would present himself and unexpectedly be detected. He knew that had been wishful thinking. But it was something that had to be done. Still, in the recesses of his mind, Theo had that gut instinct, that special feeling that the murderer had, in fact, been in the congregation. After all, it was very likely the girls knew their killer. So, it would make sense that he would be in the church.

Walking DuPree to the lobby, Theo said nothing about his instincts. As he opened the door leading to the lobby, he stuck out his hand for DuPree. "Well, we did not get what we wanted, Father, but thanks for all you did to help us at the funeral and for your time today."

DuPree took Theo's hand. It was not a firm handshake. Theo could feel his hand getting wet from the priest's perspiration. It occurred to Theo that perhaps Father DuPree was under as much stress as he was.

As he was walking away, the priest stopped and turned toward Theo. "Detective, please remember what I asked you about earlier. If I can do anything to help, please do not hesitate to call on me. I want to see this monster brought to justice."

Theo nodded and closed the door.

———————

THEO AND MOSE

Theo hurried into the office. He was huffing a bit, again choosing to take the stairs instead of the elevator leading from the parking garage to his floor. Out of breath, he noted to himself that he needed to get back on the courts or do something else to begin getting back in shape. Not only was he cognizant of his shortness of breath, but also that his belt was now holed in the first hole. If something did not change, he was going to have to go up another size, not only belts, but trousers, as well. "Good luck doing that," he had murmured to himself.

As Theo rushed in, Wilma glanced at the wall clock. This did not go unnoticed by Theo and he simply stated, "Traffic sucked," and it had. His thirty minute commute had taken almost an hour today. In fact, the traffic reporter had mentioned a recent study that described Atlanta traffic as now closing in on that of Los Angeles. Still, Theo strived for punctuality and was intolerant of tardiness, so being late irritated him. He hated to be late for anything, especially, work.

Theo had taken the file of the missing girl cold case, the one found at the park in the springtime, home with him. The girl's file had been placed on his desk for consideration as a possible victim of the Stone

Mountain murders. It had not taken him long to review, being it was so thin. The facts were quite simple. The body of a female, probably in her teens, had been found in the cove at Stone Mountain Lake. Due to decomposition, the elements and the fish and critters that inhabited the lake area, no cause of death could be established. Efforts to identify her had been impossible and the case, while not closed, had been retired due to lack of leads. In all probability, some member of the task force had come across the file and put it on Theo's desk. With his cluttered desk, Theo had not seen the file until after Wilma had completed the synopsis of the case last evening.

Theo's thoughts went back to his earlier discussion with Mose Ellard. Ellard was quite a guy, very common and simplistic, yet savvy. And he was a good citizen and a good person; he had continued to follow the case of the young girl, the one he had found dead in the lake on that early Saturday morning fishing expedition. He was upset that he had not heard or read anything in the paper about the investigation. Ellard had been right when he had said this was a time of "great sadness," an expression that Theo could certainly agree with. Theo had to chuckle to himself when Ellard had posited: "Why do killers did such things?"

Stumped for a good answer, Theo had said nothing. Mose Ellard looked at Theo and answered his own question, "I suppose the devil just drove up in a red pickumup truck and this man just crawled into the front seat and the two of them just drove off."

It was a very simplistic idea and not very likely, Theo thought, *but he did realize there was certainly a growing veil of malevolence that seemed to be penetrating society.* However, Theo just wished it was not going on in his part of the country.

Given the fact that there had been two other similar deaths at the Mountain, Theo decided that circumstantially, this matter should be added to the other two murders. He could have a serial killer on his hands. He also realized the chances of ever identifying the body of the first girl discovered by Mose Ellard were slim; however, Theo simply could not simply ignore the facts. Besides, his instincts, on which every good cop depended, told him this was the thing to do.

Picking up his phone, Theo dialed Aiden O'Brian's number to tell him about the addition of the now third victim. Getting the psychiatrist's answering machine, Theo asked for O'Brian to call him at his earliest convenience. The detective was not willing to leave any pertinent information on any answering machine.

As he was hanging up, there was a quiet knock on his door. The door opened slowly and Wilma peeked her head in. Theo motioned her in. She was holding a stack of what Theo recognized were telephone messages. Looking at him with a certain amount of empathy in her eyes, she announced, "That Hixon DuPree is on the phone."

"Tell him I'm not in and promise him I'll call him back," Theo instructed. After yesterday's call, he was not anxious to speak with DuPree.

Immediately Theo's mind went back to yesterday; and the strange telephone conversation between him and the priest. DuPree had called just after Theo had come in to begin his day. "Father DuPree, how are you? You're up and about early."

"Well, Detective, I'm in a bit of a quandary," he replied. "I really need to have some more details on the course of the investigation. I've got an entire congregation with a vested interest in the case."

Theo could feel the hair on the back of his neck rise as well as his awareness of sweat beginning to accumulate under the armpits of his shirt. Intrusive calls like this one aggravated him to no end. These types of calls generally came from the press, so while upset, Theo was taken a bit off-guard when DuPree began talking.

Theo took a moment, caught a breath, then began his response. Trying to be as amicable as he could, Theo said, "Father Dupree, I'm very aware of the situation you are in. That said, it is not the policy of this department, nor is it my policy to provide information on an ongoing investigation outside the department."

As if he had not heard a word Theo had said, DuPree came right back into the conversation, "At our meeting regarding the videos of the funeral, you may recall I was quite impressed with the number of people in the room. I think you said something about them being a part of the task force, am I right?"

Theo acknowledged that DuPree was correct.

"Detective, let me speak frankly. May I?"

"Please do!" Theo replied, trying to keep his voice under control.

"Well Detective, I can only imagine that with the size of the task force, there is a great deal more going on than you have shared with me. It is my belief that under the circumstances, you hold some obligation to share more with me than you have," Dupree said, the pitch and volume in his voice reaching a new high, his voice getting louder.

"Father DuPree," Theo said in a very stern voice, "while I understand your position and interest in the case, I am under no obligation to share anything with you regarding the investigation."

"Detective," Dupree said, sternly, "I have tried to be very cooperative with you. I went to some trouble to help you with the funeral service. You could have not gotten the freedom for your investigation and surveillance had I not talked to Reverend Bainbridge, as well as implored the Senior Warden that the congregation had some obligation to help, given the fact that two members of the congregation were brutally murdered, and further, that our congregation has suffered a blow that will take years to deal with."

Theo took a few moments to compose himself. He could feel his anger rising. He needed the few moments to allow himself to reach some balance. Further, he knew that if he allowed himself to get emotional, he would probably say something he should not say.

Slowly, he began, "Father DuPree, I do not want to turn this into some sort of pissing contest. We do have a nice sized task force and we are working with surrounding jurisdictions as well as the F.B.I. We are covering every lead that comes in. Some leads point us in new directions. That said, there is nothing substantial that we have as, of yet, uncovered. I am well aware of your situation and your relationship with the two girls and their families. Please rest assured that I will keep you informed on anything of substance that we develop." Theo hoped that was enough to satisfy the priest.

But it was not. In a cold voice, DuPree said, "You should be aware of the fact that we have some very influential people in our congregation that do hold some political power in this county, as well as other counties, plus state government. We will not hesitate to seek the guidance of those folks if need be."

"Listen," came Theo Reed's reply, "this is not my first rodeo and it certainly is not the first time I have heard from some person *who knows someone who knows someone.* Now, I don't give a fat rat's ass about who you know. We have a regimentation that we follow in these types of cases. We do not disclose everything we know, nor do we disclose the scope and nature of an investigation. Now that is the way it is."

There was silence on the other end of the line, but Theo could detect the sound of breathing. Now he felt he had perhaps gone too far. He needed to say something, yet he hated to be put in this type of situation.

"Father Dupree," Theo said quietly, "I am most appreciative of all that you have done. In fact, you have gone out of your way to cooperate. For all you have done, I am extremely grateful. I am sure you are in a difficult position and I can appreciate it. It's just that we have our way of running an investigation. Not that you would disclose anything, but maybe a slip or any small thing may come out. Loose lips sink ships. We cannot be too careful. I promise to keep you aware of everything I am free to disclose."

"Thank you," came the reply and the line went dead.

Now back in the moment, Theo looked at Wilma, who gave him a sheepish smile. "I'm sorry," she almost whispered, "I've already told him you were in."

"Jesus," Theo boomed, "why the hell did you do that?"

"You were in," she answered, then continued, "and since he is so involved in the murders, I thought you would probably want to talk to him any time he called."

"How would you like a transfer to the Evidence Room?" said Theo. He was not serious, of course, but he wanted Wilma to know she had overstepped her bounds. She should always clear a call with him before telling the caller he was available. He knew Wilma was cognizant of her duties, one of which was to protect his precious time, of which there was little. If she did not, he would be on the phone every day with every amateur detective and crackpot between Macon, Georgia and Spartanburg, South Carolina.

He had been a little abrupt with her and he knew it when she turned on her heels and walked out as he was picking up the receiver, making a mental note to apologize to her.

"This is Theo Reed. How are you today, Father DuPree?"

"I'm fine, Detective, and I hope you are the same." Not waiting for a reply, DuPree began, "Listen, I am sorry about my reaction when we were on the phone the other day. I know the pressure you must be under and I feel the same way. These murders have been a very tragic event in the life of our parish. As you can imagine, the families of the girls, as well as our entire congregation are devastated. We have stopped all meetings of our youth group until next year. I am trying to deal with both families, as well as what we feel is our parish family, so I'm feeling a bit of stress, as well. Anyway, please excuse me for my rudeness on the phone when we last talked. It was uncalled for and I am most embarrassed by my behavior."

In a tone more gracious than he actually felt, Theo responded, "Not to worry, Father. I understand totally. I know it must be difficult. Apology accepted and my apology to you."

"Well, thank you, Detective," he said. "Still, if there is anything you can pass on to me from time to time, I would appreciate it. By the way, we never heard much from all the posters the youth group and I distributed. Did you get any response?"

Theo could recall no information as a result of the flyers, but now he felt as though he must say something positive to the priest. "Actually, Father, we have had some response and those responses are being followed. If anything of interest comes from them, I will pass it on to you."

"Thank you, Detective." DuPree said softly, then Theo heard him hang up.

———————

14

ANGER

White Man hated Sundays. It was not so much that he hated being alone, he quite enjoyed the time he was alone. He was able to do as he pleased, without anybody saying anything to him, like his mother or his sister. "Cunts!" he said aloud. He had gotten used to being alone. Being alone had been a way of life for him for as long as he could remember. But Sundays, those days in the monastery where he had been placed as a young boy, were boring to him. The judge had told him, "The monks will get you in line, young man. You just behave and do as you're told. This is a new start for you. Take advantage of it."

"New start, my ass," he said to himself.

The monks had preached so much about Sunday, the day that God had rested and reflected on all he had done. Now Sundays were a day to reflect. Reflection began with morning vespers, communion, study time, evening vespers, and a little something to eat. Sunday was a time meant for families, togetherness, a sense of belonging. Well, that certainly had not been the case in his family. Sunday had never been the time he was told it was to be. He had always been alone on Sundays. Sunday was a time for him to be left out, alone, on his own.

Oh, there was time for his mother and her friends or time for mother and his sister. Never any time for him. Chores, he had plenty of time for them. "When you get the clothes washed, make sure you fold them and put them away," his mother had said to him in a commanding voice, "and try to clean your room. I wouldn't drink boiled water in that pig sty."

Then she, or they, would be off, down to the French Quarter, the music, the drinking, the good times. His mother and sister would come home and laugh about all they had done, or his mother would come home and brag about how she had "done it" with some sailor she helped get drunk, then she was able to remove his billfold from his back pocket.

In the laundry room he washed, dried and folded. As he folded he felt anger at his mother and his sister. "Who does she think I am? Fucking Cinderella?" He laughed as he visualized himself in Cinderella's dress. He thought about the first time he had a strange feeling while he folded his sister's panties. He had taken them, along with the rest of her clothes, to her room. Quickly he took off his clothes and put on the panties. He looked in the mirror on the wall. He could see the bulge growing in the crotch and it felt good to him. He lay on her bed and rubbed his hands over the cool silk. He felt himself get hard and he began to rub himself, all the time thinking about his sister. He rubbed until he felt the sensation, then the wetness.

Jesus, he thought, *now, what the hell do I do with wet panties?* The wash was done and he had no clothes for another load, so he put them under his mattress. Then at night, when he was alone in his room, he would put the panties on and rub himself again until he felt the sensation and the wet. He would take them off and put on his own shorts. One time he wondered what the wetness tasted like, so he put the panties to his mouth and sucked and tasted. As he did this, he felt the sensation again and now his own shorts were wet. Eventually, he was able to wash his shorts, but his sister's panties, he kept under his mattress. They were hers, but as long as he had them, and he could wear them and get that wonderful feeling, she would be a part of him. During that time, he could possess her. This became a part of his ongoing nighttime ritual.

White Man recalled the time his sister had come home and gone up to her room where she saw him lying on her bed, wearing her panties and rubbing himself. He had been so engrossed with his fantasy that he had not heard her. She had yelled at him, "Stop that, you little pervert," and she had begun hitting him. "Get off my bed and get my panties off you, perv!" She had scratched his legs and tugged at her panties. The panties ripped. "See what you've done, pervert. I'm telling Mom her son is a pervert."

He had run into his room, not venturing out until his mother had called him for dinner. He did not want to go to the kitchen, as he knew what she would say, but it would be worse if he did not go down for dinner.

It was obvious that his sister had told his mother what he had been doing. The tirade began as soon as he crossed the threshold. She began yelling at him, berating him, her shrill voice becoming more piercing as she got louder and louder. And her eyes, boring a hole in his face, her holding and squeezing his cheeks and yelling, "Look at me when I talk to you, you faggot bastard, just like your father." Then taking him by the hair, she had pulled him into her bedroom where she ordered him to undress. Taking a pair of her panties, she ordered him to put them on, then made him strap on one of her bras. He was too afraid to argue with her. "Sissy, come in here and look at the little faggot." He saw his sister standing in the doorway.

"There you go, you little faggot bastard. If you want to be a little girl, you might as well dress like one." His mother continued yelling, her eyes bulging with rage.

She made him come to the dinner table dressed in her underwear. He remembered staring down at his plate, not making any eye contact as she continued to berate him, calling him names. He could hear his sister snickering while the rampage continued. When he said he had to go to the bathroom, his mother had gone with him. She made him take the panties down and sit on the toilet. "If you're going to be a little girl, you might as well piss like one," she yelled, standing there while he sat and urinated. His shame was almost overpowering for what his mother was doing to him and that his sister had witnessed all this. He wasn't sorry for what he had done, but that he had gotten caught.

He waited until his mother and sister had gone to bed, until he could hear his mother snoring. Slowly relaxing, he began to feel the underwear on his body. He began to rub himself, then faster until the feeling came. When he was finished, he took the bra and panties off. Going to his chest of drawers, he removed a jack knife his father had given him years ago. He used the knife to cut the bra and panties to shreds, pretending they were a part of his mother.

"Rotten cunt," he said over and over. *God, how he hated her, hated the sight of her, skinny body, hair unkempt, sloppily dressed.* He hated the very thought of her. Eventually, he fell asleep but he dreamed of his mother all night and woke the next morning hating her as much as when he had gone to bed.

Next morning while pouring cereal into a bowl for breakfast, his mother did not even acknowledge him when she walked into the kitchen.

One night, not long after, he was in bed. The door opened and his sister came in. She was older than he and was quite well developed. She pulled the covers down and crawled into his bed. Slowly, she took his hand and put it on her breast. She began kissing him, then she reached her hand into his shorts and began to rub him. When he was hard, she got on top of him, and taking hold of him, she guided his hard cock inside her. She then began moving up and down, slowly at first, then more rapidly. She began to moan. He felt his own excitement and the thrill of that feeling. When they were finished, his sister got off of him, got off the bed and walked out of his room. She had not said one word to him.

The encounters with his sister continued for some time, certainly not every night, but at least once a week. His sister's silence eventually stopped and they began talking as their sexual behavior not only continued, but expanded. One or the other would hear of something sexual at school, in a book or on TV, and they would talk about it and try it. He loved it when she took him in her mouth and sucked him.

One afternoon when they were quite active, as well as a little noisy, they did not hear the bedroom door open. He was lying on his sister. "What in holy hell is going on?" screamed his mother. Thinking quickly, his sister screamed, "Mama, he made me do it. He raped me!"

"You faggot bastard!" his mother yelled. Grabbing him by the hair, she pulled him off the bed and kicked him again and again. Yelling at his sister to get into her room, his mother looked down at him, now curled up, his knees touching his chin.

"Go ahead and cover up, you shithead," she yelled at him. "You've had it. Now I'm going to do something I should have done years ago." She walked out of his room, cautioning him not to move.

He was still in that position when the police arrived.

He was turned over to Juvenile Justice who then placed him in a juvenile detention center where he was charged with incest the following day. Luckily, he was assigned to a social worker who took an active interest in him. She did spend time on his case and from her visits with his mother and sister, it was evident to her that there was more to his relationship with them than his mother and sister would have liked the social worker to believe.

In her discussions with the juvenile judge, the social worker learned that the judge was considering placing him into a prison system. "After all," he told the social worker, "I have no other place to put him, and it was incest."

Following her talk with the judge and hearing that the judge was limited on what he could do, the social worker began searching for a suitable alternative. She found one in a home for boys run by a group of monks. She had called the monastery, explained the situation as well as her feeling concerning the real issues, the relationship with her client's mother, the mother's behaviors, as well as what she had learned talking with the sister and other neighbors. Two days later, she received a call from one of the monks who told her that her client would be accepted in the home. This, she related to the judge, and within a week he was in the monastery. That was fine with the juvenile judge and he was so ordered into the custody of the monastery. He was to be there until he was 18. "Four years from now," he told himself. He was not sure how to feel about this, but he knew anything was better than where he had been.

Even now, years later, as White Man sat in his darkened room, he thought about when he had cut up his mothers clothes. "Rotten cunt," he said over and over. His anger began to surge. He could feel it in his body, his stomach tightening, his breathing increasing, his heart pounding. He hated when thoughts of his mother entered his conscious mind, albeit, not as often. The years had allowed him to mellow somewhat, in that the memories were not as invasive as they once had been. They were strong right now and he was not able to control his thoughts. He needed a release and he needed it now. He thought of the two girls at the laser show. He had thought of them often, leading them down the tracks and into the bushes. But now the pleasure of those thoughts was not so strong. He needed a new adventure. He was ready. He knew it was time to hunt.

———————

FOUR

White Man sat in the bushes where he could get a good view of the beach at the lake in the Park. It was mid-afternoon, not the time he generally hunted, but today, it was different. He *needed* to hunt. It was like he had no control of this urge.

He had watched the girl and her boyfriend lying on the beach. *Nice,* he thought. It was midweek, so there were very few people enjoying the sun. His spot was in the bushes on the golf course. *It was safe here,* he told himself.

Sitting on the ground, he watched as the girl and boy kissed and played around. He watched boy caress the girl's breasts. She didn't try to stop him. She even let his hands go inside the top part of her bikini, but when his hand went down to her crotch, she pushed it away. They kissed again. Again, his hand went to her crotch and again, she pushed it away. *The little fucking tease,* he thought to himself. *Shit, they're all alike, no good. Just lead some poor bastard to get all worked up, then shove him away.* "Cunt," he whispered.

Eventually, the boy got up and walked toward the concession area. White Man watched the boy go into the restroom area. Now it was time. He got up, brushed himself off and walked toward the beach, all the time keeping a close watch on the restroom. He had to work fast before the boy came back.

Walking up to the girl, he made a little noise and she turned in his direction. "I'm sorry to bother you young lady, but I seem to have lost a club. I was hitting my ball and the club simply took off from my hand. I think it came this way. I think four eyes are better then two. Might I prevail on you to help me look? If it were a ball, I would not mind, but golf clubs are too expensive to simply let it go."

God, she was so trusting, he thought to himself. Now that he was close, he saw that she was a bit younger than he thought. He guessed she was no more than fifteen. It always was amazing to him how trusting young girls could be. She didn't suspect a thing. She followed him right back to his spot in the bushes, he, pausing and appearing to look for his golf club. Once they were safe from anyone's view, he turned on her. Like all the others, she was scared to death. Her eyes were like a deer in the headlights of a vehicle at night. She was frozen, unable to move. He thought to himself, *You're toast, little girl.*

Instructing her to lie down, she obeyed, just like the other two girls had done. He knelt down over her. Putting his hands around her neck, he began to squeeze. He felt the rush run through his body as he continued to squeeze, watching the life drain out of her body. It was interesting; he could see the natural color of her body slowly turn white as she was dying. She had tried to struggle a bit near the end, but he was too strong and she was too far gone. He looked down at her lifeless body. "You got what you had coming to you," he whispered.

Sliding his body back a bit, he reached around her neck and untied the bow on her bra and slid it off. He looked at her small, young breasts. "Nice," he said. Then he undid the ties on the bottom part of her bikini and slid them out from under her. Slowly, he fingered the patch of hair. He got up and placed the bikini top and bottom in a plastic grocery sack he had brought, and then stuffed the sack down into his crotch. Picking the body up, he walked a little further into the bushes, a bit closer to the golf course. He placed the body on the ground, straightened it and slid the hands and arms across the stomach. He removed the tube of glue from his shirt pocket. Reaching down, he pushed the half closed eyelids all the way down. He applied a small amount of the epoxy. It dried quickly. He looked out over the golf course. Seeing nothing, he walked to the fairways and turned toward the beach.

Looking over the water of the inlet, White Man saw the boy who was trying to find his girlfriend. Walking to the concession stand, he asked for a Coke, then sat at a bench and slowly sipped, as he appeared to be waiting for the girl. He walked further down the beach, but he could not find her. Trudging in the sand, he continued looking for his girlfriend. Finally, he walked to the concession stand and asked the attendant if he had seen the girl.

"No," the attendant said. "I guess she left."

The boy walked towards the parking lot. It did not occur to him that something bad may have occurred to his girl. Finishing his Coke, he got into his car and headed for home.

———————

ANOTHER VICTIM

"**S**hit," the man cried out. Looking toward the other three golfers, he fussed about not being able to get rid of his slice. It was not the money; they only played for a quarter a hole. It made no difference how many lessons he took, he still hit a wicked slice. If he could just get the ball to go straight, he would be a pretty good golfer, but try as he might, every time he hit with a wood, the ball would careen off to the right. Now his ball was well into the trees and bushes down by the lake. "Fat chance of finding that thing," he said to his golf mates.

"Want to hit another?" one of the others asked.

"No," he said. "I'll just try to find this one. That was a new ball. I paid ten bucks for that thing hoping a better ball might do the trick. No, perhaps I'll get lucky and find it."

The foursome walked off the tee, got into their golf carts and began to drive down the fairway.

The cart with the unlucky golfer stopped. The driver asked, "Want some help?'

"No, I'll look around a few minutes. If I can't find it, I'll just hit another ball."

Getting out of the cart, the golfer looked around while his partner drove down the fairway. Slapping a wedge around the tall grass, he saw nothing, so he ventured deeper into the rough and into the trees. Pushing a mountain laurel bush to the side while he looked around, his foot caught on something. Thinking it was a root, he looked down.

"Holy shit!" he cried. He stared a few moments at the body of a young teenage girl. His time in Vietnam gave him the experience to know in an instant that she was dead. He had seen dead bodies all too often, both military and civilians.

He ran out of the woods, through the rough and onto the fairway. He yelled for his friends to come to him. His voice had a panicked sound. His friends turned the carts around and headed in the direction of their golf mate.

Theo was in his office talking with the Chief when he received the call. Wilma had simply opened Theo's door and nodded toward the phone. Looking at the expression on Theo's face, as the Chief of Detectives talked, it was obvious that something was wrong, drastically wrong. Theo's facial expression was one of deep concern. Sweat dripped down his forehead.

"I'm on my way," said Theo. Placing the phone on the receiver, Theo looked at his boss. "Another body at Stone Mountain," he said.

"Good God!" the Chief said.

Grabbing his coat, Theo said, "I'll call you as soon as I have anything."

"The press is going to be all over this!" the Chief cried out.

Theo said, "Right now, that is the least of my worries. I've got a madman killing young girls. I've got to find him before he does this again."

"Do you think it's the same guy?" the Chief asked.

"From what the Officer at the scene says, I'll bet you anything it's the same guy."

"What do you want me to say to the press?" the Chief asked as Theo was bolting out the door.

"Don't tell them anything until you hear from me and we can work it out. Just say there will be a press conference as soon as we have anything positive to say."

The Chief was ready with another question, but his Chief of Detectives was gone. The Chief looked at Wilma, shrugged his shoulders and walked out, a worried look on his face.

———————

17 MEMORIES

White Man wanted to get home as quickly as possible. The bulge in his crotch from hiding the bikini bottoms was now larger due to his erection. His door key was in his hand by the time he arrived.

Once inside, he made sure the door was locked, then began undressing. Sitting in his easy chair, he began fondling the bikini and rubbing it on his erect penis. Very quickly, he felt the sensation coming and his wad shot out as if fired from a cannon. The semen missed his body and shot out onto the floor. Almost immediately, he felt spent and tired.

Laying his head back, he thought of the young girl he had just killed. He was concerned that the reason she would not let the boy put his hand in her crotch was because she was having her period. When he got her into the woods and choked the life out of her, he took off the bikini bottom and he was pleasantly surprised that there was no string coming from her vagina and no pad between her legs. The very thought of menstruation repulsed him.

He thought of his sister. They had not been sexual too long when she asked him to lick her between her legs. He pulled her panties down and saw the pad.

"I'm not doing that now!" he blurted.

"If you don't, I'll tell Mama what you have been doing to me," she said.

He looked at her a moment, then said, "We're in this together. It's our secret!"

She looked at him, a sly smile in her face. "You know Mama will believe me."

He knew she was right. His sister was his mother's favorite. Mother believed everything his sister said. He knew enough now that he was in school to know that his sister let boys touch her, even in the hallways or while she was secreted part way in her locker.

"Lick me!" she ordered.

Slowly, he put his face between her legs and began licking her.

"Faster," she said, and as he did so, he began to taste the blood.

It came very fast, his breakfast and lunch gushed all over her as well as him.

"Jesus Christ," she yelled. "You little shit head, look what you've done," she said as she leaped from the bed and ran into the bathroom.

Lying on his bed, he felt his stomach heave again and more of his food came gushing out. By now, his sister was in the shower. He reached the toilet before he wretched again. He walked into his room and stripped off the bedding. He had to get his bed linens washed and dried before his mother got home.

He waited for his sister to finish showering then he went into the bathroom, showered and let the water run into his mouth for what seemed like ten minutes or more. Once out of the shower he brushed his teeth then gargled, but he still could not get that awful taste out of his mouth.

Later that night, his sister came into his room and crawled into his bed. "How's my little sick boy!" she asked.

"Go away," he said.

"Let me make you feel better," she said, slipping his penis into her mouth.

He had no idea where his sister was now. He lost contact with both his sister and mother when he was sent to the monastery

There were no letters, no calls, no birthday or Christmas cards. They simply walked out of his life. He hated them for that, yet they were his family. He really had no idea how he should feel. However, he was very aware of a current of violent anger that ran throughout his body.

Getting out of his chair, he took the bikini bottom and put it in a drawer along with some of his other souvenirs he had collected over the years.

———

ANOTHER CRIME SCENE 18

Flashing his badge and grabbing the nearest golf cart, Theo took off down the fairway toward the area where he had been told the body of the young female was discovered.

Arriving at the scene, Theo knew it was the work of the same killer as soon as he looked at the body. It was the way the body was laid out, as if she were sleeping with her arms folded across her chest, just below her breasts. A small mound of pine straw had been placed under her head like a pillow. He could see where the petechia had formed on her throat. He made a mental note to make sure the neck and all other parts of her body were scanned by a laser to look for any fingerprints. The natural oil from the body would leave prints on the skin, prints that were invisible to the human eye. Kneeling down and looking sideways toward the body, he could see the dried epoxy on the eyelids.

"Bastard," Theo mumbled to himself.

Getting to his feet, Theo saw that several officers were now present. Park police who had jurisdiction within the boarders of the park, officers from the city of Stone Mountain, county police officers, as well as several members of his own task force, had all gathered at the crime scene. Theo looked at the assembled crowd and thought to himself, *Nothing like a nice murder to bring out all the cops.* He marveled at that. It seemed like no police officer could get enough of it. They were very voyeuristic.

Walking up to the assembled members of his task force, Theo motioned for them to gather around him. "Okay," he said in a commanding, but hushed voice, "let's get the crime scene guys out here. Rope off the area where the body is and talk to the guy who found her. Also, get a list of everybody who signed up for a tee-time today. Maybe someone saw this guy. No telling how long he was here, but I'll bet you dollars to donuts this bastard watched her for a while. I can't imagine she was here alone, so get over to the beach and see if anyone saw her with another person, probably a boy about her age. Get him identified and interviewed. And one other thing, keep these other officers away from the scene; they'll just walk over everything and make a mess of any evidence."

Then realizing he had not given his men any chance to say anything, Theo asked if anybody had done any background or talked to any witnesses.

Two officers said they were eating at a pizza café in the city of Stone Mountain when they got the call. Other than the park police, these two officers were the second on the scene. Park police talked about two teens at the beach and about a young male coming to an officer to report his girlfriend was gone. The two had been at the beach. The boy went to the restroom and when he came back, she was gone. The couple had come to the park in the boy's car so she had no other way to get home. There had been no other people at the beach that the boy had recognized. The two task force officers had located and talked to the boy.

"He's clean," one of the officers stated.

Taking turns, the two officers filled Theo in on what they had learned from the boy. "Girl's name is Whitney Farr. This has not been substantiated yet. One of the Stone Mountain officers has gone to get the kid and bring him over to I.D. the body."

Theo said, "If it's his girlfriend, he'll probably go bat shit on us, so don't keep him any longer than to just make the identification. One of you stay with him, follow him home and make sure there is someone from his family with him. "What about the girl?" Theo inquired.

"Kid says both her parents work. Her dad is some sort of manager for Delta. The mom works in the optical shop at a Wal-Mart in Jonesboro."

"Any age on the kids?" Theo asked.

"The boy is 16, the girl was 15."

"Okay," Theo said. "Let's get a team out to Delta and get the dad located and notified. Stay with him until he gets home, then stay until his wife gets home. The same with the mother. If they are religious, get their minister over there. Call Wilma and let's get a grief counselor over there. She can call Aiden O'Brian, he'll know of someone trained in that kind of counseling. Stay with the parents until you get a message to leave. Find out from the parents all you can about the girl, but don't be pushy or overbearing. Shit, I don't have to tell you how to act. I have all the confidence in the world in all you guys."

As an afterthought, Theo turned to one of the female members of the task force. "Sharon, I want you to take your partner and go and get the mother. I think this requires a woman's type of sympathy. If you must, cry with her, but let's be on our best behavior."

Theo thought a few moments making sure he had all his bases covered. Then he said, "Let's get one team to follow the body to the M.E.'s office. I'll call the examiner and make sure the autopsy gets done today. If you need me, I'll be in the office holding the Chief's hand. As soon as this gets out, and it will soon, the press is going to be all over this like white on rice. I'm sure the governor will be calling and putting his two cents in, as well.

"Oh, a couple of other things, try to get everybody on the beach identified and talked to. Locate all the park employees; see where they were and what they might have seen."

Taking a step back, Theo looked at his group. He reached in his back pocket and removed a handkerchief and wiped his brow. "Folks, this case has just been ratcheted up a good bit, so be on your toes.

Looks like we have a serial murderer here. It goes without saying that when the public hears about this, all hell is going to break loose. Folks are going to see boogers behind every tree. Every soothsayer in the country is going to try to butt in. As of now, we work seven days a week. Any of you who have put in for, or have leave scheduled, well, that is rescinded. We are going to be front page news for a while. Don't talk to anybody, especially the press. Watch what you say any place you happen to be, even a diner."

As he turned to leave, Theo looked out on the lake. He spotted a boat with a camera team. He recognized a commentator from one of the local TV stations. Turning back to his group, Theo pointed over his shoulder and said in a sarcastic manner, "I rest my case."

Theo walked back to his commandeered golf cart and took off toward the pro shop and his vehicle. He knew his life would not return to any normalcy until this thing was solved and the perp was put in jail.

————————

THE PRESS BEGINS 19

*B*ack at his office, Theo checked in with Wilma before going to update the Chief.

"How did you come in?" Wilma queried.

"Through the back and into the garage. Why?"

"Look out the window," she said.

Theo walked over to her window and looked down. The front of the building was crowded with press vans. Antennae were set up so each TV reporter could make his remote broadcast. All the local TV channels had their panel trucks there. CNN had a large truck with a large antenna dish mounted on the back. There were other network reporters there, as well. Theo turned toward Wilma. "What a circus!"

"I think we better get used to it."

Walking toward the door, Theo said, "I'll be with the Chief, but don't forward any calls that come my way. I'll take care of those when I can." The last comment came as Wilma looked at Theo's backside.

As Theo suspected, the Chief had been inundated with calls. "I've had calls from all over the country," said the Chief. "Hell, I even got a call from some reporter in Minot, North Dakota. How does this stuff get out so quickly? Have you seen what it's like outside?"

"Yeah!" Theo replied.

"Theo, we have to make some sort of statement or news release. I would rather have a statement and would rather you make it," the Chief stated.

"Well," began Theo.

"By the way," interrupted the Chief, "the Governor's office called. The Governor is taking some heat on this and wants an update. What do we tell him? Then I got a call from the president of the company that has the theme park concession at the mountain. Of course, he is upset because this is going to cost them money if it isn't solved soon."

Theo was silent for a few moments, looking with a thoughtful gaze out the window. He turned to the Chief. "If I had my druthers, I would say nothing, but I realize we cannot do that. Everybody expects press conferences now and it seems to be the politically correct way to go. Shit, everything seems to be political now. So, rather than fight this, let's schedule one for late this afternoon. Chief, you can begin, by thanking everybody and continue with some general stuff about the community, about safety. Say the park is still a great place to go, you know, the usual stuff. Then turn it over to me and I'll fill the press in on what I feel we can say. I think if we schedule this sort of event every day or so, we can probably keep a better handle on the press and whatever gossip turns up. How does that sound to you?"

"Got it," the Chief answered with a short of sigh of relief. "I'll let you handle the big stuff, Theo. Will you open it up for questions?"

"Not this time," Theo answered. "Eventually, we will have to do that. I've got a few things going right now and, hopefully, some of it will all come together soon and we can have a time for questions."

"Theo," the chief asked, "what do we have? Fill me in, would you?"

Theo motioned toward the Chief's chair. "Sit down, Chief. I'll give you what we have. We've got four dead girls."

"Four?"

Theo filled the Chief in on the first girl and told him about Mose Ellard's discovery and his thinking that they should add that first girl to the list of victims.

"We have mentioned nothing about her and I don't want to disclose that right now. We have enough paranoia going around as it is." He told the chief what he knew about the other two girls, then about the murder today. "Right now, number four is at the M.E.'s office. We should have the results before too long. Chief, what we have is a serial murderer."

"Good God!" the Chief exclaimed.

They agreed to hold a press conference at 6:30 that evening. The Chief said he would send his spokesman out to make the announcement.

Back in his office, Theo made a call to Aiden O'Brien.

"Somehow, I knew you would be calling," said the psychiatrist as he answered his phone. "It's all over the TV. I just watched a retired FBI agent in Washington, D.C. give his input."

"Any thoughts?" asked Theo.

"Do you mean me or the FBI guy?"

"Aiden," Theo said, a hint of sarcasm in his voice, "if I wanted funny, I would have called Comedy Central!"

O'Brian said, "I'm sorry, Theo. The last thing you need is a wise ass. What do you have?"

Theo filled the psychiatrist in on the fourth murder. He told him of the strangulation marks and the glue, as well as the patch of pine straw used as pillow for the dead girl's head.

"Theo!" said O'Brian, "I don't think there is any question, you've got a serial murderer on your hands and he is only going to continue killing, that is until he thinks we are on to him, then he'll scoot."

"I agree," said Theo.

O'Brian said, "Why don't I come down to your place. By then, you should have the autopsy results and the crime scene and autopsy photos will be ready. I'll look at those and get right on the profile. Oh, I have begun the profile, just so you know I'm not just sitting around."

"How soon can you get here?" asked Theo.

"I'm on my way," said the psychiatrist.

"Aiden," Theo said, "don't come in the front entrance. The press is all over the place. Come in the back through the garage."

"How do I get in?" O'Brian asked.

"I'll be down there to meet you."

"You'll hear me coming. I'll be on my bike," the psychiatrist said as he was hanging up.

———————

THE PRESS CONFERENCE 20

Promptly at 6:30 p.m., Theo and the Chief of Police walked out the front door of the station. A podium had been set up with a microphone. Several radio and TV stations also had their microphones at the podium.

The Chief was the first to speak. "Ladies and gentlemen, thank you for being here. I have always believed that the backbone of law enforcement is to have a good relationship between those of us who are officers, with the press and the public."

The Chief handled himself in a very professional manner and his voice was strong and authoritive. He stopped for a moment to let what he had said sink in. *That was an excellent approach,* Theo thought. *Good on you, Chief.*

Then the chief continued, "Today we are facing a serious matter. Approximately one month ago, two young female members of our community were murdered at Stone Mountain Park. There seemed to be no decipherable motive for the murders; however we developed a task force and they have been working non stop on this matter.

"Today, another young female was found murdered, again at Stone

Mountain Park. While the first two victims were close friends, there is no indication our first two victims had any contact or even knew the third girl. Obviously, this is a matter that brings serious and real fear to our state and particularly to the metropolitan Atlanta area, but I caution you not to panic. There is no reason not to go about your business. Just be aware of your surroundings and use common sense. Please know we are working on the matter 24/7. If you have any ideas or anything that you believe might be of help to us, we urge you to call our 800 number, which is posted behind me. I know the press will be furnishing this number, as well. We are law enforcement and it is our charge to maintain public safety as well as to investigate this matter and bring the killer to trial. But we cannot do it without your help. This is a person who resides and works among us. We do need your cooperation and your help. So please do not hesitate to call us if you have any information, no matter how trivial it may seem. Now I will turn this over to Detective Theo Reed who is heading up the investigation. And I do appreciate you all. Theo!"

Impressed with the Chief, Theo walked to the podium. He looked out over the assembled crowd. There were probably around a 100 to 125 people gathered there. Some obviously were press people, but there were others, as well. Theo recognized the face of the superintendent of schools in Dekalb County and the man who managed the Stone Mountain Village, and the part of the park that featured the concessions, rides and everything that went with it.

Theo began very simply, "Thank you all for being here. I'm not going to sugar coat this issue. We have a problem and it's a big one. Someone has murdered three of our youngsters for no apparent reason other than his own perverted desires. I am reasonably sure that if not caught soon, he will murder again. We do have a task force of experienced detectives working on this. We have the cooperation of the Georgia Bureau of Investigation and their crime lab. The F.B.I. is also working with us. We have also called in forensic experts from the private sector to glean all we can from their professional experiences and expertise."

Theo took a deep breath and continued, in a more gentle voice,

"Now, we know the need for all of you to be kept aware of all we are doing and what is going on. We will continue to hold news conferences on a timely basis. Having said that, I ask for your understanding. News conferences take time and that time takes us away from the investigation. It is time we can ill afford. But I want to make two promises to you. We will keep you informed of our progress and we will get this ...," Theo stopped, searching for an appropriate way to describe the murderer. Finally he said, "deranged person. Now I'll take a few questions, but please understand I have a great deal of work to do."

A hand went up, "Detective Reed, you keep referring to the killer as *him*. Are we to take it that that you believe he is a man and there is only one killer?'

Theo responded quickly, "We have a history of this sort of thing in our country and we have a good bit of information which leads us to believe we are looking for a single male. That is not to say there aren't two individuals working together, but at this point, we see it as highly unlikely. Next?"

"What can you tell us about the victims?" asked a female reporter Theo had seen on a local TV channel.

"Really, I can't tell you too much. All three were early adolescents and all three were strangled."

"Were they sexually assaulted?"

"No comment," Theo said.

"What are the similarities in the three murders?"

"Only that they were all in the same age range and all three were murdered at Stone Mountain Park. Beyond that, I am not prepared to discuss anything else about them or the case."

"How are their families taking it?"

It was an inappropriate question, it seemed to Theo and deserved an inappropriate answer. "These were three young girls just beginning adolescence. They were all from loving families. How do you think the families are taking it?"

"Can you provide any more information on the background of the girls?"

"No more then you already know from the press!" Then Theo said, "This concludes the press conference."

He turned and walked back into the building. Several people called out to him, asking additional questions, but Theo did not stop walking. A uniformed officer held the door open for him and made sure the door was closed after Theo walked in.

Knowing he would be late, Theo had sent Wilma to the garage to let Aiden O'Brian into the building. The psychiatrist was sitting talking with Wilma when Theo walked in.

Looking at the detective, O'Brian said, "You did well. It was a nice news conference."

"Thanks," Theo responded. "Some questions just piss me off and I realized I was beginning to lose my cool so I ended it."

"As well you should have," said the psychiatrist.

"Aiden," Theo said, "come into my office. I think I've got all the stuff you need."

They walked in and Theo closed the door. Offering O'Brian a seat, Theo walked around to his chair and sat down. He took a folder and handed it to the psychiatrist. "Crime scene photos, autopsy photos and the autopsy report. Anything else you need?"

"I don't think so, Theo. Anything you want to tell me?"

"Pretty much the same scenario, except number three happened in broad daylight. She was laid out just like Paige Langford, except this one was totally nude. Instead of using her clothes for a pillow, the killer used pine straw."

O'Brian asked, "Were any clothes found at the scene?"

"Negative," Theo said. "He glued the eyes shut again. Oh yeah, and he masturbated and came over her stomach, then smeared it all over her body, just like he did with the Langford girl." Theo shook his head and muttered, "Jesus Christ, what gets into a mind like this guy?"

Aiden said, "Theo, this is bad. I'm particularly bothered by his taking the girl in broad daylight and from a place as public as the beach. It shows he's brazen and confident."

"It was almost deserted," Theo said.

"That does not matter," said the psychiatrist. "It was still daylight and there were still people around. I think our guy is getting a little anxious. He's going to do this again and more quickly the next time. But, it could be what trips him up, too. Look, I'm out of here right now. As I told you, I've been working on the profile. I should have it for you tomorrow, probably late afternoon."

"O.K., Aiden," Theo said. As Aiden started out the door, Theo called out again, "Aiden!"

The psychiatrist turned to face Theo.

"Thanks," Theo said.

"Hey, no problem," said O'Brian as he turned and left.

———————

THE PROFILE 21

Beginning work on the profile, Aiden sighed. He dreaded this. Further, he was aware that if he was honest with himself, he knew why he was reluctant to begin the profile. To do so, he had to face some issues from his past, and they were too painful to explore at the moment.

As was always the case, his conscience would take over. As much as he tried to short- circuit the process, he was never successful. When he was alone doing his work, he always found himself thinking and recalling memories of Margaret. Those memories then brought back her *frank talks* as she was so fond of calling them. This would then lead to all the reasons and events that finally led Margaret to take the kids – all three of them – two girls and a boy, who was the middle child, and leave. They had been living and working in New York, which was part of the problem, as well. He had come home from work and saw the note on the coffee table. Taking it in his hand and slowly unfolding it, it said: "Aiden, when I get to the point I no longer like the movie, I walk out. I've stopped liking the movie. Margaret."

He had been terribly lonely after the divorce. He realized he had depended on Margaret not only as the manager of the house and mother of his children, but as his confidante and best friend. But they both struggled, he with trying to share his work with her – all the horrible things that one person could do to another person, things that were unbelievable. Poor Margaret, she struggled with trying to absorb and process the terrible stuff he was trying to share with her. After a while, it was clear to Aiden that what he had to share with Margaret was simply too difficult for her to process. He knew that his psyche was building emotional guards to protect his mind, and body, for that matter, from all the carnage he saw and worked with. As a psychiatrist, he also knew that the emotional guards, his defense mechanisms, were fast becoming permanent. So, unfortunately, while they guarded his psyche, they also guarded him against his family. In a destructive way, they guarded him from his own thoughts and feelings, from examining what he had been before he married, and what had become of him since. And so he simply stopped sharing with Margaret.

Several months after the split, Aiden had traveled to Michigan to see Margaret and the children. With some hesitation, Margaret had agreed to go with him to a small resort town which had been a favorite spot for them early in their engagement, when Aiden had been able to get a few days off from his residency program. Margaret had reminded him often that she never had any quality time with him while he was a resident. They had talked about this when they were courting, so it was not like this all came as a surprise to her.

Aiden called ahead to make reservations at a lodge they had enjoyed. On the trip over and during dinner, their conversation was interrupted by long periods of silence. It being September and cold in Michigan, he had hoped there might be an opportunity for them to be intimate. The room had one bed and a couch that folded into a hide-a-bed. Margaret told him she would not be sharing the bed and he could take the couch.

Aiden left early the next morning while Margaret was still asleep. He took a local bus to Detroit and then flew back to New York. He left the car for Margaret.

Aiden had to admit he liked his new life, living alone and being responsible to no one. He had heard once more from Margaret who wrote that she had fallen in love with a wonderful man and was now married. The children loved their stepfather. She told Aiden she and the kids were starting a new life and asked him to stay out of it completely, which he had done. Perhaps his complacency was a result of not dealing with reality or with his decision to have nothing further to do with his children until they were older and could make their own decisions. He had built a wall and was not yet prepared to go past that wall.

Aiden accepted a position in Atlanta at Emory School of Medicine. Selling his New York apartment, he moved to Peachtree Road, Atlanta's landmark street, where he found a nice two bedroom condo right on Peachtree Road. It was a short commute to the Emory campus and the other Atlanta hospitals.

The condo was designed for a roommate. He used the back bedroom as his room and the front bedroom, he turned into an office. In his office, he mounted a large white writing board on one wall. On another wall, he hung an equally large poster board where he could pin crime scene and autopsy photos. He also had a large tray table where he could place photographs in the order he needed. Additionally, he had a computer set up with a projector and a DVD player he could use when he was sent CDs of the necessary photos. His desk was in the middle of the room and it was meticulous. His life may be in a bit of disarray, but he was, as he told himself and others, anal about his work.

There was one spot on his desk that was reserved for Gertrude, his Maine Coon cat. On his desk at Gertrude's special spot, was a fairly nice sized piece of mink fur he had gotten from a furrier when Gertrude was just a kitten. "After all," Aiden told a friend, "every lady needs a fur."

He had set up his office as an escape from the campus. Although he loved the campus and the college atmosphere, it was disconcerting at times to have the phone ringing or a student dropping by unexpectedly or for a set appointment. There were times he had to be at one of the hospitals that had a psychiatric wing, but he was not a regular member of the medical school faculty, so it was not a problem. The university had been very good about his needing to travel all around to do his work. They were well aware of what he did when they hired him and they were just happy to have someone with his clout on the staff.

Procrastination was not a part of Aiden's behavior. For some reason, however, it had been difficult for him to start on this particular profile. Certainly, he enjoyed the work; not that it was *enjoyable*, but necessary. The issue with serial murderers seemed to be a growing menace and helping catch them, as well as trying to understand and hopefully stop their behavior, is what he found the most enjoyable.

He had given all the events of this case a great deal of thought. He had examined all the photos and the autopsies, so it was not like he was just beginning. Now it was time to put the pencil to the paper. As Larry the Cable Guy on TV said, *"Let's get er' done."*

He put a Bach CD in the player. Over the years, he had found Bach soothing when reviewing lewd behaviors that the photos and reports revealed. For some reason, Bach gave him a sense of balance. There was no question that doing this sort of work on a continuing basis, required something to keep his emotions balanced. And with the quietness of Bach, Aiden could really get into the mind of the killer.

When he got the case well underway, and was ready to put it all down on paper, he had Elton John and Celine Dion to pick up the pace a bit as he began to take his thoughts and diagrams and conclusions to the big white writing board.

Placing the crime scene photos in order on the tray table, Aiden began to study them with the intensity a brain surgeon might give an intricate procedure. He had to make sure he did not miss anything the photos displayed. A serial murderer tends to leave certain "calling cards" at the crime scene that signify his style and behavior, indicators that shed light on the killer's thinking, his motivations and his feelings. The indicators might be the way the body was placed or displayed, where other behaviors, such as damaging the body in some way, perhaps stab wounds, sexual behaviors, the way the body was treated, or perhaps the number or kinds of wound all meant something to the profiler. While there may be commonalities in different killings, each killer had particular behaviors that set him aside from another killer. This all spoke to the mind of the murderer. Was he organized in his work or was he haphazard and disorganized in the manner in which he thought and how his mind worked?

Aiden knew, in this case, the killings were the work of one man. For one thing, it was a rare occasion that two such killers would meet up and kill as a team. Of course, this did happen on occasion. Henry Lee Lucas and Ottis Elwood Toole came to O'Brian's thoughts. These two serial killers had met in prison. Individually, they had killed alone, then spent some time together killing.

The psychiatrist could see no evidence of two killers in the Stone Mountain case. Obviously, Paige Langford was treated differently than Holly Putzier. The only real difference was that Holly had been on her period and was wearing a Tampax. To Aiden, this seemed to be a key issue. It tied in the murder of the latest victim, Whitney Farr, the one killed at the beach near the golf course. The Farr girl and Holly Langford had both been laid out, a pillow made for them and their arms arranged across their bodies as if they were resting. The eyes of both girls had been glued shut either to appear as sleeping or perhaps in repose, so the killer would not see them looking at him. The issue with the Putzier girl, the fact that she had been treated more abusively and simply left where the killer had choked the last breath out of her, had to be, O'Brian figured, due to her menstruating. The killer had to see her as unclean. When this guy was caught, the issue of menstruation and uncleanliness would certainly be one avenue investigators would need to pursue. The killer had not just choked her, but had almost wrung her neck like one might do to a chicken.

For the other girls, Paige and Whitney, the way they were laid out, the pillows, Paige's and Whiteny's clothes and pine straw as an extra for Whitney, indicated the killer saw them as different; clean, young, and innocent. Perhaps, even precious.

Aiden was positive this was the work of an organized personality. In disorganized killers, you would expect to see some level of mutilation, perhaps bite marks on the body, particularly on the breasts and thighs. No, this person was highly organized. His victims were ones of opportunity. They just happened to be in the wrong place at the wrong time. The issue was where the killings had been conducted. No question, the location was one of the killer's planning. The area was away from other people and he could spend time with them undetected.

O'Brian felt the killer, in all probability, had a sexual interest in young, prepubescent, adolescent females, so there was an issue of pedophilia. Whether or not the killer was a true pedophile was not yet clear to the psychiatrist. Aiden was certainly aware that it was possible for a man to have both a normal sexual arousal for adult females and still have a high interest in young adolescent girls or girls of an even younger age.

Going back to Paige Langford and Whitney Farr, O'Brian felt these two girls were made to appear just what they were, dead, but perhaps as though they were in a casket. The issue was that, had they been asleep, their hair would have been more tangled, they would have been on their side or stomach, and not lain out with their arms crossed. Perhaps their mouths would be partly opened while they breathed. No, this was the work of someone who had experience with dead individuals, perhaps a mortician or someone who spent time at funerals; perhaps an officiator, or an organ player.

Paige Langford had been wearing flip-flops, which the killer had arranged near her feet. Her clothes were neatly folded and laid under her head. All her clothes were accounted for, except her panties. Whitney Farr was not wearing a full set of clothes, only a bikini, the bottoms missing, presumably taken by the killer. Past experience in working such cases led Aiden to conclude the panties and bikini bottom were taken as a souvenir or a trophy. The souvenir was a reminder of a pleasant experience, a trophy to remind him of a win, a conquest.

Aiden thought about the epoxy glue on the eyes of the two young girls. *Was the act of placing the glue on the eyes pre- or post-mortem?* He concluded it was post-mortem. This was done during preparation of the deceased, so the body would look like it was sleeping.

The sexual issue was the ejaculate on the bodies of the Langford and Farr girls. The psychiatrist felt this was done post-mortem, as well, leading Aiden to believe the killings were sexual in nature. It also indicated to O'Brian that the killer was one who was not experienced in sexual behavior. Rather than engage in sexual intercourse with both girls, which would have been unpleasant if they were alive, he chose to masturbate after they were dead, then ejaculate on the body, then rub the semen over their bodies as he explored their vaginal areas. There was also a hint of anger to this behavior, as well as control. A dead girl could not resist.

Holly Putzier was another issue. In all probably, Aiden felt, had Holly not been having her period and had there been no evidence of menstruation, the killer would have treated her as he had the Langford and Farr girls. This indicated to the psychiatrist a real level of anger in the killer toward a young person and something in his past that dealt with menstruation. Whatever it was had made it easy for him to kill Holly Putzier and toss her body on the ground carelessly. There was something in his history that upset him over a female menstruating.

Looking at his now sleeping cat, the psychiatrist said, "This person has issues with women and it isn't good. He has a deep seated hatred for females."

O'Brian made the assumption, based on his extensive interviews and research in serial killers, the killer had probably come from a single-parent home, the parent being his mother. It was also his posit that there was a sister, or some significant younger female, who was the mother's favorite. This meant the killer's father had probably been irresponsible or absent. When he was home, the father was violent and probably drank a lot. Eventually, he simply walked out of his family's life. This would create a level of anger at his father for never being there to protect him and at his mother for being so abusive to him.

The boy, in this case, the killer, was identified by the mother as the offspring of the father and thus was the recipient of her anger which was shown in all types of abuse – physical, emotional and probably sexual. Aiden also felt that, at the first opportunity, the boy left home, which meant he was on the streets at an early age or was raised in some institution. The fact that the killer had taken care of Paige and Whitney by placing their bodies as though they were experiencing no trauma, meant he was probably taken in by some state or religious orphanage and taught some manners, and how to treat people with dignity. He doubted if it was a juvenile detention center, but it could have been.

There was a different and most disturbing issue regarding the Farr girl. She also had been lured from the beach to the woods. Again, this spoke to the ability of the killer to be pleasant and charm people. But the most disturbing of all was that she had been taken in broad daylight when other people were around. This was dangerous for the killer. It appeared the killer was getting desperate and this meant he would hunt and kill again, and more quickly. While the killer took time to arrange the Farr girl's appearance, he took additional time to remove clothing and place Epoxy glue on her eyes. As the killer got more desperate, he would take more chances and would mess up. But before that, if this person was not caught soon, there would be more young girls who were killed.

The killer had sexual needs that he didn't know how to – *or couldn't* – satisfy in an appropriate, normal way. He enjoyed being alone in his own personal fantasy life. He had anger towards young girls, probably women in general, yet he felt the need to be gentle with these girls. This was probably due to his ability to act normal among others. And he was angry. Very angry at his mother.

O'Brian was sure of several things. The killer was older, probably in his mid-30's, Caucasian and single. He was probably thrown out of his house by his single mother when he was a teenager, and grew up in some kind of institution, probably in an orphanage – religious or not – and maybe even in foster homes. He came from a single parent family, the parent being female. He had a deep seated anger for females and primarily directed this anger toward younger girls which indicated to the psychiatrist that the mother had a favorite child, probably a female sibling.

While the victims were random, Aiden felt the killer knew the Langford and Putzier girls and, in all probability, they knew him. Otherwise, two girls would not have willingly followed him into the woods. The girls were smart and the killer had to be a person they trusted. He was able to talk them into going with him, using some sort of ruse to persuade both girls to leave the show. Both girls obviously stayed together. There were no marks or indications the killer had tied their hands or forced them in any way to go with him. Whatever occurred seemed natural to anybody who may have seen the trio. These two girls had to know and trust their killer. When they went with him, they had no idea they were in any danger. That was a major issue in identifying this person. In public life, this individual would probably appear to have a special interest in children. Maybe it was his job to work with children.

The perp's anger was seldom seen by other people. Yet when his anger did erupt, he became physically and verbally aggressive. The three young girls killed at Stone Mountain were not the only victims of this individual. The killer had killed young girls before, and if not caught, he would kill again, and again, until he was apprehended. Perhaps he had just recently moved to the Atlanta area, and that was the reason the murders had just started.

Looking at past cases in which there were similarities, O'Brian believed the killer would want to insert himself in the investigation as a way of gaining trust with officers as a way to gain information on the investigation.

Aiden knew this person lived alone, yet had the ability to socialize with others. This was a part of his psychopathic personality. His home was a place of safety for him.

This person knew Stone Mountain Park and frequented it often. He knew how to navigate the area. There was a good chance he lived in the area. Given the fact there were so many joggers that frequented the park, Aiden felt the killer would usually wear running clothes and shoes. However, the man was not athletic in terms of running. Running would put him in too close proximity of other runners and he would probably stand out among other runners.

While preparing his profile and list of questions for suspects, Aiden wrote:

This person will probably return to the scene of the murders. Murdering the girls gave him pleasure. He will want to relive that pleasure. There must be outdoor cameras that are motion-sensitive that are available to hunters to identify trails frequented by wildlife. They could be purchased at any outdoor store. For that matter, the killer might purchase one as well to determine any police activity at the scene. Organized serial killers were very intelligent.

Aiden O'Brian was positive the killer's name was already in the task force files. Now they just had to figure out which of those thousands of names that had come up during the investigation, was the killer. When the killer was caught people who knew him would be shocked.

Aiden sat back. He then re-examined the photographs to insure he had missed nothing. He reviewed all the notes and reports. Something was missing and he could not put his finger on it. *What was it?* he wondered.

He rubbed his eyes. He was was exhausted. Then it hit him, like a bolt out of lightning! It was the eyes. He recalled a crusty old forensic psychiatrist he had worked with in New York. While working on a profile, the old man had turned to his him and said, "Aiden, never forget the eyes. The eyes are the windows to a man's soul."

That's it! thought O'Brien. Turning to his computer he typed the final paragraph to the profile:

When this person is caught and you have him locked up, look into his eyes. They will be dark and reptilian. The most powerful part of this person's brain, the secret to both his survival and his behavior is his limbic system, yet it is the most primitive part of the brain.

When confronted, his eyes will be the key. When this person is identified, people in the community will be surprised at his identity.

At last he was finished. Looking at his clock, he yawned. It was almost 3:30 a.m. He looked at Gertrude who was fast asleep. Deciding not to disturb the cat, he walked to his bedroom and scanned his calendar. He shook his head. His day would be full, with a lecture, appointments and a dreaded departmental meeting.

He lay down and was asleep as soon as his head hit the pillow. He was not aware that Gertrude had followed him into his room and had jumped on the bed and curled up next to him.

———————

AIDEN AND THEO

In between the lecture and his appointments, Aiden checked his cell phone for messages. One was from Theo asking the psychiatrist to call him. O'Brian returned the call and waited a moment before he heard the familiar voice of the detective.

"Aiden, how you doing?"

"Fine, Theo. I was planning on calling you. I finished the profile last night – well, actually this morning. I was going to call then but I didn't think a call at 3:30 a.m. was appropriate."

"Thanks," Theo said. "When can we meet? I've got a couple of things to go over with you and I'm anxious to hear what the profile says. How about dinner?"

"Theo, that would be wonderful. I've got a departmental faculty meeting at 5:00. When you get a bunch of psychiatrists and psychologists together, they all try to figure out how many angels fit on the head of a pin. It is positively a grueling time, so it will have to be a little later."

"No problem, I'm a little busy myself so, later will be good for me, as well," said the detective. "Where do you want to meet?"

"How about Manual's Tavern? It will be full enough that we will not be noticed, yet private enough that we can have a good talk. I'm free from classes tomorrow, so I may even have a barley pop or two."

"How about 7:30? Will your meeting be over then?" asked Theo.

"Sound's good, see you then," Aiden said, hanging up.

Manual's Tavern was a fairly popular, local watering hole for Georgia legislators when the legislature was in session, which would not be for a few more months. The tavern was also popular with a large group of locals, so there was always a little noise, the sound of the shuffle board, as well as the old 50's juke box.

Aiden was already there and had a mug of beer almost finished when Theo arrived and slid into the booth.

"Sorry I'm late," Theo said. "The chief is hot on me for news so I had to give him an update."

"Is there anything to update?" Aiden asked.

"No, there isn't much. Lots of leads, but nothing is panning out. I can tell you this though, visitors at the park is way down and only a handful stay for the laser show. The amusement company that has the park contract at the mountain is putting pressure on every state official they can think of. Those folks call the chief and he calls me. We really need to catch a break."

"Well, maybe I can help a bit," Aiden said. Theo brightened with this news.

The waiter came and they both ordered a frosty mug of beer and hamburgers.

"O.K., Theo, this is what I believe." O'Brian handed a copy of the profile to Theo and recapped all the main points.

When they had finished, O'Brian continued, "Theo, I think we need to put a little pressure on this guy. Perhaps a more detailed news conference where you give quite a bit of information, yet say nothing that would really tip the killer off that we are getting closer."

"Are we getting closer?" Theo asked.

"I think, with the profile, we are."

A slight smile spread over Aiden's face. He said, "Theo, we know who this guy is. He's in the case files. We can play with his mind a bit and drive him out. He thinks he is more intelligent and smarter than you and everybody on the task force. If we give out some information, raise the guy's anxiety a bit, we just might ferret him out. I think it's worth a try."

"Okay," Theo replied. "What do we do?"

"I've got it all planned," the psychiatrist said. "How long will it take you to arrange a news conference?"

"Not long," Theo replied. "I've got the press camped out at the law enforcement center. All I have to do is walk out the front door."

"This is my plan." The psychiatrist motioned Theo closer.

They talked for the next hour and a half. When they stopped, both men finished eating their hamburgers and ordered another two beers. Theo looked much happier leaving than he had when he walked in.

23
ANOTHER NEWS CONFERENCE

Walking out the front door of the law enforcement center, Theo was taken aback by the size of the crowd. The news conference had only been announced last evening. Obviously, the murders had taken on a new interest as Theo noticed a truck bearing the BBC logo, as well as several groups from other countries. He also saw trucks with logos from Canada and Mexico. The podium had microphones, not only from the Atlanta area and CNN, but from France, Germany, the Netherlands and Japan. *Good Lord!* Theo estimated the crowd at just about 100, leading him to believe there were more than just news people present.

Theo adjusted the microphone and began, "Thank you all for coming. For those of you who do not know me, my name is Chief of Detectives Theophilus Reed. I am in charge of this investigation. I wanted to talk to you today because, as some of you know, at our last new conference there was not too much we felt we could say. For that matter, there was not much we had that we could mention. Since that time, we have come a long way. First, let me give you a little history."

Pausing a moment to look over the crowd, Theo continued,

"Several years ago, Atlanta had what was identified as the Atlanta Child Murders, where several young African-American boys were murdered. The greater Atlanta area was near panic as the murders continued. A task force made up of experienced officers, men and women, with expertise in all phases of murder investigations was formed which included officers from all the surrounding cities and towns in the greater Atlanta metropolitan area. Working together and with outside help from several federal agencies, they were able to identify Wayne Williams as the person who murdered the young boys. Williams was arrested, tried and convicted and is in prison today.

"With the termination of that case, our area was able to settle down. However, the task force stayed together. With the exception of officers who may have quit, gotten promoted, or retired, the task force has remained the same. While we have not experienced any other cases like the Atlanta Child Murders, there have been times we have made ourselves available to other Georgia jurisdictions to help with missing persons, certain murders and to teach homicide investigators at the Georgia Public Safety Training Center in Forsyth, Georgia.

"As a group, we have continued to come together approximately four times a year to discuss interesting cases in our several jurisdictions and to meet with investigators in other areas where they present their problematic cases and we provide our expertise. This has worked out very well. It is this group that has come together as a task force for the murders at Stone Mountain.

"Our task force is approximately 100 strong. They operate two members to a car and are assigned leads based on their expertise. They work in shifts and the teams have groups working 24 hours a day. They will keep working until this matter is solved and the perpetrator arrested. So you can trust we are doing everything we can to find this perpetrator.

"Today, I want to bring you up to date on what we have so far. I will discuss certain issues about the investigation and about the perpetrator; however, I will answer no questions about any evidence or anything that, in my estimation, will jeopardize the case."

Theo knew full well that reporters would not listen with a sharp ear and there would be questions that he could and *would not* answer, and those questions would continue to be asked.

Theo continued, "So far, we have four victims, all adolescent females, all murdered in the same fashion. There were similarities with all four girls that have led us to believe the same perpetrator was the killer of all four girls. We have a behavioral profile of this man which has provided us a great deal of information and helped us to reduce the size of our list of possible suspects. We feel we are getting close to identifying this person."

Theo opened the forum for questions.

The first question was from a reporter Theo recognized as working for CNN. "Detective, you mentioned four victims. We have only been told about three. Can you identify this fourth girl and when she was killed?"

"She was actually our *first* victim. Her body was discovered last spring by a fisherman who was fishing on the lake. Her body was found in the water and was badly decomposed. We have not been able to identify her..."

"But why were we not told?" the CNN reporter yelled.

"At first," Theo began, "we believed this was either an accidental drowning or murder possibly of a young prostitute killing by her pimp or someone she angered. It was not until later in this investigation that we were able to add her to the list of victims in this case."

"Was your task force working on the first victim, and if not, why?" questioned the local NBC affiliate reporter.

"No," Theo replied. "While the matter of this girl was investigated, her case was assigned to first a missing person's detective, then later to a homicide detective on our task force. Later in our investigation, she was added to our list and is part of the ongoing investigation."

"Detective, I'm Herman Schlitz for German News. You said you had a profile on the murderer. Can you elaborate?"

"Yes, we do have a profile. We believe we are looking for a single white male, probably in his 30s, unmarried and in a responsible job.

He is quite familiar with the park and wooded areas. We have a much better behavioral image of who we are looking for."

Another reporter asked, "Rumor has been going around that one of the victims was treated differently than the other three girls, now four girls. Were there similarities or differences in the way some of the bodies were handled?"

"No comment," Theo replied.

The press conference went on for a short time. The questions were about details of the investigation. Theo didn't respond. Just as he was ready to conclude, a voice from the crowd asked, "For those of us who have children and enjoy Stone Mountain Park, I think I can speak for all of us that this investigation has gone on for some time. Perhaps if you worked longer and harder, the fourth girl would not have been killed. What do we tell our children and how do we know the park will ever be safe again?'

Theo said, "Sir, I can understand your concern about your children. Stone Mountain is a wonderful place to take them and I believe people should continue to take advantage of all the park has to offer. I think, at this time, and in this place, you simply have to stay together and keep an eye on your children and simply stay aware. Whoever the killer is, rest assured he will not try anything where there is a group of people or with families that are together.

"Our task force is made up of dedicated officers who have a wealth of experience in working on difficult cases. Most of the task force members are parents, as well. They have a great deal on understanding and empathy about this case. Our work is paying off. The task force members, every one of them are dedicated to bring this killer to justice. Please understand this is not a simple matter. The case is very complicated."

Another reporter yelled out, "If all the victims so far have been young girls, are young boys safe?"

Theo rubbed his chin a moment, then answered, "We have not had any male victims that we know about. I would say our killer has a high interest in females. However, this is a serial killer. Serial killers tend to move around, city to city, small town to small town, state to state. So we're checking that out."

"How do you check out something that may have occurred in a state far from here?" asked an Atlanta newspaper woman.

Theo said, "Several years ago, the FBI set up a Violent Criminal Apprehension Center where departments from all over the country would submit information to VICAP. Then, every other department in the country could compare their unsolved cases and facts with those in other parts of the country. If there were similarities in cases, VICAP would put the departments in touch with each other. We have done that."

"Is it working?' asked the newspaper reporter.

"We shall see," said Theo. "That is all for now. Thank you, ladies and gentlemen."

Theo turned around and walked inside the building.

It seemed like it took forever for the bus to show up. When it finally did arrive, there were several people waiting to board. White Man pushed himself to the front of the line trying to insure he would get a window seat, where he immediately put his bag in the next seat. Now he could sit alone and in peace.

As the bus drove off, he thought about what he had just heard. *I don't think they have shit,* he thought to himself. *They're bluffing. Those stupid bastards are just like all the others. If they were so smart and if that FBI stuff was all it was cracked up to be, I would have been toast by now. People become cops because they are lazy and can't do anything else.*

Looking out the window, he watched the people as the bus drove down the road. Eventually, the bus stopped at a red light. A car driven by a young girl pulled up next to the bus. He looked down at the girl. Her skirt was above her knees by several inches. He wondered how she might look naked. He could feel the bulge begin in the crotch of his pants. He put his coat over his lap and soon a small wet stain appeared on his trousers, right by the fly.

Shit, he thought to himself, *I hate it when that happens.*

White Man's house was not that far from the law enforcement center, but it was too far to walk. The traffic was terrible and it took almost 45 minutes for him to get to his destination. The bus stop was just a block from his house. There was little traffic on the road right now. Of course, the trains coming from the city would not be full and traffic would not increase until the 5:00 rush began. He could walk to his home without anybody seeing the wet spot.

As White Man walked, he was aware that no cars had headed to or from the park. He wondered if he needed to begin looking into find a new place to hunt.

———————————

A STARTLING EVENT

The first thing Theo did when he got into his car was to reach into the glove compartment, remove a large bottle of TUMS and pop three into his mouth. He followed that with a swig of Maloxx he kept in his car for just such situations. *Those situations* were becoming more frequent. He knew he had to make some changes in his life, if not for anything else, for his health.

The task force meeting had been held at a small banquet room just outside Stone Mountain Park and today's meal had been a culinary disaster. The salad had seen better days, the chicken tasted as though it had been processed by some tire company, the broccoli was way overcooked, and the mashed potatoes tasted like mix from a box. The rolls were hard as rocks and to top it off, the slice of key lime pie, was so small, it looked as though it had been measured with a caliper, and it had a graham cracker crust so hard he had to jam it with his fork to get a bite. In doing so, it sprang off his plate. As he grabbed for it, he knocked his glass of sweet tea over, spilling the contents all over the table.

Embarrassed, he tried a polite smile while his fellow officers ribbed him. And so it was with such events. The food was just never good. Perhaps the next meeting could be held at the jail. Jail food was monitored and was required to be fresh.

Generally, Theo had more important things to do than spend his time at meetings, but this one was important and dealt with the murders. He gave every team in the task force the opportunity to give a report.

Task forces were necessary any time there was a major case; and there was no argument about this being a major case. But in cases like this, with several well trained officers, there were egos to deal with and a level of politics which, as Theo had told Wilma, "sucked."

Adding to this was the fact that the further you went up the hierarchy, you were involved more into the administrative side of making sure the department ran well. The more he worked, the more administrative work he was required to do. Many times, he wished he had just stayed a brick detective. He missed the actual detective work, the time on the streets, the thrill of the chase, and he took every opportunity to slide back into that work, whenever he had a chance. Sadly, he realized he could never go back. It would not be allowed. If he stayed in law enforcement, his future was set in stone. There could be no turning back.

Not anxious to get back to the office and all the telephone messages he knew would be waiting, Theo exited the parking lot and drove slowly down the road that would eventually take him into the Park and onto the road that circumnavigated the mountain. Once on that road, he was careful to maintain the 25 miles an hour speed limit. The Stone Mountain park police were known to be very exact on speed limits and had never been known for professional courtesy when it came to speeding. *It was,* Theo thought to himself, *a necessary part of law enforcement at the mountain given the large crowds that were generally visiting.*

The scent of autumn was beginning to fill the air. September and October were the best, and the most beautiful times at the Mountain. Soon the trees would turn colors and the area would be awash in vivid yellows, gold, and reds with a little green from the fir trees.

It felt nice to have his car window down, and his air conditioner turned off. Looking around, Theo could see a hint of yellow, gold and red, even now. *Perhaps it was wishful thinking,* he told himself. The summer had been a sizzler in more ways than one.

Topping the road on the hill just past the Stone Mountain Inn, Theo began to drive slowly downhill. Had he been in a hurry, he might not have noticed the man walking up the hill, along the sidewalk. He was dressed in full running gear, shorts and tank top, but he was walking, not running. Giving the man a second look, Theo noticed he was wearing street shoes and black socks. He had a billed cap on his head and his ponytail was protruding from the back of the ball cap.

"Holy Mary, Mother of God!" Theo murmured to himself. He immediately slowed down, almost to a stop. Even 25 miles an hour would be too fast for this person. Heart beating like a jackhammer, Theo pulled to the side of the road where he could watch this person walk up the hill.

How unusual, Theo thought to himself. *Why would someone go to the trouble of wearing a full set of running clothes, then wear street shoes and black socks that reach halfway up the calf? That didn't match. A runner would never do that.*

Studying the man, there was no mistaking him. *It was Father Hixon DuPree!* Watching DuPree walk along the sidewalk, Theo thought to himself, *Well, just because a man wants to get in some exercise, does not mean he has to dress full tilt for it. Maybe he was just beginning his exercise program and hadn't bought the right shoes and socks yet.*

But something about the way the priest was dressed and the way he carried himself, bothered Theo. *What is it?* he thought, racking his brain. Then it hit him. "By God, he fits part of the profile! If he doesn't, then I'm Gomer Pyle. I'll be damned," Theo said out loud.

Continuing his surveillance, Theo watched, mesmerized, as DuPree stopped at a tree. Straining to see further, Theo watched him as he looked at one of the missing girls' posters. Watching as intently as he could, he saw DuPree reach up and yank the poster off the tree, fold it flat, and place it inside the front of his running shorts. DuPree then walked back to the sidewalk and continued on his journey.

Theo stayed in his parked position until DuPree had topped the hill. Then slowly, he pulled back onto the road and drove at a creeping pace to the top. Once there, he saw DuPree walking along the sidewalk with his arms swaying back and forth like he had not a care in the world.

Again, Theo had to park. He did not want to give himself away and he had no intention of stopping DuPree to talk with him. Nor, for that matter, did he want to give himself away by holding up traffic or arouse the suspicion of anyone who might be walking or running on this route. He needed to find out what DuPree was doing, and at the same time, insure he was not seen by the priest.

The game of cat and mouse went on for a mile or so until DuPree reached the playground. This was the area across the road from where Paige and Holly's bodies were found. Theo watched as DuPree left the sidewalk, walked down the embankment and into the woods toward the area where the girls had been killed and their bodies found.

Theo backed up and was able to find a small service road that led to the area where the park groundskeepers had a greenhouse and kept their lawn equipment. It was easy then for him to hide his car in the woods and get into a good place to wait for DuPree to come out of the woods.

Theo got out of his car, careful not to slam the door. Staying in the woods and shrubs on the opposite side of the road, Theo was able to keep his eyes on the path leading to the scene of the deaths, and the direction DuPree had taken. Theo held his breath, not making a sound.

After waiting about twenty minutes, DuPree emerged and continued walking down the sidewalk, away from where Theo was hiding. Giving the priest about five minutes, Theo debated quietly to himself, "Should I follow him or should I go to the crime scene and see if DuPree did anything unusual?"

The crime scene won and making sure the priest was on his way, Theo exited the wooded area where he had been hiding and walked across the road. He carefully went down the embankment and continued to the spot where the bodies of the two girls had been found.

It did not take Theo long to find the poster. Picking it up, the detective murmured, "Holy shit!" The image of Holly Putzier had been torn from the poster. Theo looked around and saw the spot where Holly's body had been found. The piece of poster was lying on the ground near that spot where Paige Langford's body had been. On the ground, wadded up.

Removing his handkerchief from his pocket, Theo picked up the wadded piece of paper. Carefully, the detective wrapped the paper in the handkerchief and placed it inside the breast pocket of his jacket as he continued to look around. The rest of the poster was lying on the ground, on the exact spot where the Langford girl's body had been found. Theo reached down and picked it up. He saw the image of Paige Langford. Looking more intently, Theo gasped. Across the face of Paige Langford was a slowly moving trail of what Theo recognized as fresh semen. *Good God Almighty!* Theo's heart thudded in his chest.

Slowly, Theo looked around the area for any other suspicious items or marks. Seeing nothing, he carefully carried the poster back to his car. Opening the trunk, he placed it inside a large paper bag he carried in his trunk. He was extremely careful not to let any of the ejaculate drip off the paper.

Slowly, Theo moved his car back onto the road and headed in the direction he had last seen DuPree walking. He did not see the priest, so he took one fast drive around the road that circled the mountain, to insure DuPree was gone. Theo then turned to take the road that would exit the park. As he drove down the road, he noticed the now familiar gait of the priest dressed in his jogging attire, along with his black calf-length socks and his street shoes walking down the road toward Dupree's home, and the location of St. Jude's by the Mountain.

Theo was simply dumbfounded by this turn of events. *Oh, my God!* Stopping his car along the curb, he watched as DuPree turned into his house across the street from the church and walked in.

Once Theo finished his surveillance, he drove until he saw a telephone booth, which were hard to find these days. There was a clank that came from the transmission of his car as he put the gear shift into park before he completely stopped. His hands trembled. Realizing he had no quarters, Theo had to run into a convenience store to get some change, all the way muttering out loud curses to the telephone company that the cost of a telephone call was no longer a dime. Once in the booth, quarter in his fingers, he inserted it into the slot and called his office.

Within seconds, he heard Wilma's soft voice, "Chief of Detective's Office, may I help you?"

"Wilma, it's Theo."

"What in the world are you doing calling me on a landline? Is your cell phone broken?"

"No, *dammit!* Listen, I want to make sure nobody hears what I have to say. When you use a cell phone, you never know who's listening."

"You're right," she said. "What's up?"

"Wilma, you still have your badge?"

"Yes," she said. "I always carry it, but I'm not sure why you gave it to me in the first place."

"I gave it to you because at some point, I may need your help. That time is now." Theo's voice sounded stressed, then he whispered into the phone, "Wilma, I've got a hunch. This is important. Actually, it's more than a hunch. You know where St. Phillip's Cathedral is?"

Wilma replied, "You mean that big Episcopal church on Peachtree Road?"

"Yeah, that's the one. The Diocese of Atlanta office is there, you know the Bishop's office. I want you to close up the shop and get down there. Use your badge if you have to. There has to be some sort of directory that gives the history or background of each member of the Diocese of Atlanta, perhaps of the entire church. I need that information. Use your charm. And for God's sake, don't let on that you know anything. Use some sort of ruse, but I want you to get all the places Hixon DuPree has been assigned as a priest or deacon since his ordination. Get a list of every place, but above all, be discrete. I don't want anybody to get suspicious, but get the information and give it to me as soon as you can. If someone comes along and asks why you are closing the office, tell them you are sick or something. Or that you have some errand to run for me. Actually, I don't care what excuse you use, just close the office and get on down there and get the information. Then go home and wait for me to call. Got it?"

"Got it!" Wilma replied.

"Good," Theo said. "Now get going and remember, don't arouse any suspicion."

Then Theo hung up with Wilma looking at the receiver with a puzzled look on her face.

Theo's next call was to Aiden O'Brian.

When the psychiatrist answered his phone, Theo burst out as quietly as he could, "You won't believe this, but I think I have our man. *It's Father Hixon DuPree!*"

"You're shitting me!" the psychiatrist shouted.

Theo gave O'Brian a full account of what he had seen: the way DuPree was dressed, that he was walking along the sidewalk and went into the area where the two girls had been killed. Theo then carefully described what he had found once he walked to the crime scene.

"Jesus," the psychiatrist said. "That's just what the profile said. And it's not unusual for the killer to visit the crime scene. He was reliving the killing and the sexual pleasure he got form it. *Wow! What now?*"

"I've sent Wilma down to the Diocese office to see what she can find out about DuPree's previous assignments. Where he's been before coming to Atlanta, that kind of thing. When she gets back, I'll call those places and see if they have anything on him. We'll also check to see if there were any unsolved murders in the areas where he's lived previously. In the meantime, I'm going to set up a 24 hr. surveillance on this guy. If he's our man, we'll do what we can to nail the bastard." Theo could hardly breathe, he was so excited.

"My God, what a break!" said Aiden. "If you hadn't been driving in the park, you would have never seen him."

Theo said, "I know, Aiden. I'll call you as soon as I know anything.

Right now I'm headed for the GBI crime lab. I'll get a rush on the DNA and any prints. When I call, I'll use the landline. I don't want to take any chance that somebody might be listening in on our conversation. So stay by your phone, your office or your home!"

"I'm at home now and I won't leave the phone," O'Brian said. "Theo, I hope this is the lead you need. You and everybody else deserve a break on this case."

"Amen to that," Theo said.

Jumping into his car, Theo drove back to the neighborhood where St. Jude's was located and the home across the street where Hixon DuPree lived. The detective was anxious to examine the neighborhood so he could set up the surveillance immediately. He would need at least two places, one stationary, and one where he could have a car where his officers could be mobile. Luck was with him. Directly across the street from the church, was an apartment complex. He hoped there would be no problem renting a place that would give his officers a direct view of DuPree's house, the church and the church office.

Theo drove into the apartment complex, perused the area, then turned to leave. This location was perfect for the surveillance, considering the distance and proximity of the church parking lot, the church office and the house DuPree occupied. Theo could not have asked for anything better. He had a great view of the entire property. He could also use the apartment complex parking lot to keep a mobile car manned, yet out of sight.

As Theo exited the apartment complex, he looked in his rear view mirror. He slowed down. Walking slowly across the road from his house to the church, as if he had not a care in the world, was Father Hixon DuPree. But now he was dressed in his clerical clothes, except for the shoes. They looked the same to Theo.

Theo knew he was safe enough. He knew DuPree was nowhere close enough to recognize him or even to take notice of the Crown Victoria he was driving.

Theo drove directly to the headquarters of the Georgia Bureau of Investigation where the GBI crime lab was located. It was several miles from Theo's office and the Law Enforcement Center. He was able to find a parking place almost in front of the building. Taking his precious cargo with him, Theo stopped by the director's office and got his blessing for a rush job.

Then, the director walked to the lab with Theo and personally asked that the DNA testing begin immediately, noting to the lab supervisor that Theo was working on the Stone Mountain case, and needed the DNA results as quickly as possible. Theo handed over the evidence.

There was always paperwork and chain of command. Everybody was aware of the fact that if the chain of command was not clearly executed, then no matter what the evidence was, it would not be allowed in court. Theo was covering all his bases.

Thanking the director, Theo rushed out to his car and drove to his office, faster than he should have, but this was important business. Theo knew this was the break he had been looking for.

He had not been in his office more than half an hour when his anxiousness got the better of him. He called Wilma at her home. "I didn't expect you to be home yet," the detective said. "Any luck?"

"It was a piece of cake," Wilma said. "They could not have been nicer. Yes, such a book does exist and yes, Father Hixon DuPree is in there with his complete history. The secretary even ran off a copy of his biography. I told her we, the police department, were thinking of presenting DuPree with a certificate for his help with children and we wanted to get some congratulatory letters from some church people in other places where he had been. She took it, hook, line and sinker."

"Wilma, you got any beer?" Theo asked.

"Yes," Wilma replied slowly. "Why?"

"Stay there, I'm coming right over," Theo said with more exuberance than he had shown in weeks.

Theo tried to hold down his excitement as he drove to Wilma's. He had only been to her house a few times, mostly on business. She owned a small bungalow in the Inman Park area of Atlanta. Inman Park was an old area of Atlanta with old, but very gracious early 1900's homes and beautiful trees, live oaks, white ash, sweet gum and some fir trees. Wilma had bought her house during an estate sale. "It had that gracious, lived-in feeling," she had said and it was just right for her and her 14 year old son. Just a two bedroom, old red brick house, well off the street, and almost hidden by a very old and large oak tree and several evergreens. But, it was beautiful and elegant like Wilma was.

Wilma saw Theo walking up to her house, almost running. Opening the door to greet him, she offered a small hug and a beer as he hurried in. She could tell he was very excited about the day's events. She had the papers from the diocese sitting on a lamp table. Walking over, she retrieved them and handed them to the detective.

Theo sat down in the first chair he saw, a Bentwood rocker Wilma had picked up at a high end antique shop. "Thanks for the beer," he said. "It has been one helluva day."

"It sure has," Wilma laughed.

Hixon DuPree's biography was not very long. Originally from New Orleans, Louisiana, he had attended a Roman Catholic Seminary. He had been ordained into the priesthood upon graduation. Assigned to a parish in Louisiana, he was there for only a small time when he transferred to an Episcopal Seminary in Wisconsin, eight years ago. He then served as a Deacon in a parish in Idaho where, a year later, he was ordained a priest in the Episcopal Church. His next assignment was as a camp director for an Episcopal Church camp in Montana. He was there for one summer. Then, there was a gap of a few years until his name appeared when he came to St. Jude's in Stone Mountain.

Wilma, reading over Theo's shoulder, asked, "I wonder what happened in Montana that caused him to leave so quickly and stay away from his church for so long? And why did he leave the Catholic Church to go to the Episcopal one?"

"Well, there's one way to find out," Theo replied. "Do you have an atlas?"

"Someplace," Wilma said. "Let me go search."

Wilma returned soon with the book opened to a section on Montana. "It was right where I last left it, on top of the bookshelf in my room," she said, handing the book to Theo.

Atlas in hand, Theo reached for the biography of DuPree and saw that the church camp was on Flathead Lake. Looking at his watch, Theo figured with daylight savings time, he had time to call the sheriff's office in Montana and talk with the sheriff or a deputy. Dialing information, he got the number of the Lake County Sheriff's Office, which was located in Kalispell, Montana.

After several rings, the call was answered by someone who talked way too fast. Theo could barely understand a thing he was saying. Finally, Theo identified himself and had to repeat it two more times before the receptionist got it right. The sheriff was not in the office, the receptionist explained.

Theo asked to speak to whoever was next in line and in the office. He was informed the undersheriff was in.

"That's fine," Theo said. "May I talk with him?"

The phone rang 5 times, then a voice said, "Sheriff Simpson here, what can I do for you?"

"Sheriff Simpson, this is Theo Reed; I'm the Chief of Detectives in DeKalb County, Georgia, a major part of the metropolitan Atlanta area. Do you have a minute?"

"Sure! Did you say Georgia?"

"Yes," Theo replied.

"Okay, what can I do for you?" the undersheriff asked.

Theo answered, "We have a series of murders here, all young girls and all strangled. The murders took place at Stone Mountain Park, which is a natural park surrounded by the metro Atlanta area and several other metropolitan cities. Our investigation has developed a suspect named Father Hixon DuPree. We know he was in your area some time ago at an Episcopal Church camp. I was wondering if perhaps you might have met him or had anything to do with him while he was there?"

"Holy shit! That's a name out of the past and one I thought I would never hear again, yet at the same time, I'm not surprised to hear it."

Theo's heart began to race. He could hear himself breathing into the phone. Anxiously, he asked, "Can you tell me about it?"

"Yeah," said the law enforcement officer. "He was in charge of the camp which is located near the south end of the lake. One day he was with one of the campers, a young girl. They were on the lake in a canoe. DuPree later told us the canoe tipped over. The girl allegedly drowned. The fact is that her body has never showed up. You know, usually a drowned body floats to the top after a couple of days; then some beach walker, or swimmer, or whoever, stumbles on it. Well, not this time and not for this girl."

"What happened to DuPree?" Theo inquired.

The undersheriff replied, "Interestingly enough, he was able to get the canoe back upright and crawl in it. When he did not show up at camp, they called us, and a search crew in a Zodiac boat found him floating around, helpless as all get out. We put a search team out, had divers go down, but hell, no luck. You know the lake is pretty damn cold and under those circumstances, the divers didn't have much luck."

"What was your read on it?" Theo questioned.

"Well," the undersheriff answered, "officially, it was ruled a drowning. When we found DuPree, he was in the canoe wet and cold, which was understandable. The lake is glacier fed and like I said, the water is as cold as a witch's tit. Had DuPree stayed in the water and not been found, he probably would have died of exposure. Fortunately for him, it was in August and although the nights get cold, they are warm enough in August that he was able to get a little warm even though he was well soaked. His story was that the girl stood up and caused the canoe to rock and tip over. Funny thing, looking inside the canoe the next day, it was never wet enough to have tipped over and gone through as much as Dupree said. Of course, it was the next day when we got a chance to look in the canoe and it had been sitting in the sun on a dock."

"Interesting," said Theo.

"Yeah, at his inquest, the coroner ruled it was a drowning. There was no indication of any fowl play and the Church was very supportive of this guy, so case closed." There was a pause, then the law officer said, "You know, I've never been convinced it happened the way DuPree said. I just had a funny feeling about that guy. I still do. It was his eyes, like you look in his eyes and know the lights are on, but nobody's home. They were just cold looking, know what I mean?"

Theo wanted to probe a bit more. "Sheriff, do you have any personal opinion in the matter?"

"You know, Chief Reed, personally, I've never been able to get over this thing. In the back of my mind, I always thought it never happened the way DuPree said. I think he killed her. I think he tied something around her neck, something heavy enough to send her to the bottom of the lake and hold her body down. In questioning some of the other camp personnel, we were told the canoe had a cement block in it that was used to hold the canoe on the bank if anybody stopped on a beach and went ashore. When we looked at the canoe the next day, there was nothing in it. Our assumption was that the block fell out when the canoe tipped. My thoughts were that DuPree probably put a second block in the canoe. That would not have drawn any attention, then he did something to the girl while they were out on the lake, then dumped her over. He jumped in the lake, but was able to get back in the canoe. It's not hard if you know how."

"What happened after that?" Theo asked.

"Dupree left the camp shortly after that. People at the camp said he was too distraught over the incident. For some reason, I was troubled by that but, hell, it was just a feeling. But there was just something about that guy. I don't know, I just don't know," the sheriff said. "You think he's your man?"

"Yeah, I think so," Theo answered. "Oh, one more thing Sheriff, were there any complaints made to your office about DuPree prior to the incident?"

"No, nothing. Everybody liked him."

Theo asked, "Did you do any background checks on DuPree?"

"No, certainly not when he got here, there didn't seem to be a need. After the event you know, you get a case, get a coroner's ruling, no probable cause and the next day, it's something else. Even if there was some suspicion, we couldn't do anything about it. Our only witness left and we had no body. We just had no probable cause to keep going," said the sheriff.

"Thank you, Sheriff Simpson, you've been a big help," Theo said.

"Glad to help. Any other questions or anything we can do, just give me a call."

Theo said, "Oh yeah, Sheriff. One more thing. The office for the Episcopal Church in Montana is in Helena, right?"

"You're right."

Theo asked, "If I need any help in Helena, who could I call in the sheriff's office?"

"Call the sheriff himself. He's a good man and I know he will help. Sheriff's name is Brad Hendrix. Want me to call him?"

"No, not at this time, Sheriff, I appreciate it, but I'll keep your kind offer in mind. Again, thank you so much. You've been a big help here." Theo hung up and looked at Wilma with a smile. "I think we're on the right track," he said enthusiastically.

"I hope so," said Wilma.

"Thanks for everything today, and the beer," said Theo. "I've gotta get going."

"Sure, see you tomorrow."

Once in his car, Theo took his cell phone and called Aiden O'Brian. The psychiatrist answered on the first ring.

Aiden smiled as he heard Theo's enthusiasm. Theo told the psychiatrist that something very positive had occurred and they needed to meet. O'Brian was deep into reading papers that were an assignment for his class on *Behavior of Murderers.* The papers had to be graded and ready for tomorrow's class.

The two agreed to meet the following day for lunch. Realizing the need to talk in some seclusion, they decided to get something from a deli near Piedmont Park in downtown Atlanta where they could talk and not be disturbed.

Things were getting very, very exciting.

———————

A PLAN FORMULATES

25

Once he arrived at his office the following morning, Theo got a telephone book to look up a number for Hixon DuPree. Not finding any listing, he called a friend of his at the main telephone equipment office in downtown Atlanta to inquire if, in, fact the priest did have a phone. As it turned out, Dupree had no account with the telephone company.

When Theo got that news, he thought to himself, *Well, scratch that idea.* He had planned to have a tap put on DuPree's telephone. These days though, many people didn't have a landline. Theo knew he did not have the probable cause to get a tap on the phone at the church.

What Theo wanted was to develop a solid case against DuPree prior to making an arrest. It had to be airtight.

The surveillance was already in place. Theo had gone to the manager of the apartment complex across the street from the church and DuPree's house. Luck was going his way. There was an apartment that was perfectly located so the officers had a good place for observing the entire church property. The apartment was directly across from the church, a perfect view showing DuPree's house, all entrances to the church, as well as a clear view of the front of the church and the church office. Theo was ecstatic. He could not have set it up better himself.

Theo assigned two vehicles that would be used for roaming the neighborhood, a white Chevrolet van and a gray Nisson Maxima. The vehicles were innocuous enough that no attention would be drawn by them in the neighborhood. Both vehicles were manned with two officers so that, if necessary, they could follow DuPree and if the need ever came, the cars could switch off so that the priest would not be aware of the same vehicle following him, if he did become suspicious.

Theo could also call on a third car which was assigned leads in the immediate area. That way, there could actually be three cars which could be used interchangeably to further avoid suspicion. One car held a team of female officers, one had a male and female, and the third had two males. While one car would follow the suspect, the other cars would hang back or follow on a parallel street, insuring Dupree, should he become mobile in any way, would not get suspicious. All the cars on the task force operated from a separate radio channel. This insured the teams could communicate more freely, and was especially important, as it was common knowledge that several of the news organizations monitored the police radios.

Theo's next stop was the Office of the District Attorney. He was hoping to see Eleanor Cameron, one of the assistant D.A's, and the one with whom his office worked with very closely. Again, luck was with him. Cameron was in her office and had time to see him. Theo walked down the hall and stopped at the D.A's office. He knocked, she looked up and smiled, and motioned him in.

Theo had known Cameron ever since she came to the D.A's office some years ago. He was impressed with her work, particularly with her skills as a prosecutor. In court, she was a "no hold's barred" person. Theo thought of the time she had prosecuted a man who had murdered a small child. In her closing argument, she had a birthday cake brought into the court room with eight candles. As Cameron lit the candles, she sang Happy Birthday, reminding the defendant, as well as the jury, that the victim would have no more birthdays because of him. It had been a very effective argument and the defendant had received a life sentence without parole.

A single mother, Cameron was tall and quite pretty. She was a strawberry blond and wore glasses which were rimless and was always dressed *fit to kill*, as his mama would say.

"Detective Reed, to what do I owe this honor? How is your big case going?"

"That's what I've come to talk with you about," Theo responded. "Do you have some time?"

"I do and I'm most anxious to hear what you have to say. Please, have a seat."

"Well," Theo said, sitting down in a chair in front of her desk, "let me fill you in." He went over the details of the case. She spoke not a word, just listened, until he got to the part about Father Hixon DuPree.

At that point, the attorney broke in, "Theo, I go to that church and my child is in the Youth Group. Are you telling me we have a child killer there and he is working with our children?"

Theo said, "Eleanor, I'm not saying anything for sure at this point except we have four girls who have been murdered. Dupree is our prime suspect and at some point in our investigation, we may need a search warrant to see what mail he's getting, and to search his house, in general. It may all blow up in our face, but I wanted you to be abreast of our investigation and be ready if the need comes that we need a warrant of some kind. I certainly had no idea you were a member of St. Jude's. You generally handle our big cases and, that being the case, I have come to you."

The attorney responded, "No, Theo, no problem. You just took the wind out of my sails. I know Father Hixon very well. I've worked on committees with him, been to church camp with him, he's been to my home for meals. He has always been such a nice, friendly guy. I'm just shocked by this."

There were a few anxious moments when neither one made eye

contact. Theo was the first one to speak, "Look, Eleanor, like I said, I had no idea. If you want me to talk with another attorney in the office, I will certainly understand."

"No! It is what it is. And I have my obligations. Under no circumstances will I not follow my obligations and, please rest assured, I will not divulge anything you have told me except to fill in Mr. Deaver, the District Attorney. I just need some time to wrap my head around this. It's such...such shocking news."

"That is all I can expect," he replied. "Again, I'm sorry. I could be wrong about Father Hixon."

"No." Cameron said, "I'm sorry. You had no way of knowing. I am surprised though – *shocked*, really – if, in fact, you are correct. That said, I will proceed on the grounds that you have reasonable suspicion that he is your man."

"If we need any information about DuPree, could you help us?"

"Theo, I will do anything I can, but given the circumstances, I will not do anything that will put my job, my reputation or this case in jeopardy. Now, if there is something that I can help you with, I want you to come to me. I'll be extremely honest with you. I'm sort of in a difficult position here and I will talk about it with Mr. Deaver. So for now, let's just leave it at that."

"That suits me fine," Theo said.

Cameron added, "I would appreciate it if all contact with this office is just between you and me for the time being. If a member of your task force has an issue, question, or whatever, have them bring it to you and you bring it to me. That way, I'll feel a bit better about this. It is uncomfortable enough as it is, considering Father Hixon is a good friend."

"I understand," said Theo. "No problem."

Cameron stood up and they shook hands.

"Thanks a lot," the detective replied.

"Just know there may be times we can speak off the record, so don't hold back on something you think is important."

"You got it," he said, as he turned and exited the office.

Theo still had time to go to his office to check for messages and take care of anything that might have come up. He was pretty sure there was nothing really important or Wilma would have gotten in touch with him. The thought of just taking a few minutes for himself sounded enticing. Theo knew he couldn't afford such a luxury.

Saying hello to Wilma, Theo walked into his office. The first three messages on his stack of telephone calls to be returned were from his mother. "Shit!" he said under his breath. He could already feel the butterflies in his stomach. *What was it?* he thought to himself. He was aware that he had not communicated with his mother since the investigation had started and he did feel guilty about that. Still, his mother would make him feel guilty.

Theo dialed his mother's telephone number. It rang until he half-expected, and half-hoped her answering machine would come on. Then he heard the familiar voice, "Hello."

'Hi, Mama, it's me!"

"Me, who?" she asked sarcastically.

Muscles tightening, Theo replied, "Mother, you've surely been watching TV and reading the paper. I'm up to my backside in a big case and just haven't had any time to myself."

"Not even time to call your mama and see how she is?"

"Mama, I've had to cancel days off and vacations for all my officers. We're working seven days a week, 24 four hours a day. This is the biggest case to hit this area since Wayne Williams. I haven't had the time to do anything else but work on this," Theo said.

"You mean to tell me, Theophilus, that you have not had one minute to simply make one phone call to me?"

With a note of resignation, Theo replied, "I suppose I could have done that Mama, and I am truly sorry for it. Maybe when this is over, I'll take a few days and we can go down to the coast. You always liked the Gulf Coast, Mama. How would you like that? You know, just the two of us. I'll rent a place right on the beach at St. George Island. Deal?"

"Theophilus, I'm not fishing for a trip. All I want is a little of your time every once in a while. I know you are busy and, yes, I do watch TV. And, I try to read the paper, but my eyes just will not keep up anymore. It would be wonderful if you could come over and read the paper to me, Theo. I would just love that."

"Look, Mama," he said, "maybe I can break away early some evening. We'll go to Piccadilly. You can get what you want and I'll tell you all about what I'm doing."

"That would be wonderful, Theo," his mama replied. "Can we do it this week?"

"No promises, Mama, but we will do it soon, perhaps this weekend. I'll call, I promise."

"Theo, there are a couple of things I want to discuss with you..."

Theo broke in, "Mama, I'm sorry. I've got someone in my office. I really have to go. I'll call you about the weekend." He hung up.

Staring at his phone, Theo felt guilty. He had lied to his mama. There was nobody in his office, but he simply had too many things on his mind to deal with whatever it was she wanted to discuss. Suddenly, his guilt turned to a big lump in his stomach. He hated that feeling and was angry with himself for letting his mama make him feel this way.

He went through the rest of his telephone messages. Most of them were from reporters he knew. Theo chose to return none of them.

Theo looked at his watch. He still had time to go to the bullpen to visit with any task force members who might be at their desks.

Walking through the bullpen, he was surprised that there were very few detectives at their desks. Looking at one of his officers, Theo asked, "Where is everybody?"

"Out working!"

Just then Theo heard his name over the pager. Reaching for a telephone on the empty, but messy desk of some officer, Theo took the receiver and dialed the operator. The police force operator told him the Chief needed to talk with him. "Put him through," said Theo.

She connected Theo with the Chief. They had just begun to talk when the Chief put Theo on hold. While he was waiting, Theo snooped in the absent detective's "IN" box. His eye caught a complaint form with the name *St. Jude's By the Mountain*. Theo grabbed the paper and began to read.

The rector of St. Jude's by the Mountain, the Reverend Bainbridge, had called with a complaint he wanted to make. Reading the body of the report, Theo learned that last Monday, Reverend Bainbridge had called the task force office to report that on Sunday, the day before, Henry Thornberry, a lay reader in the church, had reported that during the service, someone had come into the sacristy, where lay readers kept their coats in lockers, and had gotten into his locker.

Mr. Thornberry told Reverend Bainbridge that his wallet had been stolen. He said he had removed his suit coat, put his coat in the locker and retrieved his vestment's prior to the service. After the service, Thornberry returned to the sacristy, unlocked his locker and, while putting on his coat, discovered his wallet missing from an inside breast pocket. There was no question whether or not the wallet had been left at Thornberry's home as he had used a credit card to purchase a tank of gas on the way to the church.

Further, Thornberry stated he had taken out a twenty dollar bill which he gave to his wife to purchase some goodies the altar guild was selling as a money making project.

Continuing to read, Theo's interest was caught by the fact there was no evidence of a break-in. According to Father Bainbridge, the outside door to the sacristy was locked during the service. The door leading to the outside was unlocked after the service so those assisting the clergy during the service could exit the building.

When asked about keys, Bainbridge noted there were several people who had keys to all the doors in the church. He had one as did the Youth Minister. Both the senior and junior wardens had keys and the women of the Altar Guild had a key to the sacristy door.

Father Hixon DuPree obviously had a key. But surely he would not be stupid enough to use the credit cards. Perhaps it was somebody else in the congregation, maybe a kid. But unless everyone had a key to the sacristy, which Theo knew was not the case, the thief would have had to come into the chancel, cross in front of the choir and around the organ, open the door and walk in. Surely someone would have seen the person.

Theo took a piece of scratch paper and left a note for the detective to report to him as soon as he read this message. Looking at his watch, Theo saw it was almost time to meet Aiden O'Brian.

Theo parked at Manuel's Tavern and walked inside.

Looking around, Theo could not see his psychiatrist friend. He was startled by a tap on his shoulder. Turning, he saw O'Brian.

"You damn near made me have a heart attack," Theo said to his friend.

Smiling, O'Brian broke into a laugh. "Sorry, I didn't realize you were so jumpy," he said.

Theo said, "Hell, since this thing began, I've been like a long-tailed cat in a room full of rocking chairs." Both men laughed.

Luckily they found a booth in the back of the main room. It was noisy, which was good, not much chance of their conversation being overheard. The waitress came and both men ordered a mug of beer and Rueben sandwiches.

Theo began. First, he told Aiden of his meeting with Eleanor Cameron, and then brought him up-to-date on the investigation so far. He told him of his chance sighting of Father Hixon Dupree at Stone Mountain Park and of his surveillance and his viewing DuPree going down to the crime scene, then of his discovery of the poster and what he assumed Dupree had done. Theo took a long drink of the cold beer, waiting while O'Brian digested all he had revealed.

"Wow!" Aiden said as he took a long draw on his beer. "Wow!"

As Aiden was setting his mug down, Theo began again, "Now let me tell you what I learned today, just before I left to come here." Theo told of the missing billfold at the church, the fact the outside door was locked and the people who all had keys. He described the only way any unauthorized person could have gotten inside the sacristy with the outside door closed and locked.

When Theo finished, the psychiatrist was quiet for a moment, then he took another drink of beer. Finally, Aiden said, "Well, I'm not surprised that DuPree returned to the crime scene. That is not unusual for serial killers. It's classic. Doing so was a way for him to relive the pleasure he got from killing, especially Paige Langford. You'll see this kind of behavior throughout the literature, confessions and interviews of these people. Now if DuPree felt some sympathy for the Langford girl, he may have returned as a means of communicating his sorrow over what he had done. That sort of behavior is not unusual for certain killers to feel sorry for what they have done, but this feeling is never present prior to the murder, always after the incident."

Continuing on, the psychiatrist asked, "You've got your surveillance in place and going?"

"Sure do," Theo answered. He went into detail about the apartment where he had three detectives assigned as well as the roving units. Taking a paper napkin, Theo drew a diagram of the location showing just where the apartment was located and the excellent view the officers had of DuPree's house, the church and the church offices.

O'Brian said, "Theo, I'm getting a feeling that DuPree is getting a little antsy. The reason I'm feeling this is the issue with the billfold. We carry a lot of information about ourselves in our wallets. I don't think it was the need for money and I'm not so sure it was to get access to any credit cards. I'm thinking he's looking for a new identity and if he's doing that, I think he may be considering going on the run."

"Right now?" Theo questioned.

"No. If all he wants is a new identity, he will have to get a few things organized, and that will take some time. He can go to the driver's license office, say he lost his license and they will issue him a new one, right then and there. Then he will have a Georgia license with his photo and the information of Mr. Thornberry." Aiden took another drink of beer, then he asked, "Do you know if DuPree gets his mail at his home or at the church office?"

"He must get it at the church office," Theo responded. "The surveillance team has not said anything about a visit from the mailman and they log every person going onto the property. They even log the guy who mows the grass. To my knowledge, no one comes to visit DuPree."

Their sandwiches and fries came and they stopped talking a few moments to eat. Theo was not sure when he last ate. If speed of eating and size of bites was any marker, he had not eaten in some time.

Aiden watched, amused, as he nibbled on his burger and fries.

"Sorry," said Theo. "I didn't mean to gulp down my food like that. I was just starving. Haven't eaten in a while. Mama would not have approved."

"Speaking of your mama, how is she?"

"She's okay," Theo said. "She just gets a little needy at times, then gets upset if I'm not there or don't check in on a daily basis. But thanks for asking."

"Theo, I think we need to put some heat on this guy. If we can get him nervous, let him know we are on to him, he just might make a mistake."

"What do you propose?" asked the detective.

"I think we ought to have another press conference, let some things out that you have not said so far, you know, something to let him know we are getting close. To rattle him. Then, he can have a few days to chew on what you said at the press conference. Next, bring him in for some questions. We can set an office up so that you really will not have to say a thing. The office setup will tell him everything he needs to know. Put a surveillance on him that is closer than the one you have now."

Theo asked, "Will that cause him to run?"

"This is the issue, Theo," his friend said. "We all strive for balance. That is why you ate so fast tonight. Your body was telling you that you were hungry. You ate because you were hungry and thus out of balance. Now you've eaten and your balance is returning. It's the same with our mind and our emotions. You let DuPree know you're getting close to him and he'll get antsy. At the same time, his cool-headedness, his ability to reason, will go down. The result is he will begin making mistakes. That is the key to his behavior. Knock him off balance in some way. At least, that is my theory."

"Aiden, you're the best. I don't know how I will ever be able to thank you for all your help. You have been a big help in this case and you've been there to help in the past. I really owe you one."

"Don't mention it, old friend. To me, it's as much a mind game as anything. I don't exactly know why, but I love this stuff. Look, I still have some papers to grade, so I'm out of here. Keep me posted." He slid out of the booth and was gone.

Looking over at Aiden's plate with all the fries, Theo was still hungry. He pulled it over and finished the French fries, making sure nobody was watching him. Theo felt a little embarrassed, but he had to admit the fries were delicious.

———————

THE DESIGNED PRESS RELEASE

Theo had called Aiden O'Brian, and together, they wrote out the press release for the news conference which was scheduled for noon that very day. The stage was set from the beginning, to turn up the heat.

Looking out from the stage curtain, Theo could see that the auditorium in the Law Enforcement Center was full. The room was bright with lights from the TV stations. There was a buzz, almost a roar, from the voices coming from those who were seated. Men were running around the room holding wires, taping cables on the floor, getting in each other's way. Had this not been so important, Theo would have found it a bit comical.

Since the case began, it had developed a great deal of interest, then notoriety. The investigation had taken on a life of its own. Theo noticed the ever present CNN, BBC, Canadian Broadcasting, French TV, and Mexico. He saw other news people that he knew were from other countries. He could not miss the sound of other languages.

At noon, the Chief, dressed in his finest formal uniform, walked

163

directly to the podium, which displayed a bank of microphones. The room quickly fell silent.

The Chief spoke, "Ladies and Gentlemen, thank you for coming. I have a statement to read to you. This will be a simple statement. There will be no questions at this time. Later on, we will have a more detailed statement and time for questions and answers. I ask that you respect this decision.

"As you know, there have been four murders of young females at Stone Mountain Park. We are positive that all the murders were committed by the same person, a white male in his 30s. To that end, our department, along with the help of law enforcement from the local, state and federal level, have been working on this case 24 hours a day, seven days a week. I am now ready to say that through our investigation, we have an update. We have uncovered a prime suspect and an arrest is imminent. Thank you for your time. That is all I have to say."

Everyone in the room began to excitedly talk at once. Cameras were flashing, reporters yelling to please answer just one question.

Turning on his heels, the Chief quickly exited the stage, and he and Theo left the auditorium area. They wanted to go somewhere that they would not be stampeded by reporters who were sure to find a way into the building, even though all entrances to the other parts of the building, and to the stage as well, were manned by armed members of more than one SWAT Team.

Looking for a place where they would not be bothered and could get away from everything, they took a borrowed car and drove to the zoo.

———————

The statement read by the Chief was the lead story on all four Atlanta television stations that evening and the following morning, noon and night. His statement was read every ten minutes on most of the local radio stations and it was the top headline in the Atlanta papers which came out the following morning. No one could miss this update.

27
BROODING

White Man sat in his chair in his darkened room. He was nude. Several pairs of panties and a bikini bottom were resting on a table next to him. They were dry, every pair. He had seen the TV and read the paper. *Jesus,* he thought, *how could you miss the fucking news update?*

Perhaps it had been the paper. Not only was the picture of the Chief of Police on the front page, but so were the pictures of three of the victims. The third page had photos of the families of the girls. He could see the grief in the faces of the parents. It made him resentful, bitter, and angry to see the parents sobbing, caring about their children. He had *never* known that kind of love.

From the time he had been sent to the monastery, it had been going on. First, it was Father Marty who had done it. It was early morning. The two of them were preparing the altar for early morning communion. Father Marty had come to him and begun talking about how nice it was to have him at the monastery, and what an attractive young man he was. The monk's hand went down to the boy's crotch and began to rub. Just a young boy, White Man did not know what to do or what to feel, so he simply stood there.

After a few minutes, Father Marty took the boy's hand and placed it under the monk's robe and on his penis. Father Marty took the boy's hand and began rubbing his penis. At the same time, Father Marty put his hand inside the boy's pants and began rubbing his penis, as well. Before he knew it, both his and the monk's penis were hard. They continued to rub each other until they were both simultaneously spent.

From then on, it had been a continuous thing. He and Father Marty would do early morning communion together and satisfy each other before setting the communion table. They might take an afternoon walk in the woods where they would find a nice spot, take their clothes off and kiss, lick, rub and suck each other.

While he had no dislike for Father Marty, he had no like for him either. But what the boy was aware of was the intense pleasure he got from being sexual. After all, it really made no difference who it was, he could close his eyes, fantasize and he could be sexual with anyone he wanted.

Eventually, Father Marty left the monastery. That very night, Father Thad came into his room, slipped inside the covers and it all began again. Then, they too, went to the woods. Father Thad wanted to do things that Marty never did. This was all new to him. He hated the anal sex and being spanked. One day he refused and Thad got angry and slapped him. That seemed to bring all his anger to the fore. He slapped Thad back, whereupon Thad slapped him again and yelled, "You fucking little queer. Do as I say or you'll have detention for so long, you'll never get out of here."

"Don't call me a pervert," he yelled back to the monk. "You're the pervert, you shit head."

His anger was now rising very quickly. He made a fist and hit the monk square in the jaw, knocking him down. Rage filled his body and mind. Adrenalin rushed to his hands and feet. He jumped on the prone monk and hit him in the face over and over. Then standing up, he kicked the monk in his groin three times. He could hear the monk cry out in pain with each kick.

Turning around, he walked back to the monastery, leaving the monk to deal with his own pain and injuries. On the way back, he was aware that he had an erection. Once at the monastery, he went right to his room. Lying down on his bed, he thought about what had just happened and the beating he gave Father Thad. Thinking about it, he got aroused. He began thinking again about the beating and the pain he had inflicted on Father Thad. He maintained his erection. Slowly he began rubbing himself, his thoughts focused on the beating. He continued to rub himself until he was spent. It was truly a very pleasant time.

It was several weeks before he saw Father Thad again. The monk had no visible signs of their encounter. He looked at Thad, but the monk would not make eye contact. He had no idea what Father Thad had said had happened to him, nor any idea of where he had been. Of one thing he was sure, no other monk bothered him while he was at the monastery.

The following spring, he graduated from the monastery school and entered a Roman Catholic Seminary. The seminary really was not much different than the monastery. He had some sexual acting out with some of the priests on the staff, as well as members of his class. He had no question about his sexuality He knew he was heterosexual, but eventually began to think of himself as a *trysexual,* willing to try anything sexual. That was it, that's what he was, a *trysexual.* He was proud of himself to have made such a diagnosis. His main interest, however, was adolescent females. At night he would lie in his bed and rub himself while his mind went back to his times with his sister. His thoughts were both of pleasure and anger.

Now when he assisted the priest at a real church service, he would look for girls his sister's age that last time he had seen her. When he would lie in bed at night and rub himself, his mind would go to some young adolescent girl he had seen in church that morning. It was not long before the majority of his ongoing sexual thoughts were of young adolescent girls.

Finishing seminary, he realized his sexual interest was in young adolescent girls. He thought back to the times with Father Thad and the pleasure he had gotten out of beating up the monk. He recalled that incident many times. He had the power to kill the monk, but hadn't done it. That made him angry, yet the beating had aroused him. The thoughts of being sexual and then killing the monk became an ongoing nightly ritual.

Then rather rapidly, his fantasies altered a bit. He began to fantasize about being sexual with his sister and killing her. Then, the fantasies changed again, this time to being sexual with any young girl he had seen in church, being sexual with her, then strangling her and watching the life slowly ebb out of her eyes.

As time passed, he realized the Roman Church was not designed to have Youth Ministers. Working with youth was the only way he knew where he could get the trust of a young girl, then be sexual with her and eventually kill her. It would not be easy. He would have to kill them and get away with it. If he could figure out how to gain their trust and get access to them, he could figure out the rest. The *rest* he worked on at night, in his bed.

One day, while glancing through a newspaper, he read about the exploits of an Episcopal priest who was a Youth Minister. The Youth Minister took a group of children to some Central American country every summer where the kids helped with planting or harvesting crops, helped build churches and schools. It seemed to be a wonderful program and perfect for him.

It did not take him long to figure things out. He located the Episcopal Bishop's office in the city nearest to his assignment, made his appointment and convinced the bishop that he was a good candidate for ordination as a priest. He was very thorough in his presentation as to why he was unhappy in the Roman Catholic Church. Convincing the bishop was easy enough. He had been at his very best when he talked with the bishop. He was proud of his ability to sway people and convince them of his honesty.

After that, the process was not difficult, nor long. He renounced his ordination in the Roman Catholic Church and the rest was easy.

Once he was ordained, he thought to himself, *Damn man, you are very convincing, you're really good. You could tell a person to go to hell in such a way they would look forward to the trip.* He had always felt smug after that.

He had things pretty well figured out. His first assignment was to serve on a couple of Indian Reservations in Montana. That had been easy for him. The irresponsibility on the reservations was so common. He had access to many needy children, especially girls. And if he killed a girl, he would take the lifeless body to a field and leave it for tribal and federal authorities to figure out. But nobody would suspect the local priest. God only knew, dead bodies on a reservation were not something out of the ordinary. Generally, the case was given a full court press for a few days, then if not solved, the investigation languished in some folder in some drawer of a Bureau of Indian Affairs Officer or some F.B.I. agent assigned to the reservation.

When he was sexual with a young girl, almost inevitably she would be passive and do whatever he said. Such was the way of the reservation. When he put his hands around her throat and began choking her, her face would change and he would see the face of his sister or, on occasion, his mother. "Cunt" he would whisper over and over as the life drained out of the young girl.

Finally, he had "served his time" as the clergy, in eastern Montana said. He had worked along the highline, and he was now assigned as the priest in charge of the church camp in western Montana. He was a happy camper as he loaded his car, said goodbye to the dreary landscape of wheat, dirt, flat and endless wind of eastern Montana. He was on his way to the mountains, the lake and the camp.

That made him feel better, but now he had other issues. White Man needed to be very careful next time. He wondered what the Chief had meant when he said they were close and had a suspect. He had seen nothing and he prided himself on the care he took in his planning. *Really*, he thought, *the cops aren't smart enough to get me. They're clueless.*

That in mind, White Man put on a pair of panties and began to rub himself. Maybe he had one or two girls left in this place, then he would leave. Get a new life. Maybe go back to the mountains, but not Montana. Perhaps Colorado for a while, but eventually, he wanted to get back to New Orleans. The last he had heard, that was where his sister was, and she was the one he wanted most of all. It would be slow and painful for her and he would enjoy every minute.

———————

28
ANOTHER SUSPECT?

Gaylord Butts hated his name and he hated his parents for giving it to him. In fact, he hated his grandfather for having the same name and hated anyone who had ever expressed the idea to name him after his grandfather. The fact was that Gaylord Butts had a lot of hate in him. There was his father who was a career enlisted man in the army and who had been gone throughout most of Gaylord's life. He hated the fact that his father had never been around to help him through all the teasing and bullying he received at school. He had learned early that when some boy wanted to fight him, to just lie down and take it. He did not have the physique or the inclination to fight. A hit from a fist, a kick in the ribs, a torn shirt, were not so bad. It was the words, the names that did the most damage and lasted the longest period of time. Certainly his body healed more rapidly than his mind.

"Hey, happy ass," or "Maggot the faggot!" taunted him.

The teasing and taunting had not been too bad in his younger grades, but as he progressed through the elementary grades, the torments became more and more hurtful. Eventually there was the first fist fight. A name had been called, a challenge returned and the usual crowd had gathered in the school playground. The assailant's first blow had struck him directly on his nose and the blood began to flow like a tap had been turned on full blast. Gaylord was more frightened by the blood, which seemed to flow more freely than the adrenalin, which trickled through his body. He began to cry and had run away. He continued to run off the school yard, to the end of the block and around a corner. He ran into the first alley where he stayed, hidden due to embarrassment, until he knew that school was out. He was still crying when he crept into the kitchen door of his home.

To his surprise, his father was sitting at the kitchen table with his mother. They were both having a cocktail. "What the fuck happened to you?" his father challenged.

"Nothing!" Gaylord replied.

"You got in a fight, didn't you?" quizzed his father.

It was quite obvious he had gotten into a fight. There was blood all over his clothes and his face.

"No," Gaylord replied.

"No!" exclaimed his father. "Shit, a blind man could see in a minute that you were in a fight."

Gaylord finally admitted to the fight and when his father asked him what had occurred, Gaylord told him the facts.

His father became angrier by the moment. "Why, you little pussy chicken shit. You let the bastard hit you one time and you ran off?"

Gaylord could feel his eyes tearing up. The more tears, the more intense was his father's anger. "From a baby, I expect sniveling, from a twelve year old, I expect someone who will fight back, someone who will take the other kid, stomp a mud hole in his ass and walk it dry. Shit, you little baby, I'll bet you squat to pee. Go on get out of my sight, you pussy chicken shit."

Gaylord looked to his mother for support. She just shook her head and looked in the other direction.

Retreating to the security and safety of his basement room, Gaylord removed his bloody shirt and jeans. Crawling into his bed, he pulled the covers over his head and continued to cry until his sobs became sighs, then he was quiet, but he was lost in anger.

Finally, he reached under his mattress and pulled out a magazine he had found, months ago on a table near his father's side of the bed. He felt himself getting flush as he looked at the images of nude women. He stared at their bosoms, their erect nipples and the fluff of hair between their legs. Suddenly he was aware of his cock getting hard. He had never experienced the thrill of seeing this before, images of older girls, older being in their late teens or early twenties. He began to touch himself, then slowly to rub, faster, then more rapidly until he felt a pleasure unlike anything he had felt before. Slowly he began to relax. As he did so, he became aware of the sticky liquid in his hand.

As his unhappiness at school and at home increased, Gaylord found himself making more frequent trips to his bedroom. He began reaching for his magazine as soon as he woke up, when he got home from school and when he retired for the night.

Some days later, Gaylord was sitting with his parents at the dinner table. Suddenly, his mother confronted him in front of his father. Her eyes ablaze with anger, she yelled at him. She had rolled his mattress over and in doing so, had found his stash. Holding the magazines Gaylord had purloined from his father's collection, her voice getting louder and more high pitched, she ended her tirade with a piercing scream, "You're nothing better than a pervert, a fucking little pervert."

Then his father yelled at Gaylord, who had no idea his parents could be this mean. After calling him every name he could think of, his father finally yelled, "You fucking little pud pounder, get out of my sight."

Trying to stay away from his parents, Gaylord stayed in his room after school until dinner time. Sitting at the table, his parents would speak to each other, but not to him. Gaylord felt as though he was a potted plant. If his father had anything he wanted to say to him, he would address the question to Gaylord's mother, who in turn would ask him the question.

Eventually, his father shipped back to Korea. Gaylord had prayed for this day to come. Perhaps he could mend the relationship with his mother, but that was not to be. Afraid to try to slip into his parent's bedroom and raid his father's collection, Gaylord was forced to rely on his memory for visions of the images he had found so exciting.

A new family moved next door to the Butts' house. There was one child, Missy, who was ten years old. Missy's room faced Gaylord's basement room, and soon, Gaylord was caught up in trying to watch Missy's activities in her bedroom in the evening.

It happened quite by accident once when Gaylord was staring out his window with nothing particular in mind. Noticing a movement in Missy's window, Gaylord turned his attention to Missy, who had just come from a bath. Gaylord watched as the little girl's towel fell from her body. He continued watching as Missy walked to her closet, removed a pair of pajamas and put them on.

Certainly there was nothing on Missy's part that was ever intended to be erotic and, in actuality, she had no idea she was being watched. The fact was that, at this point, Missy was not even aware of sexual issues. But to Gaylord, as he watched her walking nude to her closet, it was a most exciting event. In fact, it became an event that would change Gaylord's sexual interests forever. He found that no longer needed to rely on his memories of his father's magazines. Now he had the real thing, something that was just for him alone.

As time went on, Gaylord began talking with Missy. He was too inhibited to try to develop any sort of real friendship with Missy. Their conversations were of school, the neighborhood, parents and friends. When talk did turn to parents, Gaylord was too embarrassed to tell her about his parents, so he made up fictitious relationships, telling her of amazing feats of his father in the military. He told her of hunting trips with his father, their times at professional football games and how much he liked the Atlanta Falcons. He told of trips to NASCAR races and exploits of hiking and wrestling. In reality, Gaylord had no interest in any of these activities.

In fact, Gaylord had no interest in anything other than his sexual adventures that played in his mind two or three times a day. He found school boring. He had been able to dodge the bullies. Perhaps it was because he was getting older now and the bullies had found younger kids to haze. Probably the main class that he hated and the one that provided the stimulus for him to leave school was P.E. In the shower room, he would listen to other boys talk of their sexual exploits. When they were not bragging, they were teasing Gaylord. After all, he was very thin and wimpy-looking. His face was covered with acne which had never been treated by a doctor. His hair was unkempt and his clothes were dirty with food stains. Gaylord actually had no interest in clothes, choosing instead to wear the same clothes day after day. His teeth were yellow and some blue was starting to form around his gums.

The P.E. teacher was a football coach. Gaylord knew the coach enjoyed watching the other boys teasing him, flipping towels at him and putting athletic balm in the crotch of his shorts. In fact, Gaylord felt the coach was actually encouraging the boys to taunt him. The first time the teasing had occurred, his balls had begun to burn as he walked home. By the time he arrived at his home, he thought his crotch was on fire. He ripped his pants and shorts off as soon as he was in his room. Only then did he see the traces of red balm. This made him angry. What made him angrier was his cock and balls were so sore, he had to stop his nightly rubbing for three nights.

The following day in P.E. the kids were calling him red ass. Walking down the hall to his next class, he saw a number of jocks with their girlfriends leaning against a bank of lockers. As he walked by, they all began to laugh. Gaylord could feel his face flush. He knew the boys had told the girls.

Gaylord had never been a very organized individual. He never developed any of the teenage interests or dress fads. He simply lacked any interest in them. In fact, he never developed any interest in anything, not a vocation, his future, a love interest. Truth be told, his only interest in the opposite sex was Missy, but he knew it would be fraught with peril to try anything with her.

On Missy's birthday, she had a sleepover and three other girls spent the night. Gaylord watched as they took turns bathing and dressing in their night clothes. He watched, fascinated, as the girls brushed and played with each other's hair. They laughed, talked and listened to music, not once even realizing the bedroom shades were open and that anyone was watching.

Eventually, the girls tired of this play and began a pillow fight. Watching the action, Gaylord became more and more excited as the girls slung pillows at each other, allowing their pajama tops to ride up, exposing their small and undeveloped breasts. Eventually, Missy's mother came in, put a stop to the combating girls and pulled the shade down.

Eventually, Gaylord told his mother he was quitting school. She gave him no argument because, as she told her friends, "Gaylord lacked a brick or two of having a full load." What she did tell him was that he would need to find a job and stay gainfully employed. He would need to get some transportation. After all, he was now sixteen and old enough to be on his own. It was a relief for his mother. Now there would be no more calls from the school attendance officer, the school social worker or school guidance counselors. *Jesus,* she thought, *those folks could be a real pain in the ass.* They did not care about the kids, only the money they received from the state, the amount of which was based on school attendance figures.

To say that the relationship between Gaylord and his mother had deteriorated was an understatement. After leaving Korea, his father had dropped out of the family, for all intents and purposes, volunteering for any foreign assignment he could, his trips home shorter and less frequent.

Gaylord got a job as a bus boy at a local restaurant. When not busing tables, he was washing pot and pans. The restaurant was a very busy, popular place and Gaylord was kept busy during his shifts. Tips were shared among the other help and eventually, Gaylord was able to buy a junker of a car. As a sign of freedom, he threw his bicycle in the Chattahoochee River and bought a 1992 Ford Escort. It was clean when he drove it off the lot of the used car dealer, but within a week or two, the car was dirty and the inside crowded with sacks and napkins from McDonalds and Taco Bell. The windows became cloudy with residue from cigarette smoke and an occasional puff or two on a joint. Adding to the collection were empty plastic bottles of

Mountain Dew. He loved Mountain Dew. It gave him a bit of a high from the large amount of sugar and caffeine in the drink. Apparently, he failed to notice the sugar from the drink was advancing his tooth decay problem.

He got older and Missy grew as well. Gaylord really did not think much about Missy's growth. But as she got older, he began to lose interest in her. What he did notice were the younger girls, around nine or ten, who came into the restaurant with their parents. He enjoyed looking at them.

Gaylord had no skills relating to girls or dating, or even going out with a group. His knowledge was gained from the magazines he read, which by now had become a sizable amount of pornography. He knew his collection was safe from his mother. She no longer paid any attention to his room. In the past she had come in to collect his dirty laundry for washing, or to get his bed linens for cleaning. Now that was all in the past. The result was that unless he did his own wash, which he never did, his clothes and bedding simply became more dirty and gritty.

While he enjoyed looking at the pictures of the nude women, he was more enthralled by other parts of the magazine where men would write in for advice about their sexual relationships or fantasies. Some of these were ripe with sadism and masochism. The stories were just plain exciting, and a new and wonderful source of his own fantasies.

Soon Gaylord was spending a great deal of time in his fantasy world, grabbing young girls, taking them into the woods and forcing them to bring him pleasure.

GAYLORD ON THE MOVE

*C*learing a table after some customers had finished breakfast, Gaylord happened to notice some photos on the Metro page of the Atlanta newspaper. The photos were of some girls who had been killed at Stone Mountain Park. He took a moment to scan the story, then putting that part of the paper in his pocket, he went about his job.

When he was through with his shift, he stopped by a McDonald's for a burger and fries. Taking the paper out of his pocket, he read with interest the history of the investigation to date. At age 17, he was more interested in the sexual part of the murders than the fact that four girls were younger than he was.

Once back in his car, he drove home. Entering the house, he asked his mother, who was sitting at the kitchen table smoking a cigarette and drinking coffee, if she had heard of the murders. "Where have you been all these weeks?" she replied. "Hell, it's been all over the TV. If you would get your sorry ass home once in a while, you might just learn something."

Looking at the clock, Gaylord saw it was almost time for the early news. Sitting down in a chair in the living room, he turned on the TV hoping there may be something about the murders on the news. He was not disappointed. A reporter told of the news conference, then gave a summary of the investigation. Again, the images of three girls were shown on the screen. Knowing what he had read in the paper, Gaylord wondered what had happened to the fourth girl. Noticing his mother had come into the room, her coffee now replaced with a glass of wine, Gaylord asked about the fourth victim.

"I'm not sure," his mother answered. "They have been very quiet about that." Then she went on, "It must be a real sicko who would do something like that. I hope they find him and string him up by his balls." With that she drained the wine in her glass and headed back to the kitchen for a refill.

Gaylord headed down to his room in the basement. He took the paper out of his pocket, got in bed and began looking at the photos of the three girls. He could feel himself getting hard and began fantasizing about being in the woods with them and raping each one, while each girl watched and cried in horror. It was a very satisfying night. He repeated the fantasies the following morning, and it was just as satisfying as the previous night.

From then on, Gaylord carried the photos in his back pocket. On every break at work, he went into the men's room, took out the photos, began his fantasy and began rubbing himself. Eventually, he did not need the story or look at the photos of the girls, his mind stored his story and the images.

It was now almost an ongoing fantasy and one evening driving home from work, Gaylord began fantasizing and began rubbing himself. The traffic was heavy and slow. Well into his fantasy and rubbing, he saw a huge eighteen-wheeler stopped in front of him. Slamming on his breaks, his car skidded to the right. Fortunately, he missed the truck, but his car had now skidded into an adjoining lane. The car in the lane in which Gaylord had skidded was able to stop in time.

Taking a deep breath, Gaylord slowly eased off the break and continued his drive, but very slowly and more attentive. His heart was pounding to the point he was afraid he was going to die. He pulled off the Interstate at the next exit and stopped at the first fast food place he saw. He did not place any order; he just sat in the parking lot and waited for his body to calm down. He told himself he would save those particular times for when he was not on the road.

Gaylord's fantasies continued, but not in his car. It was not the murders that interested him so much. He had never thought or fantasized about a murder. His fantasies were simply of having control over a young girl. Now the thought of murdering some female was invading his fantasies. Finding a girl and *doing it* at Stone Mountain Park now consumed his fantasy life.

To Gaylord's disorganized way of thinking, having sex with a young girl was simply a matter of driving to the park and picking out his choice. That was as far as his planning went.

He had continued his now almost constant fantasizing about the three dead girls. His magazine collection now included *Teen* magazine as well as *Parent* magazine, all with photographs of young girls. He was beginning to formulate a plan of grabbing a girl at the park. Truth be told, Gaylord had not been to Stone Mountain Park in years. He had given no thought to where he would go when he arrived, where he would go once he found and grabbed a girl or how he would carry out his fantasy. Actually, Gaylord Clapp was mentally and emotionally incapable of developing any plan that was in any way complicated.

Finally the energy and desire building up inside him simply became too much. He called in sick to his job, got in his car and began the 45 minute drive to the Park.

THE CHASE

The surveillance teams were in place in the apartment as they had been for several days. Other members of the team had been at the park every night to watch the crowd just in case DuPree decided this was the night to hunt once again.

On every occasion, Theo had been on the park ground, accompanied by Aiden O'Brian. Theo had arranged with the Sheriff to have O'Brian sworn in as an auxiliary member of the county sheriff's department.

Theo told O'Brian, "These days you can never be too prepared. Every ambulance chasing attorney is out for a buck and looking for folks who are down and out and who have been arrested with any hint of force used."

On this night, all the teams were strategically placed. There was even a team in the ticket booth so they could observe pedestrians walking into the park, as well as individuals in cars entering the park. Theo and Aiden were parked at the museum building which was at the top of the great lawn where those watching the laser show would sit.

About 7:00 p.m., Theo received a call on his radio. "Chief, I think Eleanor Cameron just entered the park."

"Are you positive?" Theo questioned.

"I'm pretty sure. I was with her this morning in her office."

"Was she driving?" Theo asked.

"Yes, sir, she looked right at me as though she had never met me."

"Was she alone?"

"No, she was in a black van and there were several kids with her. I didn't get the make or any tag number since I knew who she was," the officer said.

Still on his radio, Theo spoke to all his officers, "Okay, did you all hear the report? Eleanor Cameron is in the park with a load of kids. Keep an eye out for her. She's probably taking the kids to the show. If you see her, just keep quiet and do not, I repeat, *do not* engage her in any conversation or show any sign of recognition. Our man belongs to her church!"

As Theo and O'Brian were talking about Cameron coming to the park with young children, knowing full well the inherent danger, a call came over the radio.

"Heads up, he's out of his house, walking on the road toward the park."

"How is he dressed?" Theo asked, knowing the call was from the apartment by the church.

"He is wearing all black, shirt, trousers and shoes. It does look as though he is wearing a clerical collar," said one of the officers from the apartment.

Theo called his teams, "Okay, attention all teams. Suspect is out of his house walking towards the park. Team at the entrance, you should be able to see this guy walking up to the entrance. Get a good eyeball on him and a thorough description of him. Units at the house and church, stay where you are. Roving teams, you can come up the entrance and park. Keep alert so you can pick him up, but stay parked until he is inside the park, then walk behind him. There will be enough people walking that he probably will not notice you. Let me know as soon as he gets into the park. Team at the entrance, listen up. When you know he is entering the park, leave your position and get in with the crowd walking into the park. Follow him and keep your tail on him until he either stops or settles down. You can probably get pretty close since you will be in a crowd of people."

"Air one?" Theo said to the roving police helicopter.

"Roger that," the pilot said.

"Have you been listening to what's going on?"

"Ten four."

"Do you have a visual on the suspect?"

"That is affirmative," the pilot answered.

"How many are you?' Theo questioned.

"Just me and my copilot who is doing the observing."

Theo's entire nervous system was on alert. The years as a cop had taught him to stay very calm is situations like this. Experience had also taught him that in high profile cases there was no room for error. Even though his desire was to be on the ground and in the action, he knew he was in his right place. He had chosen the members of his task force very carefully. He knew their capabilities and had all the confidence in the work and skills of each and every one of them.

All of a sudden a call came over the radio. "Hey does any body have a location on our man? We've lost him," yelled one of the officers DuPree from his home.

"Fuck!" Theo blurted out.

And just as quickly, another officer said, "Air One, we've got him."

"So do we," replied one of the officers in the booth. "He's just about fifty feet from the entrance. He's walking in the middle of the road like he has no cares in the world."

"Okay," Theo said. "Let's remain calm. Just let us know if you lose him. We've got plenty of people on him."

It was silent a few moments, then, "He just entered the park."

The teams reported in on a regular schedule and everyone knew where DuPree was.

Both Theo and Aiden were startled when a call came in. "Okay, he's met up with Eleanor Cameron. She acted as though she was expecting him, jumping up and hugging him. The kids with her, are hugging him now."

"Jesus Holy Christ!" Theo yelled. "Doesn't that woman have a lick of sense? I just spent an entire morning telling her about this scumbag. She obviously didn't believe a word I said."

Then speaking into his radio, he instructed his teams, "Get as close as you can without anyone noticing. Keep your radios out of sight and the volume down. You all have portable units to send and receive so make sure you use them and talk in a whisper."

In just minutes, the laser show began with a thunderous blast of music. It was now dusk and the lasers were brilliant on the side of the mountain.

The show had not been on for five minutes when a call came in. "He's up and he has a kid with him. They're making their way through he crowd. Our man is holding the little girl's hand. She looks to be about 8 years old. I think they are going to the train terminal. It's hard to keep him in sight. Jesus, there must be a million people out here."

Theo looked at the psychiatrist. "How you got this figured?"

Quickly O'Brian posited, "I don't think he is going to do anything to this girl. The girl is with Cameron and DuPree knows what she does and that she must be aware that there is a huge investigation going on. He's no dummy. My thoughts are he's being very attentive to the people around him to see if he can spot a surveillance, and at the same time, prove he's innocent by doing nothing at all to any of the children."

Taking his radio, Theo instructed, "Keep the subject and the girl in sight, but back off a little. Our man may be looking to see if he's being followed."

At that time, another voice came on the radio, "A woman just ran up to the concession stand where a park police officer is standing. She's pretty hysterical, claiming someone just grabbed her little girl and ran off. As much as we know right now, the perp is white, early twenties, messy and dirty looking."

"Holy Christ!" Theo said looking at O'Brian.

The psychiatrist said, "Theo, that's not our man. That's another one."

Looking at his friend, Theo responded, "I can't ignore this!"

Another team came on the radio. "We have a visual on him. The perp has the child and is running toward the park entrance."

"Which park entrance? There are three or four entrances to this place," Theo yelled.

The officer said, "He's running in the direction of the main entrance, but I don't think he's going to leave the park. The bastard's fast as hell, though. He's almost at the Barbeque Shack."

"Get him!" Theo yelled.

Then another voice said, "We just talked to Eleanor Cameron. It's her daughter our suspect is with. She made a comment last Sunday in church that she was going to take some kids to the laser show and DuPree just invited himself."

Then the officer asked, "Do you want us to nab DuPree?" "Jesus! Negative," Theo said. "Let's not use proper names. Remember loose lips sink ships." Theo was quiet a moment and then instructed, "The team that is with our suspect now, please, just stay on him. You can get a little closer but do not give yourselves away."

Then another voice came on the radio, "He's cut off at the track and running toward the path leading up the mountain. Jesus, it's hard to see."

"Okay, everybody, just stay as you are," Theo said in a calm voice. "Let's not forget why we're here. Keep an eye on our man. I'm joining the team that's monitoring the kidnapper. Air One, can you pick me and my partner up?"

"Affirmative, we can set down in front of the booth at the main entrance."

"We're on our way," Theo said. "Someone, get the park police to cordon off the area where Air One is going to land."

Starting his car, Theo hit the accelerator, throwing O'Brian back in his seat and leaving rubber on the road. Theo grabbed his radio, "Team at the entrance, there's a service road that leads up to the top of the mountain. Get up there and start looking for this guy. Near the top of the mountain, the trail ends and you almost have to crawl, so your viewing area will be larger than just the path. You'll have more area to observe, so be on your toes."

In the distance, Theo could hear the whine of the chopper blades. It set down just as he and O'Brian were arriving. Both men jumped out of the car and ran. Theo ordered the co-pilot into the back seat and instructed O'Brian to do the same, then Theo took the co-pilot's seat. Looking at the pilot, Theo yelled over the whine of the rotors, "Let's go."

The pilot pulled back on the stick and the helicopter took off.

Once they were up, the pilot gave Theo a headset. "Now you can hear everything and stay in touch. Just push this button," the pilot said, "and you can talk to anyone on the detail."

The searchlight on the helicopter was more powerful than Theo imagined.

The pilot said, "I've got the light on the trail. We should pick him up any second. If not, I'll fly a short grid. There are a million places to hide the first mile of the trail."

That said, it did not take the pilot long to beam the powerful light on the young man, carrying the girl up the trail. He was holding the child by her arm, almost dragging her.

Theo got on the radio and reported their location. By this time, his men had gotten the sky team moving and several teams were headed up the mountain.

While the man with the child ran, he would stop periodically, look up at the chopper, and hold his arm over his eyes in an attempt to see.

Theo toyed with the idea of getting the pilot to land near the top so he could get out and run down the mountain toward the man fleeing with the young girl. As he was getting ready to ask the pilot to land, Theo and the pilot noticed simultaneously that the young man had left the trail and was running, his victim in tow, toward the side of the mountain where the carvings were located.

Sitting in the back, O'Brian thought about what this must all look like to the people watching the laser show. It must be quite a sight.

Meanwhile, Theo was concerned as he watched the man and girl wander past the retaining fence and ease along the now almost perpendicular side of the huge granite rock. He knew that if they got too close to the edge, they would not be able to hold their footing and would fall down the mountain onto the rocks below. The man and girl continued on, getting dangerously close to the slick edge of the mountain. Suddenly the man began to slip.

"Theo yelled, "No, no, no!"

Fortunately the man was able to stop his slide. The little girl looked up. Theo could see the fear on her face.

The man turned back toward the fence. He reached out for the fence which marked the dangerous section of mountain. It was a no trespassing area. Slowly, he began inching both himself and the little girl up the side of the steep slope, being quite careful, but his hold began to give.

Theo told the pilot to get as close as he could to the man and girl who were now holding onto the fence. Then, Theo opened the door of the helicopter, which was now hovering above them the kidnapper and child. Slowly, the pilot was inched the chopper lower and closer to the ground.

Theo crawled out on the runner, right hand stretching out, left hand holding on the door of the helicopter. O'Brian crawled over into Theo's seat and stooped down, reaching his hand toward his friend. Grabbing Theo's left hand, O'Brian held on with all his strength. At the same time, the co-pilot maneuvered himself into a position and snapped one side of a pair of handcuffs on O'Brian's wrist and the other on Theo's wrist, insuring a stronger support between the two men.

Both the man and the little girl had their arms stretched toward Theo and were mouthing the words, "Help!"

"Get me closer," Theo yelled to O'Brian.

The pilot inched the chopper closer.

The prop-wash was blowing dust around, causing the fence to shake from its anchor in the granite on the mountainside. The man and his captive began to slip.

Theo made a lunge at the girl. He could feel the hands of the little girl encircle his hand. He managed to get a good grip on her arm and pulled with all his might. Theo could feel Aiden's grip on his upper arm. Slowly, Theo was able to hoist the girl on the runner. Carefully, he maneuvered himself and the little girl toward the door. O'Brian and the copilot got them inside. Once he was sure everybody was inside, the pilot began to gain altitude.

"You're safe now," Theo told the little girl. "We're the police." She was crying and shaking. She had just been through a terrible ordeal, and Theo would have to talk to her when they landed.

Theo looked out toward the man who had taken the girl. Perhaps they could rescue him, as well. But maybe not. As he was watching, the powerful prop-wash forced the fence to completely give away. The fence and man rolled down and off the face of the mountain.

Theo and his team in the chopper knew the man was gone. Turning toward the co-pilot, Theo thanked him for using the handcuffs to insure a stronger hold. Then the detective said, "Now get these fuckers off my wrist." The co-pilot complied, and soon Theo and Aiden were rid of metal wraps on the wrists.

The pilot landed in the parking lot near the barbecue stand. Theo placed the little girl into the arms of her weeping mother. "Oh, Detective, thank you so, so much! Was that the murderer?"

"I don't think so," said Theo. "I'll explain later. Right now, your little girl needs to go with this officer to the ambulance, where she'll be examined by an EMT. He has just arrived. The little girl was pronounced in good shape, thank God, except for a few scratches. Theo told the mother that he would need to talk to her and the little girl later. She said that would be fine.

Not taking any time to recover himself, Theo ran to his car, got on the radio and checked on the status of Eleanor Cameron and Father DuPree Hixon. He was told DuPree had taken the girl to the restroom and had stood outside while the girl went in. Then, they returned to their spot and sat with Cameron and the rest of the children. They watched the show and looked at the helicopter at the top of the mountain. It was like the audience didn't know which show to watch.

The laser show had continued. When it was finished, Cameron and Father DuPree walked to her car. When she had everybody in and accounted for, DuPree hugged her and she returned the hug. She drove toward the entrance of the park and Father DuPree began his walk home. Unbeknownst to the priest, he was watched all the way and once in his house, the surveillance team there took over and reported when the lights went out.

Finally, Theo had a moment to try to digest just what had happened. It all seemed to hit him at once and he began to shake uncontrollably. Aiden O'Brian walked up to his friend and put his arms around him. Although he felt like collapsing, Theo continued to stand.

Whispering in his ear, the psychiatrist said, "You did a hell of a brave thing tonight, my good friend. I've seen a lot in my years, but nothing as courageous as what you did."

"But we lost our guy," Theo said. "Maybe I'm just getting too old for this kind of thing"

Aiden put his arms on Theo's shoulder. "Theo, Dupree was not going to do anything tonight, certainly not with Eleanor Cameron by his side. He's too smart for that."

"Then, why?" asked the detective.

"He's smart." said O'Brian. "He has to know the park is being watched like a hawk. He came tonight to see what he could learn. Also, he came to show that he is one of the good guys. He was there with children, and nothing happened to them. He's trying to find out if he's a suspect, and what the police are doing. He was looking for a tail or some other indication that he or some other person may be a suspect. Could be that he thinks he's in the clear now, and with the chopper, that we got another guy. Now, my friend, you need to get home and get some sleep."

The psychiatrist took a small bottle of pills out of his pocket and handed them to Theo. "I've been watching you for a few days. Perhaps it's my own surveillance. Take one of these each night for a week.

There's nothing addictive and nothing bad about them. They'll just help you settle down and sleep a bit better."

"Thanks, Aiden," said Theo. "I could use a good night's sleep."

Both men got in the car. Theo drove O'Brian to the law enforcement center and waited until his friend had gotten on his Harley and driven off. Then, slowly, Theo drove home. He told himself, "Tonight was a bitch." And indeed, it was.

———————

DEBRIEFING

"Well?" the Chief said, taking a sip from his morning coffee. In front of him stood both Theo and Aiden. "What happened?"

Theo and Aiden looked at each other, waiting for the other to start.

Finally, Theo began, "What we had last evening was a copycat."

"How do you know he was not our real killer?" asked the Chief.

"The person last night was a 23 year old white male who lived in Marietta. We got that from his billfold after the body was taken to the M.E.'s office. Kid named Gaylord Butts," said Theo.

"Gaylord Butts!" exclaimed the Chief. "Who the hell would put that on any kid? I can only imagine what his life was like."

Theo went on, "We did go to his home. He lives with his mother. His father is in the army, but has pretty much stayed out of the lives of his family for some time. Mom says dad and son had a strained relationship."

"I don't find that strange," the Chief replied. "Go on, Theo."

"The kid was a busboy and dishwasher at a popular mom and pop diner, specializing in family dinners, mostly soul food. They described him as a real loner. For that matter, so did the mother. My thoughts were as long as he didn't bother mom, she was satisfied. Anyway, he called in sick for work yesterday. Searching his clothes, we found his billfold. Going through it, we found several newspaper photos of our victims: numbers two, three and four. Going through his bedroom, we found a lot of magazines, mostly Teen and Parents types of magazines."

"What the hell was he looking at that Teen stuff for?" asked the Chief. "That certainly is not pornography. If it is, we will have to investigate every pediatrician in town."

Clearing his voice, Aiden said, "Perhaps I can shed some light on this. My thoughts are that Butts was a pedophile, or at least he had strong pedophilic interests, particularly in young girls. Pictures of young girls are not found in *Playboy, Hustler* or any of those magazines. He had pictures of young girls that had been cut out of legitimate magazines that focus on children. These were stuffed under his mattress. For him, these were, in fact, his form of pornography."

"Why the hell didn't he get real child porn on the Internet?" the Chief asked.

"Chief," O'Brian replied, "this kid was a real disorganized person. Not very bright. He didn't get along in school and quit as soon as he could. I'm not sure he even had enough interest or savvy to turn a computer on. He has no friends, he's messy. My God, you should have seen his room. Never in my life have I seen such a filthy place. It was a roach farm. His mother said she told him when he quit school that if he wanted to be on his own, he could do his own washing and clean his own room. It appears he didn't do either. The room was just unbelievably dirty. Looking at his sheets, they were so covered with dry semen that they were as stiff as a board. My thoughts are he had no interest in the Internet or computers, so the idea of going on the Internet to get child porn never occurred to him. His car, I mean, it was as bad as his room. He had garbage like uneaten tacos, fries all over the floors. There was mud and fast food wrappers all over. This is classic for a disorganized person. He goes to kidnap a child in an area teeming with people and takes the child up the mountain. In his mind, going up is the only route to escape. But every mountain has a top, so where does he go from there? He had no real plan. The child was not picked up, he just saw his opportunity and grabbed her."

"How's the perp's mother taking it?" the chief asked.

Theo replied, "She did not seem too overwhelmed. She cried a bit and was cooperative to an extent. She seemed to put more on her son than on her husband. My bet is there was some real shit going on in that house when the dad was home. This was a skinny kid, rotten teeth, face like a pineapple, dirty clothes. I'd bet you anything it was a bit of a relief to the mother."

There was quiet for a few moments before the Chief turned to Theo. "You were quite the man last night. Folks are calling you a hero."

Looking embarrassed, Theo replied, "Now that I look at it, the whole thing scares the shit out of me. If I had had time to think, I probably would not have reacted as I did."

"Well," the Chief said, "It was a brave thing to do. You saved that little girl's life. No doubt about it. I'm proud of you, and I'm putting you in for a citation. But Theo, brave as it was, it was also a stupid ass thing to do. I'm of no mind to look for a new Chief of Detectives."

"Thanks, Chief, I appreciate that, but it certainly is not necessary, and I promise not to put you in a position of having to replace me for a few more years. Er...a...is there anything else?"

The Chief said, "No, go home and get some rest. Both of you."

Their next stop was to see Eleanor Cameron. As Theo and Aiden walked in the door of her office, she looked up and said, "For some reason, I thought you might show up today."

"What the hell were you doing with Father DuPree?" Theo asked.

"It was sort of a Catch-22 situation," she replied. "My husband is out of town, and the girls had been hounding me to go to the laser show. Father Hixon heard the girls talking at church and sort of invited himself." Looking at Theo, she said, "This was before you talked with me."

"But..." Theo began.

Look," she said, interrupting him, "I knew what was going on. I knew I was safe. Father Hixon would not do anything with my kids; he's not dumb. Don't forget, I've prosecuted a few cases for you and your other detectives. I recognized some of your men. I felt I was probably the safest person at the laser show. Am I right?"

"Yeah," Theo said.

Cameron continued, "I guess all that stuff that was going on last night at the show was your chasing that jerk who tried to abduct the little girl?"

"What did you think when you saw it?" Theo asked.

"I wasn't sure," she answered. "I knew it had something to do with the police. You guys are the only ones around here with a spotlight on your chopper. The laser show was still going when the man fell. I'm not sure anybody knew what was going on. I will tell you one thing, when that chopper showed up with the searchlight, Father Hixon stopped watching the show. His eyes were fixed on the chopper. That really got his attention."

"Did he say anything to you? Father DuPree, I mean," O'Brian asked.

"Not a thing," she said. "When the show was over, he was like his old self, friendly with the children and very helpful getting everybody in the car. I told him if I had the room, I would give him a ride home. He thanked me, but said the walk was good for him. That was it, period, end of story."

Both men stood up. "Thanks, Eleanor," Theo said, "I'll be in touch."

"Theo," she said, "you did have me under a close watch last night, right?"

"Right" he said. "You were surrounded."

As they left, he was sure he saw relief in Cameron's face.

———————

ANOTHER SORT OF DEBRIEFING

When he arrived at his home, Father Hixon Dupree was distressed. Something *big* had gone on at the park. *Was it just a coincidence that the police helicopter was there and something was going on?* He certainly had no inkling that anybody suspected him of doing anything. *Still,* he thought to himself, *perhaps I need to lay low for a while. I've got my toys and they work just fine.*

Still, he was a little jittery. He needed to work off some energy. Going into his bedroom, he removed all his clothes, then walked down the stairs to his basement. Before him were his free weights and his weight machine, an elliptical apparatus and a treadmill. He needed a good workout. Looking at himself in the mirror, he was proud of his body. *Oh shit, here it comes*, he thought with a hint of a laugh. Looking in the mirror, he saw the erection. *"I do need a workout,"* he said out loud.

As he began his workout, he kept wondering why the police helicopter had been at the park.

He spent about an hour in his basement. It was a long and hard workout. He had a lot to think about and some decisions to make.

Working out always allowed him to clear his mind and think more decisively. The deciding factor was the helicopter. He could come up with no reason why that chopper had been near, or at the park, at that specific time. The chopper was a major distraction with its loud engine noise and the rotors whirling. Surely, it was not there just on the whim of the pilot. Walking up his stairway from the basement, he could feel the breeze coming beneath his kitchen door. The breeze felt good on his hot, sweaty body.

Walking into the bathroom, he turned the shower on and left it at cold. He loved a very cold shower after a good workout.

Finished, he toweled off and wrapped the towel around his body. Walking into his living room, he turned on the TV. *Might just as well watch some news,* he thought to himself. He let the towel drop to the floor and slid into his leather armchair. The cold leather felt good next to his skin.

As he was sitting down, he was immediately drawn to the news anchor who told of the adventure at Stone Mountain Park. There was a photograph of the now deceased kidnapper, as well as a photo of his mother's home in Marietta. The anchor stated that Butts' mother refused to be interviewed. Sitting in his chair, he said out loud, to the news anchor, "No! You dumb bastard."

So, that was it. But listening to the story, he was still not sure why the chopper was there in the first place. This was indeed a puzzle. He turned to make sure the rubber-backed curtains were fully covering his windows, both in the front room, then his bedroom. Finally, he got into his bed, but sleep did not come as quickly as normal. The helicopter was still puzzling to him. He decided he would sleep on it and make a decision tomorrow.

When he awoke, his decision was made. He showered again, as it was a part of his morning routine, shaved, dressed and walked to the church office feeling quite content.

THE REAL CHASE BEGINS

33

The first thing Theo did on his way to the office was call Aiden O'Brian. When O'Brian answered, the two men talked briefly about the previous night. Then Theo asked the psychiatrist a question that had been bothering him since he woke up. "Aiden, I'm feeling that perhaps DuPree may know he's being watched. We may have given away our ace card last night. Do you feel the same way?"

"Theo, I don't think there's any question about it. He has to know after last night and all the activity, the chopper and all, especially with everything that's in the press. In fact, I would not be surprised to see our man try to get out of town."

Theo asked, "Any chance you can take the day off and spend it over here?"

"I've got a lecture at 10 this morning. It's an hour-long class. I'll come over as soon as I can."

"Good," Theo replied, "I'll see you then."

Theo called the surveillance team watching the house and church. "What's going on?" he asked. "Anything?"

"Not much. Our man left his house and walked over to the church. We haven't seen anything since then."

"Good. Let me know if there is any change; I don't care what it is," Theo instructed. "By the way I'm getting a message out to all the task force in a minute, so listen up for it."

"Ten-four."

Theo got on the radio and instructed one of the officers from the surveillance house and the officers in mobile units covering the church, to come in to the law enforcement center immediately. He also asked for all units who were not immediately on any important lead to do the same. Following that, he looked at his stack of ever increasing phone messages. Gathering them up, Theo walked into Wilma's office. She was busy at the computer.

"Wilma," he said, handing the stack over to her, "I can't get these taken care of until I don't know when. Call these people, see what they want and try to head off any problems. Just put them off until I can get them contacted or handle the questions yourself. Just don't tell anybody anything. Questions from the press you can refer to the Information Office. Got it?"

"I'll do what I can," she said.

"Good, thanks," he replied walking out the door. Turning he said, "I'll be in the conference room."

By this time, most of his officers on the task force were in the room. Theo took a chair in the front row, turned it around to face his officers and said, "Well, last night was interesting, wasn't it?"

There were several remarks all erupting at the same time. Theo smiled. Then he said, "Y'all have been doing a wonderful job. You've been away from your families too long. Your sacrifices have been above and beyond. I have a hunch we're closing in on our man. I think, after last night, he cannot help but feel that something is going on. My gut and Dr. O'Brian's experience tell us DuPree may be getting ready to leave. So, for God's sake don't slack off. We need to be *heads up* from now on. Not that you haven't been, but, well, you know what I mean. You are all good experienced officers. Questions?"

One officer raised his hand. "Theo, any possibility that last night's guy was the one?"

"No. He was just a copycat."

Seeing no more questions, Theo dismissed his team and returned to his office to wait for Aiden.

The psychiatrist was in Theo's office by 12:30. Hungry, he had stopped by a deli and brought sandwiches. As both men ate, they discussed the case, with emphasis on the profile. Aiden had mentioned the multiple times DuPree had inserted himself into the investigation, putting up the posters, cooperating with the filming of the funeral and his coming to view the photos and video of those in attendance. When he brought that up, the psychiatrist asked Theo, "Say, do you, by any chance, have a video of the press conferences?"

"Sure," Theo replied. Getting up from his desk, he opened his door and asked Wilma to get the videos. "What do you want them for?" the detective asked.

"I'll bet you anything that if we can see the crowd well enough, we'll find DuPree."

Wilma brought three videos in.

"Thanks," Theo responded with a smile. She smiled back and told the men if they needed anything else, to let her know.

Theo had a portable video player in his office. Inserting the first video, the screen came to life. Putting the video on slow motion, both men scanned the audience.

"There he is," Theo yelled. Jumping up, he pointed his finger, almost blotting out the face to where he was pointing. As both men looked, it was quite obvious it was Father Hixon DuPree. "Son of a bitch," Theo whispered.

They looked at the other two videos and just as expected, they could find DuPree in each one.

"That's one way he could keep up with the investigation. I'll bet the last press conference scared him just a bit, especially when the Chief said they had a suspect in mind," O'Brian said.

The conversation was interrupted by a transmission by one of the surveillance team. It was the team from the apartment. "What's up?" Theo asked.

"Not much. There's no apparent church meeting or anything, but two women parked in the parking lot, went up to the door that leads to the sacristy, unlocked the door and went in. Can you get any information on what they're doing?"

"Just a minute. I'll get back to you." Picking up the phone, Theo punched in seven numbers. Aiden could hear the answer, "District Attorney's Office."

"Eleanor Cameron, please, this is Theo Reed."

"Just a moment, Detective Reed. I'm ringing her now."

Cameron picked up on the first ring.

"Eleanor, it's Theo."

"Nice to hear from you. After last night, I was not sure you would ever speak to me again."

"Not so. As you said, you were caught in the middle. No harm done and it all turned out fine," Theo said.

"I'm sure this is not a social call, Theo, what's up?"

"Look," he responded. "One of our surveillance units just saw a car park in back of the church and two women got out and went in. As near as my men could tell, there's nothing going on. I can't call Father Bainbridge to find out. That's your church. Can you help?"

Cameron said, "I'll bet those women are on the Altar Guild. They get the altar ready for Sunday services. Let me make a friendly call to the secretary. I'll get right back to you."

"Thanks," Theo replied and hung up.

Looking at O'Brian, Theo asked, "You really think he's going to take off?"

"I'd bet money on it," the psychiatrist said.

They were both quiet for a few minutes, each man deep in his own thoughts. The silence was broken by Wilma. "Theo, it's Eleanor Cameron."

Theo picked up the phone. "Eleanor, what you got?"

"Just what I thought," Cameron answered. "The two women are

there to set the altar as well as polish some silver and some brass. They'll probably be there around two hours, I would suspect."

"Thanks, Counselor," Theo replied.

"Anything else?" she asked.

"That's it. I'll call you as soon as I have anything." Theo hung up.

Both men finished their sandwiches and making small talk.

Finally, O'Brian asked Theo about his mother.

Shaking his head, Theo said, "She's fine, better then she thinks she is." Then he told of his last communication with her and his promise to take her to St. George Island when things quieted down.

"If the requirement is when things settle down, I imagine your Gulf Coast excursion will be some time away," Aiden said jokingly.

"Naw," the detective said, his head shaking, "I've really neglected her. I hate to say this, but sometimes old people are really a pain in the ass. I mean she's my mama and I love her, but she just can't understand why I have no extra time."

"It's not the issue of not understanding the time, I think it's just a point of growing older and not having a lot to do. She wants more time with you and that's where she concentrates. Coretta is away becoming a doctor and you are all she has. Getting old is a lot about coming to terms with your aging and then having to deal with the finality of your life. Old age is a tough stage to be in. Next to adolescence, I would say it's the second most difficult stage in which to navigate," the psychiatrist said to his good friend.

Theo was not excited to go into his mother issues, so he took his radio and called the apartment. The response was immediate.

"Parker here."

"This is Theo. Where's Dupree?"

"Still at the church."

"The two ladies still there?" Theo asked.

"No, they left about an hour ago. Only difference is, there were three ladies when they left. I checked and we all thought we saw two ladies, not three. I don't know where that third lady came from. But no DuPree," Officer Parker said, somewhat hesitantly.

"Parker," Theo asked, *"what other woman*? What the hell is going on? What did the third lady look like?"

"She was taller than the other two women. She had on a pants outfit and was wearing a hat and dark glasses."

"O.K., stay on it and stay in touch. Don't wait for me to call," Theo commanded.

"Ten-four."

Hanging up, Theo gave the phone time enough to disconnect, then dialed the DA's office again.

"Theo Reed here, I need to speak with Eleanor Cameron, please."

"I'm sorry, she's in a staff meeting."

"Look, this is important. Please get her for me, and please do it now."

In less than twenty seconds, Eleanor Cameron came on the line. Theo told her what had happened. Cameron said she would call the church and get the story.

Hanging up, Theo looked at Aiden. "What do you think?"

"Right off the top of my head I would say our man is the third woman. Look, by now, DuPree has to know he's being watched. You have not mentioned any contact from DuPree in several days. A couple of weeks ago, he was calling you like he was your best friend. Now you don't hear a thing from him. I don't know what he told them, but he disguised himself and took off with the women."

Picking up the phone again, Theo called security at Atlanta Hartsfield-Jackson International Airport. Asking for the Director of Security, he gave the information, scant as it was. "I'll get more to you as soon as I have it," Theo said and hung up. His next call was to the Atlanta Police precinct at the airport. Talking to the lieutenant on duty, Theo did the same thing.

Wilma knocked and opened his door just as he was replacing the receiver.

"Eleanor Cameron" was all she had the chance to say.

Theo said, "Eleanor, what you got?"

"Theo, I got the names of the two women. There were only two women scheduled. Nobody at the church knows anything about another woman. I spoke with Father Bainbridge and he knew of nothing. I tried DuPree, but he's nowhere to be found." She then gave him the names and addresses of the two women who were on the Altar Guild.

Armed with that information, Theo got hold of the two roving units and directed each unit to a woman's house. "As soon as you interview them, get back to me on my radio. I'll be in my car."

Theo could feel the sweat dripping under his arm and on his forehead as his nervous system went into high gear. Grabbing for the phone, it slipped out of his grip. "Fuck," he yelled.

Aiden said, "Hey, buddy, slow down a bit. Just take a couple of deep breaths. You're going to get it all done." He placed his hands on Theo's back, gave it a few rubs and Theo began to relax.

"Thanks Aiden," he said. "I'm glad you're here."

Then yelling for Wilma, who was in the door in a flash, Theo said, "We think DuPree is trying to give us the slip. I've called the airport. I need you to get all the task force members in here and get them organized so they can get on this now. I have two task force cars on assignment right now. The others will know what to do and who to contact, car rental, and everything. Notify the highway patrol. Dr. O'Brian will be with me in my car. We're on our way to the airport."

Grabbing his suit jacket, Theo was quickly out of his chair with O'Brian was right behind. As they were running to the car, Theo looked at his watch. It was almost 5:00. "Shit," he said, "we're going to hit the damn Atlanta traffic."

Once in the car, Theo put his portable blue light on the top of his car. With the light flashing and siren blasting, they roared out of the parking garage and in two turns, merged onto Interstate 285, the highway that serves as the beltway around Atlanta. It was bumper to bumper traffic. "Just our fucking luck," Theo said. He turned to O'Brian. "Still have your badge?" he asked.

"Right next to my heart."

Theo gave a somewhat forced laugh.

As they were driving, the voice of Parker radioed in from the apartment, "Chief, I just came from his house. DuPree is gone. I mean he is nowhere to be found. Father Bainbridge has no answer either, and is too overcome to be much help. The junior warden did show up and let me in DuPree's house. You would not believe that place. The windows are all covered with some sort of rubber-backed material. I mean, *all* the windows in the house. He has a place to work out in the basement. I looked in some of his drawers and found loads of panties."

Theo said to Parker, "Look, you can't do much of that stuff without a warrant. Get your ass down to the DA, get hold of Eleanor Cameron; she's the ADA who is handing this case. Get a search warrant now, then go back in the house and do what you need to do. Search every place, attic, and crawl space, every place. I want that place thoroughly gone through, not a crumb untouched."

———————

DUPREE ON THE RUN

At first, Hixon DuPree was not too worried. Then last night and the helicopter. It was not there just to help direct traffic. "That fucking Reed," he said to himself. This place was different from all the cities and towns he had been in. He had not expected the enormity of the investigation until he had begun going to the press conferences. He knew there were men assigned when he went to try to help with the funeral photos and video, but since then, the investigation and the number of investigators had grown.

When that Butts kid took the little girl, it had seemed to him that cops were coming out of every place in the park. Obviously, he had not recognized any of them from the times he had been to task force meetings. He was bothered by the fact that he was so unaware of just how close the police were, not just in the park, but in the investigation. There had been a couple seated on a blanket right next to him and Eleanor Cameron. He had noticed during the start of the show that the couple were kissing and rubbing each other's back.

My God, he thought, *surely they were not cops.* There had been a pesky teen walking around selling some sort of glow in the dark trinket. When the "shit hit the fan," the teenager had dropped everything, ripped off his apron and had run toward the depot. At that point, DuPree knew the person had not been some zit-faced kid; he was an undercover cop in disguise. *How did they know it was me?* he wondered. *I know I didn't make any slips. I spent time with that dickhead Reed and he never acted strange when I was with him, not one damned time.*

Even though he had worked out hard and enjoyed the workout, he still had a feeling he could not describe. In all his other encounters he had not felt this feeling, a sort of foreboding. But he was smarter than they were. Of this, there was no question in his mind.

Earlier, after the last press conference, he had been thinking about getting out. The following day he had removed the key to the church thrift shop and gone over there. The store was just a four minute walk from the church. He made sure it was a day the shop was not open. He went during the daytime, but he knew that if he was seen, he had his story. After all, he was a priest of the Women's Guild who operated the store and he did belong to that very parish.

Once inside, he had gone through every bit of women's clothes. He was pleasantly surprised to find a good variety that would not only fit him, but would work for him. It was not like he had never worn women's clothes before. He had done so, and in fact, had quite enjoyed the feel of them on his body. So, he was certainly aware of what size would work for him. He also knew what clothes made him look more feminine and less like Hixon DuPree.

Quite quickly, he had found a black polyester pantsuit that would do nicely. Next he took a gray sweater set, pullover and cardigan. He would not need the cardigan, but he took it just in case. "What the hell," he said to himself, "it's free."

He had his own wig at home, as well as some black low heel pumps which he had gotten at a large and tall shop a couple of years ago. He topped off his find with a string of costume pearls. Putting the items in a plastic grocery sack kept behind the counter for customers, he slipped out the back door and was back at his house, where he dropped the items off and was back at church before anybody knew he was gone. All this would fit nicely in a leather tote bag he had stolen during a Christmas Eve church service last year.

He had awakened early this morning, and had slowly had begun to rub himself. As he always said, jerking off made him feel good, relaxed and more in control. Years ago, he had said that jerking off was his drug of choice! As he rubbed, his fantasy began as a vague image before it became more real. The image of Paige Langford came into his mind. It became like an out of body experience where he was up high, over the body of the little girl, yet watching himself slowly squeeze the life out of her. He watched as the little body squirmed, her hands pulling at his hands, the hands that were choking the life out of her. It was as if the other girl, the dirty one, was not there at all. He watched himself take his swollen cock in his hands, rub it and squirt on her body. He watched as his hands painted the little girl's stomach with his sperm. He quivered with relief and was aware of his wet and sticky hand. Now he was calmer, back in control. And life was good.

—————————

THE CHASE CONTINUES

In very slow traffic, and experiencing how difficult it was to find a fast lane, Theo got a call from one of his teams. The police officer working on that team, had gotten in touch with one of the Altar Guild ladies. The woman, Mary Loukes, had just dropped her friend and church volunteer partner off at her home. She and Ginger Havens had been at the church earlier preparing the altar for next Sunday. They had also taken some time to polish some of the silver, as well as some brass candlesticks. As they were putting away the silver, a woman had approached them. Loukes said that neither she nor Ginger Havens knew the woman, but found her face very familiar; however, they could not place the woman or recall where they may have seen her. Loukes said the woman told them that she thought she had an early afternoon appointment with the rector, Father Bainbridge. She arrived at the church office only to learn the priest was at the cathedral for a short meeting with the bishop. He would not return until later in the afternoon. The woman said she guessed she was mixed up about her appointment.

Neither Loukes nor Havens had given any thought to how the

woman gained entrance into the church, although the only door open to the actual church building was the door leading to the sacristy. Further, they had not thought about the fact that the church office was in one building, some distance from the actual church.

Pleading lack of money, the woman had asked the two women for a ride to the nearest MARTA station, Atlanta's subway system. The woman also said she was leaving that very afternoon for New York to visit family and would return the following week.

Loukes related that she and her friend had felt sorry for the woman and having nothing else planned, they had offered to drive the woman the extra half an hour it would take them to drive to the airport. Besides, there was a nice new café in College Park, a town that bordered the airport and they thought it might be nice to stop for a glass of wine.

Once in Mary Louke's car, with their passenger in the back, both ladies tried to draw the woman into conversation, but she had remained quiet, answering only in short phrases. For the most part, she had appeared to the ladies as inattentive. Perhaps, they decided later, she had a lot on her mind. That was probably the reason she had come to visit Father Bainbridge.

At the airport, she asked to be dropped off at the south terminal. Once they arrived at the destination, she had immediately jumped out of the car. She thanked the ladies for the ride and almost instantly was swallowed up by the crowd at the airport. Both ladies had estimated it was around four in the afternoon when they were there. Neither lady paid any attention to the fact the other lady was carrying only a small, carry-on bag.

Theo got on the radio, which was on a separate channel from the regular channel for the department. He ordered one team to maintain liaison with the Atlanta PD at the airport, another team to work with Delta security, and given the fact the lady had gotten off at the south terminal, the location for Delta airlines, the largest carrier at the airport, he had a team work with that airline's security. He ordered two teams each to cover each of the six concourses. Theo also ordered a team to make contact and work with AirTran security. After all, they were the second largest carrier for Atlanta and had a large route with stops or destinations to several cities, especially three of the four New York airports. The officers assigned to the several concourses were to walk up and down the concourse and look for any person dressed like that woman. Clearly this was a very small needle in a very large haystack. One thing Theo and Aiden were sure of, the *woman* was indeed Hixon DuPree.

Once out of the car, DuPree walked directly into the terminal. The terminal was extremely crowded with large lines at the various Delta ticket counters. Instead of getting in line, he turned away and walked toward the exit doors leading to ground transportation. At the end of that walk, he turned right into another area that served MARTA, Atlanta's public transportation system. Calmly, he walked to the ticket booth and purchased one token. He then walked through the turnstiles, took the escalator to the top and boarded the train which would take him back to Atlanta.

Theo was getting more upset with the traffic jam, driving only a few yards, then stopping then a few more yards. He knew it was a rare day when there was not a traffic accident someplace on the beltway. At best, the airport was a thirty minute drive from his office, providing the traffic was cooperative.

Today they had been on the road almost forty five minutes and had gone barely two miles in spite of his blue light and siren. Both he and Aiden were quiet with their own thoughts, both realizing how important it was to catch this killer of children. He could not be allowed to escape and live to kill again.

DuPree looked at his watch as the MARTA train pulled out of the station destined to travel through several stops in Atlanta, then continue its route to the outlying suburbs. He smiled at himself.

You've done well, he thought. Looking out the window he saw an Atlanta PD car speeding down a major road, blue lights flashing. He could even hear the siren. He wondered if they were looking for him. *Surely,* he thought, *they know I've left. But, they have no idea who I am.* He chuckled at the thought of the two women. The Loukes woman had given him several strange looks, like she knew him, but could not place how. DuPree recalled that he and Loukes had worked on a Lenten luncheon a few months ago. Surely the clothes and make up had done the trick.

Not wanting to arrive too early at the train station where Amtrak ran, he got off the MARTA train at the High Museum stop. Then he could either take a bus to the train or walk, it really was not that far. He hoped the train was on time. Again, he took the escalator to the top, then calmly walked toward Symphony Hall, which was located next to the museum. The door was open. DuPree walked directly to the women's restroom. Fortunately, it was empty. He stepped into a stall, locked the door, then began changing his clothes. He took out a pair of well worn men's jeans, a long sleeved shirt and a baseball cap with an Atlanta Braves logo. Once dressed, he put the women's clothes back in the bag. He went to the row of sinks and scrubbed the makeup off his face.

Deciding to walk to the train station, he pulled his baseball cap down so his eyes were almost covered. Not wanting to arouse any suspicion, he set off with a moderate speed walk.

As he approached the station he looked carefully in order to see if there were any vehicles that looked like unmarked police cars. Seeing none, he walked into the station and up to the ticket counter. He asked the clerk if the train was on time.

"She's running a bit behind today, about an hour away, still in Alabama," the clerk said. Looking at the board which contained the schedules, DuPree was able to figure out this train was headed east to Washington, D.C. He would rather the train was going to New

Orleans. There was only one train per day and the train to the Big Easy would not run until the next day, then it returned the following day headed for Washington.

The clerk said, "Need a ticket?"

"Yes, one way to Washington, D.C. please and I would prefer to have a room. Is that possible?" DuPree asked.

"We can do that, trains are not very crowded."

After purchasing his ticket, DuPree was uncomfortable waiting around the train station. Taking his carry-on bag, he hurried across Peachtree Road to a bookstore where he could wait and watch for any strange happenings that might indicate he was in jeopardy. He would be glad to get on the train. It would be light when the train arrived, thanks to daylight savings time. DuPree figured if he could get to Washington, he could then head up to New York and get lost in the city for a time. He would take another route from Washington to the Big Apple; perhaps he would rent a car or maybe even take a bus. When things cooled off, then he could get to the Big Easy.

Now all he had to do was keep out of sight until the train arrived. Once on the train, it would not take too long to get into South Carolina. Then he would feel safer. He smiled as he thought of all the police officers and that Reed jerk running all over the airport.

For some reason, Aiden had a very real unsettling feeling in his stomach. *This was natural,* he thought, *given the fact that DuPree had slipped his surveillance and was now back on the run.* Wondering what he could have done to prevent this, what he should have seen that he had not, was causing the psychiatrist a great deal of concern. He was not surprised at Dupree's womanly disguise. He had known about the killer's fetish for women's underwear and transvestism would certainly be another element, but he had not seen it earlier and had not included cross-dressing in the profile. Of course, this could be the first time Dupree ever dressed as a woman, and more out of necessity than an emotional desire.

The psychiatrist began mulling over all he knew about the killer, like Dupree's motivations and behaviors. What O'Brian needed now was to formulate in his mind how DuPree would think now that he was at the airport. *What would DuPree do? How would he act? Would he purchase a ticket? Would he maintain his disguise? Where was he likely to go?* They knew so little about him. *It's the behavior,* he told himself. *Study the behavior.*

Serial murderers were actually quite insecure people. Despite their outward façade, they felt powerless unless they had control of a situation. *So what was DuPree trying to say to himself?* Aiden asked silently.

Aiden was unsettled, but it was not from what he knew; it was from what he did not know. O'Brian felt he had the key; he just needed to figure it out.

Lost in thought, O'Brian was unaware of the traffic jam. He could hear Theo swearing, trying to maneuver the Crown Vic down the highway, trying to change lanes and questioning the birthright of every person who would not let him make his moves as well as every person who would speed up, not allowing the detective to change lanes or those who cut him off.

Glancing at the clock on the dashboard, Aiden saw that it was now just past 6:00 in the evening.

Once he was in the bookstore, DuPree sat at a small table and rummaged through his tote bag. He had enough money. Once he got to D.C., he would buy a new set of clothes. He also had Henry Thornberry's billfold. He knew that, by now Thornberry would have reported his billfold stolen and his credit cards gone. He still had Thornberry's driver's license and his military identification. He decided to keep those. *Who knows, they might come in handy sometime.* Getting up from his chair, DuPree walked into the men's room. He washed his hands, then took a towel and dried off. Reaching into his pocket, he took the stolen billfold, wrapped it in his used towel. Then he reached into the used towel depository, pulled the other used towels up about half way and placed his towel holding the billfold in the hole he had made in the towels. *Now,* he thought, *it would be difficult for anyone to find.*

He returned to his seat. Looking at his watch, he figured he had about twenty minutes before the train arrived. He would wait ten minutes, then make his way across the street and down the ramp to the train. Once on the train, he felt as though he would be safe.

Atlanta Hartsfield – Jackson International Airport had gone into its red security alert. Atlanta PD officers, now armed with faxed photos of Hixon Dupree, as a male and a police artist's depiction of DuPree, dressed as the women had described him, patrolled the ticket counters of all the airlines in both the north and south sections of the terminal. Officers were posted at the four escalators leading to the level to go to the concourses. APD officers were stationed outside both the north and south side of the terminal. Theo's officers were riding the golf type carts on every concourse. Atlanta PD had officers on Segways patrolling the atrium, food court and any other place in the terminal where a person might try to be inconspicuous.

Both Delta and AirTran security had taken it upon themselves to alert all the other airlines in case DuPree tried another airline. Immigration had been contacted to determine whether or not DuPree had a passport, and the foreign airlines had been notified just in case. Delta had posted photos at every gate. It had been a Herculean task and it had been done quickly and quite easily.

"Control," Aiden O'Brian said over and over to himself. DuPree felt powerless unless he was in control and he could not operate unless he had some control over the events in his life. "He has to be in control," the psychiatrist said softly to himself. Aiden knew that serial killers like DuPree, those whose thought patterns were organized, needed to be in control. In doing so, they might change their modus operandi to thwart the police or to gain more control over their situation, what ever the situation may be. Like a bolt out of the blue, Aiden had his answer. Of course, it was very simple and it made sense.

"I'll be damned," O'Brian blurted out. "Theo, it's not the airport, it's the train station. DuPree is going to take the train!"

"What the hell are you talking about?"

"Its control, Theo. DuPree has to be in control. He has no control at the airport. He's got no ticket; he'll be standing in line to get a ticket. Lines at the airport are long as hell. Then he has to make it through security. Those lines are long, as well. Then he has to wait in one area for his flight. He can't do it, not under these conditions. He's going to take the train, I tell you."

Theo looked intently at Aiden. They had been working together for some time. And Aiden knew all about serial killers. His own instinct, however, was to try the airport. An airplane had to be the fastest way out of Atlanta. DuPree had no car. Theo was not sure the man could even drive. He was not one to hitchhike; he definitely would not take a bus. DuPree was a bit of a sophisticate.

For a moment Theo hesitated, not sure how to respond. All his years of police work told him to go to the airport. Now he had to decide whether to set aside his instincts and trust what his friend was telling him.

"Theo," O'Brian yelled, "we haven't got time. Get us the hell out of this mess and to the train station." O'Brian, his red hair beginning to stand on end, was looking more wild than normal.

Looking his friend in the eye, Theo responded, "But the women, they took him to the airport. An airplane is the most logical way for him to get out of town."

Upset with himself for not seeing it earlier, O'Brian yelled impatiently to his friend, "Goddammit Theo, I know what I'm talking about. The sonofabitch is going to take the train. Look, I've lived with this bastard for days. I've eaten with him, showered with him, and slept with him – in my mind – since this whole thing began. I'm angry with myself that I didn't realize this earlier, but I know what I'm talking about." He ran his hands through his shock of red hair, almost frantic.

"Theo," he said, "the trip to the airport was a stroke of luck for Dupree. It was luck that gave him the opportunity to throw us off. He has no control at the airport. The entire process is too long for him, the standing in line for a ticket, security, time at the gate. He can't deal with that. He has too little control. There's no security at the train station and he can leave the train damn near any place he chooses. Theo, trust me!"

Theo realized he needed to trust his friend. He looked at his watch. It was now getting close to six. Hopefully, if he could get off the Interstate and on some side streets and curbs, they could make it. Mind made up that they were on the right track, Theo was like a New York taxi driver. It was a carnival ride for Aiden, but Theo was able to eventually make it to the shoulder of the Interstate. Driving through trash, kudzu vines and small piles of asphalt, he made it to the next exit where he literally forced his way in front of a car and plowed ahead.

Once on the surface streets, the blue light and siren had more impact on drivers and pedestrians, as well. Grabbing his radio, Theo called in to the dispatcher. When his call was acknowledged, Theo asked to be put through directly to the chief.

In a few moments the chief's voice said, "Theo, what's up?'

Responding excitedly, Theo announced, "Chief, DuPree is headed for the Amtrak station. I'm on my way there now. Traffic sucks and I'm not sure how quickly I can get there once I hit the downtown traffic. We need some officers at the station ASAP."

Theo knew he was asking the chief to digest a lot. Then the chief replied, "What happened at the airport?"

"The airport is still on," Theo replied. "I've got Aiden O'Brian with me and he is convinced DuPree's trip to the airport was to throw us off. I'm still having my officers monitor every airline there, so now I need some officers at the Amtrak station."

"Jesus, Theo, we've got everybody but the Russian army at the airport. Let me see what I can do."

"Chief," Theo said loudly, but being careful not to scream, "we need some officers at the train station, stat!"

"Theo, I'll do all I can if it means I have to go there myself."

"Thanks chief, I'll keep you informed," Theo said.

Then using his cell phone he called Wilma.

"Where are you?" Wilma said as she answered her phone. "I've got big news for you."

"What is it?" Theo retorted.

"GBI called; they have a match on the semen samples. No question about it. The samples match DuPree. Based on that, Eleanor Cameron drew up papers for a search warrant for DuPree's house. They found a lot of stuff, including a small case that would fit in a pocket. The case contained some Epoxy glue. With that, Cameron issued an arrest warrant for Dupree."

"Okay, Wilma," Theo replied. "We, O'Brian and I, think DuPree is trying to leave town on the train. We're headed for the Amtrak station right now. The rest of the task force is at the airport covering everything there. I'll keep you posted. Close up the office, but make sure you keep your cell phone with you."

"Theo," Wilma cried, "take care of yourself."

"I'll be in touch," the detective said.

Driving like a maniac, Theo brought Aiden up to date on what Wilma had told him.

It was getting close to the time the train was supposed to arrive. Seeing nothing alarming, DuPree left the comfort of the bookstore and ventured outside. He stopped by the side of the building and looked around for any evidence of any law enforcement officers. Seeing nothing suspicious, he went to cross the street. The traffic was very heavy and was slowed by the number of streetlights on Peachtree Road. When the traffic stopped, DuPree dodged in between cars and made it to the curb on the other side of the street. He walked into the train station. Walking up to the ticket counter, he asked how long before the train arrived.

"Be here in about fifteen minutes," the clerk said.

Handing the agent his ticket, DuPree asked if he could explain just where he would be on the train.

"You're about halfway from the front, two cars from the dining room. The next car is the lounge car and the end of the train. You have a sleeper, just like you asked for."

DuPree was sure the agent had not even looked at his face. "Impersonal ass," the priest mumbled. The agent gave no indication he had heard DuPree's comment.

DuPree had a few minutes. As train stations go, this one was extremely small, not at all like train stations in other cities. Under most conditions, he would have liked a big station with lots of travelers around so he could hide, but now this was just right. He could see everybody. Nothing appeared out of the ordinary to him.

Soon enough, DuPree heard the whistle of the train and soon, he could see the undulating movement of the front headlights. He walked to the end of the ramp, then down the stairway to the lower level ramp where he would board the train. He stepped back as it slowed, coming into the station.

Theo had no idea what to expect so he called the dispatch office and asked the location of the helicopter. He was informed the chopper was at Peachtree-DeKalb airport getting fueled up. Theo told the dispatcher to have the chopper fly to Brookwood Train Station. "There is a large condo complex across the street. Have him set down there and wait for me. If anyone has any questions or problems, direct them to the Chief," Theo directed.

Still some distance from the train station, Theo maneuvered the car with a steady hand. Blue light spinning and siren blaring, he drove from street to street, going through areas Aiden had never seen before. It was nice being with someone who knew the city so well.

Eventually, as Theo suspected, he got into heavy traffic on Peachtree Road. Interstate 85 cut through downtown Atlanta and Peachtree Road had a bridge that spanned the highway. Traffic came to a halt. Looking at his clock, Theo realized the trip had taken him almost an hour.

Theo could see the Brookwood Train Station from where he was sitting. Just as he was ready to abandon his vehicle, the cars began to move. Getting closer to the station, Theo strained to see if the train was there. It was not. "Let's hope the train is late," Theo said to Aiden.

Once at the station, Theo drove the car over the curb and came to a grinding stop on the sidewalk. He threw the car into park before he was even stopped.

With Aiden right behind him, Theo ran to the station clerk, badge in his hand. Paying no attention, the clerk was busy with some paper work. If he knew Theo was there, he certainly gave no sign of it. Theo was growing more impatient. Two hours of frustration with traffic and now missing the train was about all he could stomach. His anger was growing with each second he was ignored. Growing more impatient by the moment, Theo began thumping his fingernails on the counter. Still the clerk was impervious. The shear frustration came to a head. Finally, Theo had had enough. Reaching through the window, and following an old football practice, he exploded with a little *jersey justice*, grabbing the clerk by the shirt and pulling him tight to the counter. Holding his badge in the face of the agent, Theo whispered to the now white faced agent, "When's the next train, you little piss ant?"

"Crescent for New Orleans will be day after tomorrow," said the petrified agent whose feet were about one foot off the ground.

"When was the last train through this station?" Theo hissed.

"Crescent going the other way to Washington, D.C. and New York left about twenty minutes ago."

Realizing he now had the clerk's complete attention, Theo released the hold on the man's shirt.

"Was there a white female who bought a ticket on that train?" Theo asked.

"I sold several tickets to people, black and white. Fuck man, I can't look at everybody. This is AMTRAK, we got no money and little help." The agent tried to straighten his shirt.

Theo gave the agent a menacing look. Not wanting to get "collared" again and seeing the officer was in no mood for anything but short accurate answers, the agent replied, "I don't recall any white lady buying a ticket prior to the train coming in."

"The last ticket you sold, who bought that?" asked Theo, now a little less aggressive.

"Man wearing a Braves baseball cap bought a ticket about an hour, maybe less, before the train came in," the agent replied. "He bought a ticket to Washington, D.C. Got a sleeper."

"Did he look like this?" Theo asked, holding a photo of DuPree.

Taking the photo, the clerk said, "I think the man probably does favor this picture."

"Where does this train stop next?" questioned Theo.

Now all business, the agent replied, "The train makes several very quick stops all the way to Charlotte. Gets there about 1:30 tomorrow morning. first step is Gainseville, Georgia. Train will be there in half an hour. The next big stop is D.C."

Theo turned toward O'Brian, mouthing "Fuck" and shrugged his shoulders as soon as they were out of listening distance. A dejected look on his face, Theo looked at his friend. "Shit man, we were this close." He held his two hands just a few inches apart. Then he said, "I've got to get on that train."

O'Brian put his hand on Theo's shoulder, pulling him around so they were facing each other. "While you were talking to the clerk, I got a train schedule." He smiled waving a paper in front of him and Theo. "The agent was right. The train will not make any stops for any length of time until it gets to Charlotte, but there are places along the way where the train stops. Maybe we can work out some plan."

Theo thought a second, then said, "It can't be done. The damn train will be in South Carolina in a couple of hours. I need to get on that train, but unless we can get to it before it is out of Georgia, I'll be out of my jurisdiction."

As they continued walking toward Theo's car, O'Brian remarked, "Look, we need to get on the train far enough ahead that we will not cause any commotion or arouse suspicion. DuPree is going to be super vigilant until he feels totally safe."

Once outside of the station, both men could hear the whine of the helicopter rotors cutting through the air. Looking up, they saw the chopper descending to the parking lot of the condo complex across the street. "How the hell did he know to come now?" O'Brian asked.

"Oh," said Theo, "I asked for it earlier. I thought we might be in for another chase."

Theo looked at the busy Peachtree road traffic. It was hard to talk over the noise. Yelling in O'Brian's, ear Theo screamed, "I'm a law enforcement officer in pursuit of a fleeing felon. Give me that train schedule. I need to find a good place ahead of the train so I can get aboard."

O'Brian yelled back, "I'm still a sworn deputy, I'm going with you. We need to get on the train as soon as possible, but without DuPree seeing us or getting suspicious. We want him to be able to settle down a bit, to think he got away."

Stopping at his vehicle, Theo reached in and grabbed his cell phone. He hesitated a moment, then opened the glove box and took out a pistol in an ankle holster. Looking at O'Brian, he said, "I don't know what is going to happen, but you may need this," handing the gun to his friend.

Theo turned to a uniform officer, threw him his car keys and yelled for him to deliver the vehicle to the law enforcement center in DeKalb County. Then both men began running across the street, both dodging traffic, brakes mashing, horns blowing, and a few irate comments and fingers. Once across, they ran around the corner of the building and to the waiting helicopter.

Theo talked to the pilot, then directed the copilot into one of the back seats and O'Brian into the other. Then Theo took the seat next to the pilot.

Once in the air, Theo got on the radio and was patched through to the chief. Theo told him what was happening and asked him to call South Carolina and North Carolina authorities and let them know what was going on.

They settled inToccoa, Georgia as the place to board the train. Then Theo told the chief, "Make sure that no officers are at any stations and no officers are to board the train. We're pretty close now and I don't want our man spooked." The chief promised to call South Caroline authorities and pave the way.

There was a small discussion about authority for Theo and Aiden to conduct business outside their jurisdiction. The chief realized that no matter what he said, Theo was on his way. Hesitantly, the chief acknowledged his Chief of Detective's request.

Hixon DuPree settled into his sleeper. Immediately, he pulled the curtains across the window. Sitting on his bench, he slowly pulled a bit of curtain at the lower corner making a very small area where he could see what was going on and who else might be boarding the train. Noticing nothing unusual, only a few scurrying passengers, he let out a sigh of relief, and let the curtain go.

Slowly, the big silver train began pulling away from the station. DuPree looked around his sleeper room. It was small and not exceptionally clean. Although he had been in a hurry to board and get to his room, he had not been able to ignore the condition of the cars and the engine. They were dirty with thousands of miles of dirt and grime. The inside of the cars were not much better. *Too bad,* he thought to himself. Trains in other parts of the world were better kept and fun to ride, especially in Europe and the United Kingdom. In the United States, they were a dying breed and a nuisance.

He stayed in his seat, the door to his room closed and locked. Pulling the curtain open, he watched the buildings slowly pass by as the train maintained the required thirty five mile an hour limit while going through the Atlanta area. He looked at the amazing collection of graffiti on the walls of most of the buildings. He smiled. Graffiti was the same the world over: the size, the lettering, everything. He wondered, *How is this accomplished? Certainly the artists are not all world travelers.*

Slowly the train began picking up speed. The buildings of Atlanta were now in the distance. The train was traversing through suburbs, woods and less populated areas. Slowly he began to relax a bit. A deep sigh came from his mouth. DuPree stretched his legs and lay his head on the cushion of the seat. Looking out his window, he saw that it was dusk.

Just before the helicopter took off, the pilot handed helmets to both Theo and Aiden. Using hand motions to communicate over the loud noise of the engine, the pilot insured both men were hooked up to the machine's speaker system so they could talk during the flight. Theo brought the flight crew up to date and gave them his plan. Both Theo and Aiden found out that speaker systems were very necessary. Helicopters were not designed for pleasant conversation; the engine and rotors were too loud and it was rocky.

Theo directed the pilot to Taccoa, Georgia. *As quickly as possible!* That was the second stop for the train. Since the train was running late, the actual schedule was good only for where the train would stop. Times were no longer real. The first stop was Gainesville, Georgia, but that would be a short stop and they would not make it in time. Toccoa was the last stop in Georgia and they had to board the train there.

O'Brian was absorbed in the disappearing skyline of Atlanta.

"Aiden," Theo said, "the chief is notifying the railroad. We'll get on the train at Toccoa. We'll split up. I'll board up front and get in the engine. You get on at the rear of the train. DuPree does not know you and will think nothing of you getting on the train. The railroad will have radios for us to communicate. The conductor will have eyeballed our man by then. We'll give DuPree time to sack out, then we'll hit him. Aiden nodded. He had to admit, he was a bit nervous, yet excited at the same time.

As the crow flies, it was a relatively short distance from Atlanta to Toccoa, a small town in the north Georgia mountains. The pilot set the chopper down in the parking lot of the high school. A police car was waiting for them to rush them to the train station. Thanking the chopper crew, Theo and Aiden climbed into the waiting police cruiser and were rushed to the station.

Once at the station, they talked a few minutes about their plan. Theo took his cell phone and called the chief. Arrangements had been made with AMTRAK security and jurisdictional matters had been handled with both South and North Carolina, as well as Virginia and the District of Columbia. The chief had said the governor had been making those arrangements. Both men were armed, Theo with his department-issued Glock automatic pistol, O'Brian with the small Smith and Wesson five shot snub nose Theo carried in his car just for backup.

Theo would ride in one area of the train, while Aiden would stay in the back. The conductor would walk the train a few times to spot DuPree and insure he was not on foot.

They did not need a major search of the train. That might cause panic and something could happen if another passenger got involved. That they did not need. "Whoever spots him first, let the other know," said Theo. "I don't want anybody hurt on this."

O'Brian nodded.

Off in the distance, they could hear the whistle of the approaching AMTRAK entering the yard limit.

Turning toward his friend, Theo said, "Get to the end and keep out of sight. I'll go up to front and let the engineer know what's going on and I'll stay with him. Get on as soon as the train stops. Someone will be there to greet you, probably a steward. As soon as we get our radios, we'll be back in touch."

Theo turned to walk away, then stopped, turned and said, "Aiden, thanks, man, but be careful!"

Aiden smiled and gave him a thumbs up. He didn't want Theo to know how nervous he was. *God! He would be facing the killer!*

Both men then walked to their designated places on opposite ends of the platform. Excited and scared, Aiden hoped nobody could hear his knees knocking. In the distance, he could see the twirling strobe lights of the train.

The train seemed to stop for just a moment. DuPree wondered why it needed to stop at all. He assumed it was just a mail pickup. He decided to stay in his room until he knew the train was in South Carolina. Then he might venture out for some exploration and perhaps a whiskey or vodka in the club car. He was not much of a drinker, but perhaps this might be a special occasion. Maybe just one very, very dry martini. The bigger question, however, was whether or not to go in as a male or female. *Oh well,* he said to himself, *I have some time to decide that. Besides, it would be a lot of work to try to dress like a woman while on the train. There wasn't much room to maneuver around.*

Looking out his window, he could see nothing. He could ask the conductor or one of the stewards whether they were in South Carolina, but he did not want to call attention to himself. He was quite certain he was safe. He chuckled at the thought of all the action that must be going on at the airport in Atlanta. He did feel a slight flutter in his stomach. *Should he be worried?* he thought. *Nah, but perhaps a martini would be just the thing for him.*

The engineer greeted Theo in a very matter of fact way, not friendly, not hostile. Theo had no idea what the engineer or any of the crew had been told. The engineer sat in his seat, another crew member sitting across on the other side of the locomotive. This man simply nodded to Theo, not bothering to say a word.

"Conductor will be here in a minute," the engineer said, turning away from his array of gauges and rods.

Theo smiled and said, "Thanks." Outwardly, he appeared calm, but on the inside, though, his nerves were all a twitter, and his heart was racing.

The engines powered up. Theo could feel the vibration as the engines RPM's increase as the engineer eased off the brakes. Trains had always held a certain fascination for Theo ever since his father had given him his first Lionel Electric Train for Christmas. Over the years, he and his father had added to his collection until a section of the basement had become an intricate rail system. Theo had spent hours with his trains. Eventually, after the murder of his father, the train set had been taken down and placed in boxes.

Theo had always wanted to get a room where he could set up the system once again, but like so many other things on his of things to do list, the train simply stayed on the list. *Someday,* he always told himself.

Mesmerized, Theo looked out the big windscreen as the train speeded toward South Carolina, its first stop at Clemson. Theo took the train schedule from his pocket. After Clemson, the train would stop in Greenville, then Spartanburg, then on to North Carolina.

A door opened and the conductor walked through. The conductor informed him, "There's a small catwalk along the engines so we can gain entrance to the other cars. Mechanics need room to work on the engines at times and they certainly can't tear an engine out."

Theo nodded and smiled.

The conductor continued, "Your partner is in the back in the crew room. Now, who are you looking for?"

Theo gave the conductor a succinct summary of the details of the events leading up to DuPree getting on the train. The conductor did not recall any woman of that description getting on the train, but stated he would be going through the list of passengers and those who had sleeping accommodations. That way they could probably figure out if DuPree was, in fact, a passenger, and if he was dressed as a woman or a man.

As he was leaving, the conductor said, "Damn, I almost forgot." Reaching inside his coat, he unhooked a small radio from his belt. "This is yours," he said. "Your partner has one, too. Now you two can talk. I'll let you know what I find out." With that the conductor opened the door to the catwalk leading to the engines and was gone.

Theo looked at his radio, turned it on and called Aiden.

"I'm here."

"Aiden, the conductor's going through the train roster now and will check to make sure our boy is here. Just stay in your seat until you hear from me," Theo instructed.

"Roger that."

"Are you doing okay?' Theo asked.

"I'm fine," the psychiatrist said. "A little nervous, a little excited. Good, overall."

Looking out the window, Theo was giving this matter a lot of thought. *I can't let this thing get screwed up. I need to stay on my toes.*

He was not worried about O'Brian. His friend had taught some of his officers specific tactics regarding hostage negotiation and had taken part in the training of the SWAT team. And Aiden was fit and clear-headed. He could take care of himself. But Theo knew, DuPree was smart, as well. This was certainly not the first time the priest had been in a situation involving police. What Theo did not know was how DuPree would act under stress. Theo did not want any passengers getting hurt and wished he had more time. He wished there were more officers on the train for backup.

When DuPree was positive the train had passed into South Carolina, he took his bag from the carrier above his head. Slowly he began to sort through the contents. He knew he could not take any chances.

He was certain that damned Detective Reed, by now, would have figured out that he had not taken any plane out of Atlanta, and would be working furiously to find him. He had no idea how long it would take Reed to discover he was on the train. Perhaps never, but he could not take the chance.

Reaching into his bag, he took out a black nylon sheath dress he had rolled up and placed in his bag earlier. Removing a wig and the rest of his outfit, he slipped the dress over his head and onto his body. It was a long dress and came down to just above his ankles.

"Good," he said, "no calves showing." At the sink, he took a comb from his bag and began working on his wig, the hair was short and choppy. Placing the wig on his head, he looked at himself, and smirked, "Well, it's not exactly Liza Minnelli."

Taking a razor and shaving cream out of the bag, he shaved his face. Then he applied a proper amount of make-up. Fortunately, he did not have a heavy beard. Looking at himself again, he thought, *I really don't look too bad.*

He had one more item in his bag. Lifting his skirt, he strapped the holster to his calf. He took out the pistol, a twenty-five automatic, moved the slide back, then forward, and put the first round into the chamber. "Just in case," he said aloud. Leaving his bag on his seat, he was careful to notice just where the bag lined up on the design of the cloth of the seat. "Always paranoid," he whispered.

With one more glance in the mirror, he puckered his lips into a kiss and said, "Okay, darling, let's go explore and get that martini."

With that, the woman opened the door of his compartment, and began walking toward the rear of the car.

Hixon DuPree found the club car with no trouble. Fortunately, there was a single seat in the back of the car. He could sit there, enjoy himself and spot anything, or anyone, suspicious in the area.

Once seated, he looked around, catching the eye of the bartender who came over to the table. "What will you have ma'am?"

"I'll have a Bombay Sapphire gin Martini, dry, two olives, *up*, please," he said in his softest voice.

DuPree took time to look around. There was laughter across the aisle where four college age girls sat directly across from him. All four were wearing sweatshirts with some sort of college stuff emblazoned on the front. *Probably going to some sort of convention,* he thought to himself. The second time he looked their way, all four girls acted as though they were trying to stifle laughs.

"Fuck them," he said under his breath. *Cunts,* he thought to himself. *If they only knew, they would be scared shitless. To have his secret, his power to instill fear in others, to kill, made him feel invincible.* He began to feel tingly all over, and was aware he was getting hard. "Whoa," he whispered, thinking, *I don't want to go to all this trouble to look like a woman only to have a hard-on give me away.*

The waiter brought him his drink. Hixon DuPree said, "If you don't mind, I think I'll run a tab."

"Fine by me," the bartender replied.

Lifting the cold martini to his lips, he took a sip. *God, that tasted good.* Sitting back, he began to relax. It had been some tense hours since that night at the mountain. He wondered about Eleanor Cameron. Surely, she knew by now. *I'll bet she nearly shit her pants,* he thought. He had to stifle a small giggle. *And that shit, Detective Reed, must have pissed all over himself.* It proved his point; he was certainly smarter than most cops, certainly more so than the cops who had entered his life in the past.

Sitting there relaxing, DuPree watched the activities in the club car. There were not too many people there. He was a bit surprised. The four girls across the aisle from him, another couple near the middle of the car, and yet another couple at the far end of the car. The bartender and waiter were engaged in an animated conversation at the bar.

Suddenly, Dupree's attention was drawn to the door at the end of the car. The conductor had entered and was walking through the car, toward the area where DuPree was sitting.

The clergyman, trying to be as unobtrusive as possible, watched as the conductor approached. The conductor seemed to be a bit more attentive to his passengers as he walked through the car. He did not stop and speak with them, but appeared to be scrutinizing each one. DuPree told himself that he was just being a bit too hyper-vigilant. Still, he had to be ready for anything.

After the conductor left, Dupree felt a little better. The conductor hadn't seemed to pay much attention to him, but he still felt a little uneasy. He was not sure why, since things had gone very well for him, as far as his getaway was concerned. He had seen nothing to arouse his suspicions. Perhaps he should not begin to question things now, but in the event there was a problem, he did not want to be trapped and unable to get away. Maybe it was best if he stayed where he was. If he left, and the conductor came back soon and he was gone, this could arouse more suspicion, if in fact there was any suspicion in the first place. He was, however, aware of the fact that he stuck out like a sore thumb, a woman alone in a club car. He needed to be less visible. He needed a plan.

As he sat there, DuPree focused on the four college girls sitting at the table across from him. They were deep in conversation. He could hear bits and pieces, but the more he listened, the more it became obvious they were talking about Washington, D.C. They seemed to be talking about their friends, often breaking into laughter. He noticed two of the girls were wearing sweatshirts with Greek names across the front. Another girl's sweatshirt had University of Alabama on it and the last girl was wearing a shirt that said FIJI. DuPree wondered what "FIJI" meant. They were probably heading to a sorority event in DC.

DuPree decided that if he could sit with the girls and get involved in talking with them, he would not be so conspicuous. Slowly, he began to formulate his plan.

———————

As well as he could, given the circumstances, Theo was enjoying the ride. It was a little boy's dream come true. The engineer had explained the handles and gauges of the engine. The locomotive did not have the smell of burning oil that was in the old oil fired engines. But there was a smell of grease and heat present. Somehow, Theo found that comforting. The control board of the locomotive was not as complicated as he had imagined, certainly nothing like the massive array of instruments and controls on an airliner.

His concentration was interrupted by a call from Aiden O'Brian. "Theo, the conductor is here. He's been though the train and looked at the manifest. No familiar names, but a sleeper was sold to a man who made a late purchase in Atlanta. The conductor went by the man's room, but he didn't knock or hear anything. There is a single female sitting near the back of the club car. Conductor said she does not fit the description of the person in the sleeping car, but he had not seen her prior to the Atlanta stop. When he went by her, she was obviously sitting down and had her glass to her lips so it was a little difficult for him to judge by description," the psychiatrist said.

Theo thought about checking her tickets but was told that once a ticket was presented, there was no reason to check again. Both men agreed to do so might arouse suspicion.

Thinking for a minute, Theo asked Aiden to ask the conductor if it might be possible to make a visit to the room of the woman the conductor had seen in the club car.

The conductor nodded, and O'Brian said they could do it.

"Okay, I don't want him to arouse DuPree's suspicion, but we need to find out if the woman is him or not. My hunch is that it is DuPree. As soon as the conductor knows anything, have him get in touch with me on the radio. In the meantime, I'll head back into the train to meet him, then, if it is positive, we'll develop a plan."

The conductor told Aiden that he would check immediately. Aiden felt if the conductor went back through the club car, then returned in a few minutes, it just might arouse suspicion, so he directed the conductor to do his check, then walk toward the front of the train and meet Theo.

———————————

Dupree heard the door of the car open and he turned toward the noise of the train wheels on the track that came through the open door. He watched the conductor walk the length of the club car and exit to the next car. DuPree decided it was time for him to make some new friends. Slowly, he got out of his seat, drink in his hand, and crossed the aisle to the table where the four girls were seated. They stopped talking as DuPree approached at their table.

DuPree smiled and said, "Kappa Kappa Gamma, I see. I'm a Tri Delt myself. Bet you're on your way to a convention? I loved it when I went to those. Of course, it's been a long time since I was in college. My, how time flies, ya know? But I do miss those days. You all seem like you're having so much fun. Mind if I join you? What are you drinking? I've got the next round" As he talked, DuPree, looking very much like the female he was dressed to be, slid into the seat next to the girl with the FIJI tee shirt. The four girls were so startled that DuPree had sat down and already asked the bartender for a round of drinks, they were speechless.

Realizing he had caught them off-guard, DuPree quickly engaged them in conversation by correctly guessing they were, in fact, on their way to Washington, D.C. for their annual sorority convention. *Hell, his Youth Group experience really paid off.* He smoothly maneuvered them into talking about themselves and their sorority, their college and social life. *Girls just loved to talk about themselves.*

Soon, it was like they were all good friends. One big happy bunch.

———————

"No one came to the door," the conductor said to Theo as they met in one of the forward cars. The detective listened intently as the conductor related that he had knocked several times on the door. When nobody answered, the conductor took his passkey and unlocked the door and looked in. All he saw was a carry-on bag on the seat. The passenger was not in the room. He told Theo he had been too scared to look into the bag. Instead, he closed the door and made sure it was locked.

With the conductor standing with him, Theo, called O'Brian. He told the psychiatrist what had transpired when the conductor went to the room. Theo related that the conductor had stated there was a single woman in the club car and she appeared to be alone. She had different colored hair than DuPree and was wearing a black dress. The conductor could not describe the dress any more than what he had seen in the short time he walked by the woman.

"Do you want me to go look?" Aiden inquired.

"No. I want us to go into that car at the same time from both ends, but I need to get a look in the room first. I don't want the conductor going back into the club car again. We can't be seen and I don't want to arouse any suspicion. I'm going to get in the room, have a look, then I'll get back to you."

Turning to the conductor, Theo asked if he could let him in the room.

"No problem," the conductor said. "Follow me." He seemed to be enjoying himself. It wasn't every day they had a suspected murderer on the train. Scary, but exciting.

Walking through the train to the sleeper car, Theo was aware that what he was going to do was illegal – conducting a search without a warrant. But hell, Theo felt justified in doing the search. He would deal with the consequences later, but he knew there would be no defense for what he was about to do.

Finally, after walking through two cars, the conductor stopped at a door. He unlocked it and Theo stepped inside. Theo found the light switch and turned it on. It was a very small room. Immediately, Theo's eyes saw the carry-on bag on the seat. He looked very closely at how the bag was positioned on the seat. He wanted to make sure he left the bag in the same position as he found it. He did not want DuPree to get suspicious and notice things had been disturbed.

Kneeling down, Theo slowly and methodically pulled the sides of the canvas bag open. His eyes were immediately drawn to the black nylon fabric. Reaching into his pocket, he removed a Maglight, which he turned on, then placed in his mouth. Slowly, he felt the fabric, and found men's clothing and the baseball hat with the Atlanta Braves logo. Feeling further down, he felt some hair. Shining his light, he saw a wig. *Bingo!*

An icy chill rolled down his entire body. The hair on the back of his neck stood up. DuPree was here on the train and was probably the single woman in the club car. Sweat dripped down his forehead onto his nose. His heart raced a thousand beats per second. Theo closed the bag, positive he had not disturbed anything. He knew he had to find out exactly where DuPree was sitting. Again, he made sure the bag was in the same position as when he found it. He put his Meglight in his pocket, turned out the light and left the room.

Theo asked the conductor, "Where can we go to talk and still be out of sight?"

"There's a porter's room in the next car. They keep linens and stuff there. We can use that room."

"Great," said Theo and they began walking toward the next car.

Aiden O'Brian was troubled. Things were going too quickly for his analytical, academic mind. He was not used to the fast pace that had propelled him from his campus office, to Theo's car, then the helicopter, and now the train. He was an analytical person and needed time to think things through. True, he had some time on the helicopter and had given himself quite a bit of time in Theo's car. Just the same, he was uncomfortable. And nervous. And scared.

Aiden knew Hixon Dupree was the killer of the three young girls at Stone Mountain Park, and for that matter, was probably the one who killed the first girl found in the lake in the spring. And no telling how many more that had gone undiscovered. Aiden was stone cold certain of that.

And now, DuPree was on the same train, just yards from where he was sitting. But the big question in his mind was how would DuPree respond when he realized what was happening. *Would he become violent? Did he have a gun? Would he shoot? Would he run? What would he do?*

Aiden knew things were about to come to a head. He could feel the pistol Theo had given him, but he wasn't fond of guns, at all. Obviously, there was more to be done, but an arrest was now almost certain.

His mind racing, Aiden needed a few minutes to think. He needed to get into the mind of the murderer. Taking a few moments, he leaned back in his seat, took several deep breaths and meditated. Meditation was something he had begun in medical school and it had helped him tremendously, especially during times of stress. It took away the clutter in his mind and he was calmer.

He knew Father Hixon DuPree was smart, and an organized person, a killer who planned things out. And he was intelligent enough to formulate good, sound plans. So far, there was no hint that DuPree was beginning to unravel, or that his thinking pattern was beginning erratic.

O'Brian was reminded of Ted Bundy, a famous serial killer from years ago. Bundy had been organized, as well, and planned everything out but his victim. But in the end, when he knew he was being chased, he began to unravel. Once fastidious about his appearance, he became unkempt and even dirty, and in Florida, killed a young girl and hid her body sloppily beneath some trash. Eventually, he was stopped by a local Florida police officer for driving erratically. The stress, the lack of sleep, the running and the high intensity of his thoughts and emotions drove Bundy to deteriorate. Cunning as Bundy had been, he had turned into a man whose irrational thinking and physical behavior caused him to make big mistakes. He became a man out of control. None of that was evident in DuPree right now.

No, the psychiatrist, thought to himself, *DuPree is smart and very aware of his surroundings. He feels in control right now, but pushed into a corner, he will respond. He will not give up and that makes him very dangerous.*

Taking his radio in his hand, Aiden called Theo and said, "Theo we need a plan. DuPree is not going to give up and just walk away with us. He's going to fight. He could have a gun, and could be dangerous."

"I know. We need a plan to outsmart him. I went into DuPree's room, and sure enough, there was a bag of female clothes, plus what he was wearing when he bought the train ticket. He's in the club car, I'm sure of it. And he's dressed as a woman. The conductor has seen him. What's your analysis?"

"When he realizes we're about to get him, I think he'll respond in a physical way. He could have a gun, we don't know. I know this, he's not going to surrender. He'll do anything he can to escape. The idea of being confined in a jail cell will be unbearable to him. Don't forget, this man is strong. Remember his workout room? I think we're better off getting him while he's confined on the train. If we stop again and he thinks he's close to getting caught, he'll run, and he'll be fast and gone before we can catch him. And, no telling where he'll end up and what sort of carnage and violence he'll leave in his wake."

"Hell," said Theo. "I believe you're right, Aiden." He turned to the conductor and said, "When's the next stop?"

"Clemson, South Carolina in about 45 minutes," the conductor answered.

Theo came back on the radio and said, "Aiden, get ready. I'm not letting this bastard off the train. I've sent the porter into the club car with a stock of cherries and olives for the bar. Stand by a sec, the bartender's just coming back."

After a few moment, the detective's voice was back on the radio. "Okay, he's sitting with four college girls around a table on the right side of the car, as you walk in. He knows me, so it will have to be up to you. He won't have any idea that you're anyone other than another passenger getting a drink. As soon as you see him, go ahead and place him under arrest, but be quick. When I see you walk in the door, I'll get in there and be with you in a flash. He's with those girls. We do not want a hostage situation."

Aiden's throat tightened and his heart hammered in his chest. Hair bristled on the back of his neck and his knees knocked together. He told Theo, "I need to take a leak first."

"Go ahead," Theo replied. "Aiden, you'll do fine and I'll be right there. Let me know when you're ready and we'll get started."

O'Brian wished he had his friend's confidence. His fingers could hardly unzip his fly. Afterwards, he called his friend, "Okay, I'm ready."

"Good. The porter said DuPree's in the corner. He's sitting around the table with four girls. Fortunately, he's sitting next to the aisle. He arranged his seat so he can see anybody who walks in. You'll have to move fast. Give me a minute to get to the door at the other end of the club car. I'll let you know when I'm in place."

Aiden nervously made his way to the front of his car. He opened the door and stood on the platform just outside the club car. He knew what DuPree looked like. He had studied the man for weeks.

Hixon DuPree was no fool. His instincts told him something was amiss. As inconspicuous as the conductor had tried to be, it was obvious to DuPree that the man had been looking for him and had spent too much time scrutinizing him the two occasions he had walked through the car. DuPree had become very attentive to who came and went in the car. He had not seen anyone who looked like a cop, but still, he knew something out of the ordinary was going on, and he did not like what he was feeling.

It was obvious the girls at the table had no idea he was a male. He had been able to engage them in conversation, had bought a couple of rounds of drinks for them. He had switched to soda. The girls had become quite comfortable with him, treating him like an older sorority sister. He had always had a way with girls and these four were no different.

During the evening, one of the girls had gone to the restroom and he had maneuvered his seat so that his back was not against the wall. When the girl returned, she took his old seat, giving him some shelter. If anyone came for him they would have to reach or point across the body of the girl who was now sitting in his aisle seat.

Dupree took a napkin, given him by the waiter, and slowly began brushing the table in front of him. Then he allowed the napkin to drop to the floor.

"Oops," he said and reached down to retrieve it. As he reached down, he felt the holster strapped to the calf of his leg. He unbuckled the strap around the hammer of the revolver. Now all he had to do was reach down quickly to his leg, draw the gun and fire.

The lights of the railroad club car were dimmed a bit. He was happy for that. It might make it more difficult for anyone to spot him.

"Okay, Aiden, let's go," said Theo on the radio.

Aiden O'Brian grabbed the handle of the club car door and pushed it. It took just a moment for his eyes to adjust to the dimness of the car. Aiden saw the table of women. He had spent too much time on this case not to recognize Hixon DuPree.

The other girls were happily talking and laughing. They took no notice of DuPree as he looked at the psychiatrist entering the car. Their eyes locked on each other immediately.

O'Brian, almost touching the girl on the end, turned in the direction of the table where DuPree was sitting. His voice quivering, he yelled, "Hixon DuPree you're under arrest!"

He could hear Theo running down the aisle.

By now the girls had stopped talking and were staring at Aiden like he was some kind of madman.

Aiden and DuPree had not taken their eyes off each other. Dupree's eyes were cold and vicious, the expression on his face blank and composed with only a faint smile.

Everything moved in slow motion. Aiden saw DuPree reach down. He saw a gun coming up and pointing at him. At the same time Dupree reached across the table with his other hand, to the girl sitting next to him, and grabbed her hair, pulling her body across his.

The girl screamed and the shrill sound pierced Aiden's ears.

O'Brian heard Theo yell, "Drop the gun, DuPree, it's over!"

DuPree's expression never changed. Turning his face to Theo, he calmly said, "Quite the contrary, Detective Reed. Try anything and the girl gets the first shot."

By now, the other girls were clutched together, crying and screaming.

DuPree had his captive by the hair with his pistol at her forehead. "Please!" she screamed.

"Shut the fuck up," Dupree said.

Aiden focused his attention momentarily on the priest's eyes. They were the eyes of a predator, cold and emotionless. The eyes of a psychopath who had no feelings for anyone else. He was a diamondback rattlesnake coiled defensively, and ready to strike.

Aiden trembled. He looked at Theo who now had his Glock pointed at DuPree's head.

DuPree's just smiled. "Okay Detective, now just back off" he instructed. "No one has to get hurt here."

Motioning his head at O'Brian, he said, "You, get over by your partner."

Aiden walked over next to his partner.

"O.K." DuPree said. He looked at the girl who was in his clutches and commanded her to get up slowly. "Don't try anything cute with me."

Dupree's eyes focused on the conductor, who was standing in the doorway where Theo had entered. "Conductor, get this train stopped right now. Don't fuck with me or the girl gets killed. I'm in charge now."

Theo, his eyes never leaving Dupree, pushed down the impulse to charge DuPree.

Dupree said, "You were right, Detective Reed, it is over, but not the way you planned."

The blackness in DuPree's eyes burned with hate. Any sign of the Youth Minister's good natured personality was gone.

Dupree hissed, "Now, you mother fucker, I'm in control." He

looked at the conductor and screamed, "I told you to stop this fucking train! Now!

The conductor looked at Theo and asked, "What do I do now?"

Theo said, "Do as he says. He's right; he is in control."

Taking his radio in his hand, the conductor called the engine room, and gave orders to stop the train.

The engineer radioed back, "What's going on? I can't just stop the train. We're behind as it is."

The conductor yelled, "Stop the fucking train. Do as you're told."

DuPree, seeing that everybody was following his instructions, relaxed a bit. Looking at Theo, he commanded, "OK, put your gun down and you and your partner, back out of the car."

Slowly, Theo backed up.

Against his better judgment, Theo lowly he bent down and laid his automatic on the floor of the railroad car. He saw no other way out of the situation.

In the excitement, Aiden O'Brian realized he had forgotten to take his gun out of his waistband. DuPree apparently figured he was unarmed. Slowly, O'Brian moved toward Theo and the conductor.

DuPree, keeping his eyes on Theo, grabbed his hostage by the shoulder and said, "OK, my dear, now let's get up. Slowly, now."

They both stood up. As they did, the train lurched forward and started slowing down. The train was stopping, just as DuPree had ordered.

Once they were both on their feet, DuPree pointed his gun to the young college student's temple. His left arm was now around her neck, his right, holding the gun. Looking at the other girls, Dupree said, "You three get back, as well." Trembling, the girls slowly inched their way towards Theo.

At the same time, Aiden O'Brian moved closer, behind the conductor.

As the train rounded a curve, the motion and the application of the brakes caused a forward jolt. The girl in DuPree's arm lost her balance and fell.

Realizing he had lost his cover, DuPree pushed the girl in front of Theo, then grabbed the door release and jumped through the doorway, into the next car.

Aiden O'Brian was the first to respond. Grabbing his revolver from his waist, he threw himself in the direction of Hixon DuPree. By the time he opened the door to the next car, he could see DuPree fumbling with the side exit door, trying to get it open. He'd be able to jump off the train if he got that door open. And then he'd be gone in the wind.

The train was continuing to slow down, but was still moving at a fairly good clip. The psychiatrist knew that if Dupree got off the train, they would never find him in the darkness of the subtropical forest of pines and palmettos of South Carolina. And this area was swampy and known as a haven for copperheads, moccasins, rattlers and alligators, not to mention mosquitoes and God knows what else.

Dupree turned and saw red haired man headed his way. Dupree aimed his gun and pulled the trigger. The train lurched again, forcing Aiden to lose his balance. The bullet from DuPree's gun sailed over Aiden's head, barely missing him.

Dupree turned to open the exit door.

Aiden, used the floor to steady his grip, and pointing his gun, pulled the trigger.

But DuPree was too fast for him. With superman strength, he managed to pry the door open so he could leap out into the darkness and safety.

"Shit!" Aiden shouted.

The train had not quite stopped. It was still traveling about 30 miles per hour. Aiden ran to the rear of the car where the door was located. By now, the door was almost closed again but something was holding it open. Afraid that DuPree was hiding in the door-well, and might fire again, Aiden got on his hands and knees, and crawled to the door, his gun in his hand.

As he crawled, Aiden could hear the train slowing to a stop.

Slowly, Aiden edged toward the door.

His gun ready, Aiden slowly crawled to the doorway. The door was partially opened. The view of the gravel whizzed by as the train continued stopping.

Aiden got to his feet and looked at the door. Something caught his eye. It was a woman's shoe, a black pump, wedged in the doorway, holding it partially open. *There was still a foot in the shoe! Good God!*

Pointing his gun in the direction of the door, Aiden pulled it open. It was easy to do now as the train had released the lock on the door as it stopped.

"Jesus," O'Brian said out loud, "he must have been one strong son of a bitch to get that door opened."

In the doorway, Aiden looked down and gasped.

Trying to piece together what had happened, Aiden surmised that Hixon DuPree had turned to shoot O'Brian. At the same time, Aiden shot at him. The psychiatrist was not even aware he had pulled the trigger. O'Brian's hollow-point bullet had pierced Dupree's leg and the bullet hitting and shattering the tibia then ricocheting to the femur and shattering it as well as tearing muscle and ligaments.

The slowly moving train was shuddering and vibrating. DuPree had caught his foot in the door, and due to the electric power of the automatic door, he couldn't recover. As the train lurched forward, DuPree had hit his head against the side of the door. The flesh and bone was no match for the metal and the power of the railroad car. A second lurch of the train tore muscle and tendon in the neck.

DuPree had been knocked outside the train, but his foot had been caught in the automatically closing door. The body had been slammed beneath the train and the railroad ties, which banged against Dupree's head, bringing the priest to a quick death. By the time the train stopped completely, O'Brian had jumped off the train to look for DuPree. He found the body, lying under the train. It was obvious that Hixon Dupree was dead.

Gasping, Aiden felt a hand on his shoulder. His friend, Theo, was at his side.

"Are you O.K." asked Theo.

Aiden nodded, but he was shaking.

When they got the body out from under the train, they saw that the entire left side of the top of the head was gone. There was blood all over the face, but strangely enough, Dupree's eyes were still open. His eyes still had that black, empty, menacing, reptilian look. Aiden shuddered.

Neither man said anything.

Aiden walked to the end of the car, bent over and vomited.

———————————

36 FINAL

Once Theo and Aiden were able to leave the scene, it was a quiet ride back to Atlanta. Earlier, the Chief had ordered the helicopter to pick him up, then fly on to Clemson, South Carolina to pick up the two men and return them home. *It had been a helluva an evening* Theo thought to himself.

One never knew what might arise – a difficult question from a reporter or a question about police procedure. The Chief of Detectives and his buddy, the psychiatrist, had been through enough and the Chief could handle the press or any other issues.

Aiden was in a state of shock. He was surprised after all the gore he had seen in photos in the past, as well as a few crime scenes he had visited during his career. He thought his mind would have been better insulated. He guessed that was not the case.

All the way home, he kept replaying the death of Hixon DuPree over and over in his mind in slow motion. It was like a scene out of CSI: DuPree exiting the club car, DuPree shooting at him, him reaching for his revolver and returning fire. DuPree opening the train door, the image of the shoe containing a foot and part of a lower leg, then the actual sight of Hixon DuPree, dead. It was a sight that the psychiatrist would never forget. It would be with him forever.

They figured Dupree had been dragged by the train for almost two miles before the train came to a full stop. Hixon Dupree was almost unrecognizable, except for his eyes.

When questioned about what had occurred, Theo posited the man was terrifically strong, strong enough to pull the door open. As he was ready to jump, he had to deal with the pain in his leg, as well as get in a position to jump. As he did this, he lost his hold on the train and the door slammed shut just as DuPree jumped, catching his foot and leg in the door. The impact of the fall, and the fact his leg was caught in the closed door forced DuPree to the ground. With the train still moving, and his lower leg caught in the door, he was unable to free himself. Trapped in the train's door, his head smashed along the railroad ties.

Horrendous as it was, Theo believed DuPree had died very quickly. The pain had to have been excruciating, but death had been swift.

It had taken several hours for the crime scene to be processed, and passengers and crew interviewed by the South Carolina Law Enforcement Department. The train track was not reopened for regular traffic hours, thus upsetting commerce on the entire east coast.

Funny, Theo thought, even in death, *DuPree exercised some level of control.*

While Theo appeared unfazed, Aiden had gone over to the ambulance, where the four college girls were being tended to. He spent several minutes with each one, then walked to the other side of the ambulance, where he sat down on the ground, head between his legs, and wept. It had been a bitch of a day and night.

Aiden was unaware of the sun coming up. Had he looked, he would have seen a southern sun, coral red and clear.

Aiden felt a hand on his shoulder. He looked up to see his friend. Theo had a big smile on his face.

"Hey, big guy," Theo said, "you're a hero. Jesus, you tag along and in no time, you steal my thunder."

Slowly, Aiden looked up and began to smile.

"It *was* a helluva night, wasn't it?" said Aiden

"You bet, old friend." Reaching his hand down, Theo offered helped him up. "Come on, old man, I'll help you up. The chopper's ready to leave."

Both men were silent on their way back, exhausted and lost in their own thoughts of the last few hours, oblivious to the rattle and whirring of the helicopter.

———————

During the trip back home, and for the next several weeks, the events would play again and again in the minds of both men: the search in Atlanta, the flight to Toccoa, the train ride, the confrontation and eventually, the death of Father Hixon DuPree, Youth Minister, serial murderer.

Once out of the helicopter and back in Atlanta, Theo turned to his friend. "Aiden, you did a hellofa job through all this. I can't tell you how much it means to me that you helped me. You're the real hero."

Aiden said, "Thanks, Theo, coming from you, that is a compliment. You know, at some point, we need to talk about all this. With all the experiences I've had in my years in forensics, I still need to deal with the fact that I helped kill a man last night. Even though he was a murderer, I played a part in taking a man's life."

"I know, my friend," Theo said. "You'll feel better in time. The first time is the roughest, and the reality is that this will always be a part of your history now. Asshole that he was, Father Hixon DuPree was still a human being. I'm positive he had to have had a terrible upbringing. Too bad we'll never know. To have known his mind would have been a treasure of information. Especially for you, in all your psychological analyses and profiling."

"It's one for the books, that's for sure," said Aiden.

When they arrived at the parking garage, Aiden put his hand on his friend's shoulder and gave it a squeeze. Then, he walked down into the garage toward his Harley. He was anxious to feel the wind on his face and get home to see his cat, Gertrude. He needed to hear her purr as she sat snuggled on his lap. He was bone tired.

Theo got in his car. His first call was to a florist. He ordered a dozen red roses to be delivered to Wilma. That done, he called his mama.

"I guess you know it's all over?" he said when she answered.

"Yes, I've been watching the news," she said.

"Mama, I need some pork chops, some greens and black-eyed peas. I also need cornbread and plenty of sweet tea. Can you help me out?"

"Theo," she replied, "I always have a place set for you at the table. I was just gettin' ready to fry up some pork chops and I've already got collard greens on the stove with some black-eyed peas. Cornbread just came out of the oven and the tea's outside brewin' in the sun. And I've got the purtiest peach cobbler sittin' on the stove. Ready for you, son."

"I'm coming over, Mama."

Right now, Theo needed some TLC and there was no better place to get it than at his mama's house. And later, maybe tomorrow, he'd take Wilma out to dinner and a movie. He wasn't getting any younger.

EPILOGUE

Nothing moves quickly in the South. And so it took almost a month for the body of Hixon DuPree to be returned to Georgia authorities. It required some work, but Theo finally was able to locate Dupree's sister in New Orleans. He called her to tell her of her brother's death. "What happened?" she asked. Theo gave her a short version of Dupree's history.

"Serves him right!" she said then she hung up.

Theo had gone by St. Jude's by the Mountain. The rector had been caught off-guard when Theo asked if the church wanted to deal with the body of Hixon DuPree. He would have to check with the vestry, was Reverend Bainbridge's answer. Eventually, Father Bainbridge did call him back, and reported that the church did not want to be involved.

When the priest tried to explain, Theo interrupted, "That's okay, Father, I'll take it from here. I understand."

And so the county undertook one last expense in the case of Hixon DuPree. They buried him in a nondescript pauper's grave. At the service, those attending were the Police Chaplain, Theo Reed and Aiden O'Brian.

As they walked away, Theo stopped by a small gravestone located on a grave close to Dupree's grave. Theo had made arrangements to pay for the stone out of his own pocket. He squinted at the words, then read out loud, "Jane Doe. Died at Stone Mountain."

Looking back at the location of the fresh grave of DuPree, Theo shook his head at the irony then he ran to catch up with Aiden. They were going to play tennis later. Aiden was helping him get back in shape. Then, Theo would pick up Wilma and they'd head over to his mama's for dinner where his sister was visiting for a week.

For this brief moment in time, life was very, very good.

It was not the best of times for Mose Ellard. It was beginning to get cold; winter was just around the corner. Mose had enjoyed the fall. It was his favorite time after spring. He loved the trees showing off their brilliant colors which ranged from bright red to a glowing gold and brilliant yellow. Interspersed were some evergreen trees illuminating their green needles which added another level of color to the mountain area. Now, however, the leaves were mostly gone and the trees had begun their winter rest. He saw several squirrels attacking the acorns which had fallen from the oak and ash trees, their, cheeks bulging, rushing to their nests in the trees to stock up for the coming winter.

If anybody had noticed Mose today, they would have been surprised. He unloaded his johnboat and pushed it to the water. The boat was strangely bare for a fishing boat. There was no rod and reel, no tackle box, no container of live bait and nothing to put the fish in after they had been caught. The only thing in the boat was a white box about eighteen inches long and three inches square.

Stepping into the boat, Mose took his paddle and began paddling across the cove. He felt a chill and stopped a moment to put on his denim jacket with the red plaid fleece lining. He put on his gloves and placed a stocking cap on his head. *Funny,* he thought, *it hadn't seemed that cold* when he was getting the boat out of his pickup truck.

Finally settled, he again took his oar and began paddling. When he reached the spot, Mose stood up, then took off his hat and removed his gloves. Reaching into the white box, he removed the single red rose. He looked at the rose for a few moments, then stepped to the front of the boat and looked down into the water, now clear as the water flowers and moss had long since settled to the bottom of the lake.

He thought of the body of the young girl he had found there so many weeks ago. Tossing the rose into the water, Mose whispered, "This is for you, honey. It's a shame what you had to go through, but I know your soul is soaring in a new and lovely place." Then sitting, he donned his hat and gloves, took his paddle and began his way back to his truck. He was anxious to get back to the vet clinic and be with his animals.

———————

FOR TIME AND ALL ETERNITY

Don't miss Henderson's next book coming soon. Mary Grace Suddeth, a South Georgia southern belle graduates from the Medical College of Georgia. Wanting to spread her wings she chooses the University of Utah to complete her residency in Anesthology. Soon she meets Heber Smith a young dermatologist. They fall in love and eventually decide to marry. Heber informs her that they will have to be married in the Mormon temple where she will be "sealed" to him for time and all eternity. If not they will not be together in eternity. Then he takes her to southern Utah to meet his parents. That night he also tells her his parents are polygamists. Thrown for a loop Mary Grace tries to recover only to find her husband is leading another life as well. She develops a paranoic mission which starts her life on an emotional roller coaster. This story has some strange twists including the Mormon rule of "blood atonement." The book promises to be a "stem winder."

ABOUT THE AUTHOR

Born and raised in Idaho, Mr. Warberg, writing under the pen name Brent W. A. Henderson graduated from Idaho State University in 1961 with a degree in English. He taught high school English in Pocatello, Idaho for three years. Following that, he began graduate school at Utah State University, but left to begin a career as a Special Agent with the F.B.I. where he stayed for 25 years. During his time in the Bureau, he was trained as a hostage negotiator and as a profiler in unknown subject cases involving serial rapists, child molesters and murderers. He cooperated in the research that the F.B.I. was conducting on serial offenders. During his time in the F.B.I. he received a Master of Science in Special Education with an Emotional Distrubance Option from Montana State University – Billings.

Following his retirement, he and his family relocated to Atlanta, Georgia. Mr. Warberg attended the University of Georgia and obtained a Master of Science in Social Work. He received his license a Licensed Clinical Social Worker and worked as a therapist with psychiatrist Gene G. Abel, exclusively treating sexual offenders.

After several years as a practicing therapist, he attended the

American International Institute of Polygraph in Atlanta. His internship was completed in England where he took part in a research project polygraphing sexual offenders on probation. This project took him to England on two more occasions. He was a member of the faculty which taught the first polygraph school in England at the University of New Castle, New Castle Upon Tyne, United Kingdom.

A polygraph examiner for twelve years, he only tests sex offenders who are on probation or parole. He has conducted tests on sexual offenders in Georgia, Connecticut and New York. He continues to do such tests. In addition he has co-authored numerous peer-reviewed journal articles and book chapters all dealing with sexual offenders.

Mr. Warberg and his wife Mary currently live in a cabin in the Blue Ridge Mountains of North Georgia. They share their time and space with two Shelties, Sally and Ruby. They have two married daughters, one living in Georgia and the other in New York. The Warbergs enjoy spending time with their grandchildren, as well as spending time in the nature that surrounds their cabin.

This is Mr. Warberg's first novel.

CPSIA information can be obtained
at www.ICGtesting.com
Printed in the USA
LVOW12s0058230916

505838LV00001B/4/P